Acknowledge[illegible]

I would like to express [illegible] ya, for her unwavering support throughout the process of writing this book. Her encouragement has been invaluable.

I also want to thank my mum, Pushpa Arya, for always believing in my writing ability.

Special thanks to Diana Dorell for her exceptional developmental editing and guidance, which greatly enhanced the flow of this book.

I am deeply appreciative of Monica Srivastava for her meticulous proofreading and editing work, ensuring the book met the highest standards.

Finally, I want to thank Rizwan Mirza for the brilliant cover design, which brings the essence of this book to life.

Ebook ISBN: 9798230888437

Paperback ISBN: 9798307281291

Hardback ISBN: 9798307324981

Traveller

Amit Arya

Traveller

Chapter One

Sashin had always been sceptical about anything to do with psychics, clairvoyants, or mediums. As he made his way through Piccadilly Circus, he looked around at the droves of people and felt somewhat exposed and vulnerable. A creeping feeling of doubt began to enter his mind, and he felt his stride slow down almost to a standstill.

The reason why Sashin was traipsing through central London is because his sister Reshma, who had become very accustomed to her newfound interest in spirituality, attending various courses on psychic development and learning to crystal dowse, had used her angel cards to do a distance reading on him. The card that her reading had uncovered was that of the wanderer, one without goals or direction. The result of the reading had concerned her and she urged Sashin to see a renowned psychic by the name of Doreen Dorell, who was based in New Park Road, about twenty minutes from Piccadilly Circus. Sashin deliberately chose to walk the whole route from Piccadilly rather than take the tube, as he wanted to use the walk to think about the decision he had made to see Doreen.

Visions of the impending encounter whirled through his mind, and he was conscious that the more he tried to imagine what would be said, the more he expected an inaccurate and meaningless evaluation of his current life situation. He tried not to think of what Doreen would say and instead took in the surroundings of London.

Looking at his iPhone, the navigation showed he was now at the beginning of New Park Road. He turned into the road and found number fifteen. Sashin was met with a white door, upon which was a brass knocker – it reminded him of the Victorian era which only made him worry even more.

'Great, a psychic living in the past,' he thought.

After three knocks, the door opened. A White lady with brown curly hair stood before him. She was in her forties and slightly shorter than Sashin, who was five feet, nine inches.

"Hi Sashin, come in."

"Thanks," replied Sashin.

"Hope you found the place okay."

"Good old iPhone," joked Sashin, waving his phone.

He was ushered into the living room where there was a coffee table in the middle of the room, with a sofa on one side and a chair on the other. At the back of the room stood a dining table and a clothes stand nearby, with various garments hanging to dry including black and red frilly underwear.

'Oh brother,' thought Sashin.

"Make yourself comfortable on the sofa. I'll be back in a minute."

A scented candle burned on the coffee table with a distinct smell of vanilla. Meditation music played in the background. Sashin sat down and sank back into the sofa. Whilst waiting, he found himself becoming drowsy, and his eyelids began to feel heavy. His thoughts were incoherent, and as soon as his eyes began to close, he was coaxed awake by Doreen's voice.

"Sorry about that. I just had to get my tarot cards."

"That's okay. I was getting comfortable like you said," replied Sashin.

"Don't nod off, as you'll be no use to me asleep," chuckled Doreen.

"I will be recording this session. If that is a problem, let me know now. You will get the recording as part of the reading."

"That's fine," replied Sashin emphatically.

Doreen sat on a chair opposite Sashin. She closed her eyes and began to breathe deeply. She held out her arms in front of her, with palms facing towards Sashin.

Breathing out rapidly, Doreen began to speak.

"I'm sensing a really strong Egyptian presence; it's so strong it nearly pushed me off my chair. Do you like Egypt, the culture?"

"Yes, I have an interest in the history of Egypt."

"There is a strong connection that I'm getting with a person or place in Egypt. Maybe it was a past life, but I'm not sure," said Doreen hesitantly.

Sashin sat quietly, not sure what to say in response to Doreen's reading. He felt there was an element of truth in what she was alluding to regarding his fondness of Egyptian culture, but in the back of his mind he questioned whether Doreen had picked a random subject and taken a lucky punt.

She spoke, which interrupted his thought pattern.

"Hold out your hands."

Sashin held out his hands, and Doreen placed her hands on his, closing her eyes she began to take deep breaths again.

"I sense that you're a little lost at the moment, if that makes sense. You're not quite sure what direction to take in your life, whether to do this or that. You're kind of just taking each day as it comes. There is a lot of drive within you though, and I feel like you have done well in your life. You're the type of person that if you put your mind to it, you can do anything. I'm getting academic achievement."

Sashin just nodded. He didn't want to confirm anything or reveal too much to Doreen. He wanted to see just how good she was, whether she was genuine or a fraud.

"Do you dream a lot, Sashin?"

"Doesn't everyone?" replied Sashin in an unemotional tone.

"I mean, do you have vivid dreams like you are in faraway places or meet people that you don't recognise from your waking life? And when you are awake, do you feel drained at times?" Doreen further questioned.

Sashin sat up, he looked more alert. Doreen had gained his attention by asking about dreams. Only one resounding question crossed his mind. 'How could she possibly know this?'

"Yes, I do have dreams like this. Sometimes it's in a familiar place even though I haven't been there, and sometimes the dreams are just weird, of strange places and very weird," Sashin paused.

"What is it?" asked Doreen.

"Just one disturbing dream I had," replied Sashin nervously.

"What happened in the dream?"

"I was in the Victorian era. Everyone was dressed in, well, Victorian dress. I saw a man wearing a tall hat, and he murdered this young woman. He just slit her throat, and there was blood everywhere. I went to confront the man, and he got into a horse-driven carriage. I got into the carriage and started shouting at him, questioning him about why he murdered the woman. He didn't make any eye contact with me, just smiled, in a creepy way. He got out of the carriage, I followed, and he immediately grabbed me by the throat. I saw his face and it started to change; it was hideous. He told me to stay away and then hinted at something to do with it not being the right time and that my time would come. His touch burned my throat. He let go and walked off. When I looked at my reflection in the window of the carriage, there was a burn mark on my throat. Then, I woke up."

Doreen's complexion changed – the colour in her face was replaced with a pale hue.

"You are an astral traveller. And from what I am sensing and what you have described, you have no control over your ability to travel. Many people spend years trying to astral travel and you seem to have the ability to do it without even trying. I'm picking up that this started to happen to you recently – it was dormant within you until now," shared Doreen.

"What does this even mean?" asked Sashin.

"It means that you will need to learn a bit more about the subject so that you don't get hurt. Sorry, I don't mean to make you feel uneasy. It's just that on the astral plane there are good and bad energies. If you just travel willy-nilly, you can bump into all kinds of beings that can drain you of your energy. Anyway, let's move on. If you want to know more, you can do some more sessions with me, and I can teach you some techniques to help you. Let's get your tarot cards done now, and see what comes up," continued Doreen with an unconvincing smile.

Sashin knew Doreen was just trying to make him feel better.

For the next twenty minutes, Doreen conducted a tarot reading. She laid out the cards on the coffee table and turned over various cards. Sashin seemed unable to fully concentrate as his mind was transfixed on the conversation he had a few minutes earlier regarding the dreams.

Two tarot cards had been selected, 'The Lovers' and 'The Fool'. Doreen explained that 'The Lovers' card represented making decisions using the heart and a gut feeling rather than the head. This made Sashin feel at odds as he tended to always make decisions based on logic rather than a feeling. As for 'The Fool' card, Doreen's explanation of this card was of embarking on a journey, which could be spiritual as much as physical.

"I appreciate the tarot card reading, but how can this help me with my current situation?" asked Sashin.

"Try to make decisions based on intuition, on how you feel, rather than always trying to overthink things. If you go with your instincts, you will pick up on opportunities. If you experience coincidences, go with it and take it in," replied Doreen.

Doreen finished the tarot reading and asked Sashin if he wanted a cup of tea, which he declined.

"It's time I got back to Kingston," said Sashin.

"Is that where your sister lives?" asked Doreen.

"How did you know that?" he said.

"I picked up on a strong female influence in your life, also a healer."

"Yes," replied Sashin.

"It was lovely to meet you," said Doreen with much enthusiasm.

Sashin walked back to Piccadilly Circus feeling much lighter, and he felt the meeting was not quite as bad as he had envisaged. There were questions he ruminated on that echoed through his mind.

The tube station was buzzing with people, from tourists to commuters on their way home. After battling his way onto the tube train, Sashin found a spot near the doors and pulled out his phone. He had no signal, so reluctantly put his phone back into his pocket. As he did, he caught the reflection of a woman in the carriage door; she had long black hair and looked

Mediterranean. He found her strikingly beautiful. As he stared, she caught his glance, and he immediately turned his head. Sashin could not quite remember where he had seen this woman before. He frantically went through images in his mind, but it was no use. He felt he knew her, but was it just someone who looked like a person he had met in the past? He stopped trying to remember and turned around to catch her gaze again. She looked at him, he smiled, she gave a weak smile back, and Sashin nodded.

'You muppet Sashin,' he thought to himself.

It was dark when Sashin had arrived at Kingston; he caught a taxi to his sister's house. When he got to the front door, he saw the silhouette of his sister, who had opened the door. She stood smiling intensely.

"How did you get on?" asked Reshma.

"Alright, not too bad," replied Sashin.

"Not too bad? You just saw one of the top psychics in the country!"

Sashin took off his shoes and walked into the living room. The large cream sofas looked extremely appealing after all the travelling. He sat down, laid back and closed his eyes.

"Come and eat first," offered Reshma.

As Sashin got up and walked towards the kitchen, he saw a poster on the wall in Reshma's office. It was new; he had never seen it before.

"Nice isn't it? I got it online. Have a read – this will actually help you, Sashin."

Sashin took a closer look to see a picture of a person sitting down with crossed legs and coloured orbs down the centre of the body. The orbs were chakras, and beside each one was a description of their function and meaning.

As they both sat down to eat, Reshma eagerly began to fire off her questions.

"So, what did she say?"

"Basically, she said that I was a bit lost and..." Before Sashin could finish, Reshma interjected.

"I told you, didn't I? I got that as well from my reading."

"She went on to talk about finding direction, trusting my intuition, and something about astral travel."

"What did she say about astral travel?" said Reshma, her voice raised in pitch.

"About my dreams, she picked up on it. I can astral travel without really trying. She seemed to know that I have been having dreams which I found harder to work out, the other stuff she could blag about, but not the dreams. I'm not going back, £30 for the reading, if you go several times, that's expensive," grumbled Sashin.

"It was worth going, Sash. Astral travel is a major thing. The fact you can do that without trying is amazing. People spend years trying to do what you can. You have to do what I keep telling you – meditate every day and do chakra balancing."

"Yes, I know. It's just that it's hard," said Sashin, turning his head away in discomfort.

"You don't believe it, *that's* why it's hard. But at least you went, which is a start," replied Reshma.

"Oh yeah!" exclaimed Sashin loudly.

"What?" asked Reshma.

"She mentioned that I have a strong connection with Egypt."

"Oh, that means you have to do the next thing now," said Reshma, nodding her head.

"What's that then?" replied Sashin.

"Past life regression. I know a lady named Sarah who lives in Croydon – I checked her site out, she's really good at regression," said Reshma.

Sashin nearly spat out his juice. "You've got to be kidding me. Then what after that? Colonic irrigation?"

"Stop it!" said Reshma angrily.

Sashin refrained from making any further comments and proceeded to finish his meal in silence.

A few years after Reshma got married to Ketan, it became apparent that Ketan had developed a drinking habit, which he tried to justify as a way to alleviate the stress at work. A symptom of the frequent and heavy drinking were bouts of anger which resulted in them both arguing many times. However, as Reshma was physically fitter than Ketan, he did not dare try to push her around in any way. These episodes had left Reshma weary. Sashin had rationalised that maybe Reshma turning to spirituality was a way of dealing with some of the turmoil early on in her married life. There were times when Reshma could be very emotional, and Sashin felt helpless that he could not do a great deal as he lived on the other side of London in Hendon. He was conscious of when he had crossed the line and did not want to upset her. He knew that she was only trying to help him with her newfound wisdom in the white arts.

The door clanged open as Ketan walked in and put his keys on the kitchen worktop.

"Hi Sash, how was your reading?" Ketan asked.

"It went alright. I gotta get going. I'll tell you all about it when you come down in a couple of weeks. I will leave the recording of the session with you both. Bring it with you when you come over," replied Sashin.

When he got back home, Sashin took out the piece of paper Reshma had given him, with titles of videos he could find on YouTube for meditation and chakra balancing. He used his phone to type in the first title 'Solfeggio Frequency Meditation', and the music started. Sashin got comfortable on the floor, closed his eyes and began his first bout of meditation in weeks.

The sounds varied from high-pitched frequencies to ocean waves and chanting. Thoughts danced through Sashin's head, and all kinds of random images appeared. He became irritated at the calamity of his mind. Soon, there was an array of colours that appeared out of the darkness, and then just white, like a blank page expanding. He felt himself falling asleep, trying to pull himself back awake. He felt comfort in not trying. Soon, he was completely asleep.

Chapter Two

A pastiche of coloured images flashed through Sashin's mind, and he was unable to clearly make out what he was seeing. Somewhere in his subconscious he was aware that he was in a dream, but it was a vague feeling. The flashing images took prominence, garnering all of his attention. Many of the images appearing rapidly were dark, and he felt himself narrowing in on a particular one, a mountain range. He approached the mountain from a height, slowly descending down to the bottom.

It was dark over the mountain, and as Sashin finally came to a standstill at the foot of the mountain range, he saw a stone staircase in the distance to his right. The steps seemed to lead down to a temple-like structure. He proceeded on with caution, looking around and noticing how dark and dank this place he had come upon felt. At the top of the stairs, he heard screaming coming from the temple. He looked ahead intensely to see what was happening, but he could not see anyone beyond a number of stone pillars. Sashin ran towards the temple and saw an opening which he rushed through.

Once inside, he stopped abruptly. Before him was a wall. As he looked down, he saw an opening across the expanse of the bottom, which Sashin made out to be approximately four feet high. Sashin crouched down onto his hands and knees and saw that the opening was the entrance to the main temple hall. There were several people, including children, sitting or on their knees due to the ceiling being so low. Sashin swiftly made his way forward. A group of ladies sat in the middle of the hall facing a shrine of white marble statues. The ladies were in distress, and one of them looked at Sashin. He immediately recognised her. The lady was Jyoti, and she had passed away a year before due to lupus. She was a family friend who had lived only a few doors away from Sashin's parents' house, a frequent visitor who used to have chats with his parents over tea.

"Jyoti? What's wrong? What is this place?" asked Sashin.

Teary-eyed, Jyoti struggled to speak, managing to get out a sentence after a few short breaths.

"Sashin, what are you doing here? We are trapped; we came here to get away from those things."

"What things?" replied Sashin.

Jyoti pointed behind Sashin. He turned to see a shadowy figure fly past the opening to the hall. His eyes widened with disbelief.

"Right. Everyone out of here *now*!" shouted Sashin. He began to usher people out of the hall.

The people started to leave through the opening looking at Sashin in relief, some touching his shoulder on the way out. As Sashin backed up towards the opening to exit, there was a scream from one of the children who had made her way out. A force pulled Sashin back. He quickly turned his head through the opening to see the shadow figure had taken hold of the child. It was black, and the edges of the being were like wisps of dark smoke. Sashin thought the being to be a spectre; its face was partly human, grotesque like a gargoyle's.

Sashin struggled to free himself from the grasp of another spectre. He was pulled with great speed out of the temple towards the mountain. Once at the bottom of the mountain, the spectre pulled him up. Sashin looked below him to see the drop to the ground growing wider and stopped his struggle to get free as the idea of free-falling to his death did not seem like a sensible alternative. Once at the top of the mountain, the shadow being dropped Sashin, who landed on his back. The jolt from the fall caused him to feel disoriented. He got up and staggered, quickly looking around as he gained balance to see several other shadow entities walking like normal humans. They stopped and then vanished away like mist in the wind.

Someone approached him wearing a robe with a hood that concealed the person's face. As the figure got closer, a hand pulled down the hood. Sashin caught sight of the exposed face. He recognised the man from his earlier dream – he was the 'Jack the Ripper' imitator.

"It's you!" shouted Sashin, pointing to the man accusingly.

"I wondered what had become of you, Ahmenemat. I have been looking for you for a long time. I sensed you and here you are. You are different now, like a lost child in an unknown land. Why is that? How the mighty have fallen."

"What are you talking about?" responded Sashin angrily.

The man lunged forward and attempted to grab Sashin by the neck. Sashin moved backwards in response. The robed man jumped up and over Sashin with superhuman agility, landing on Sashin's back. Sashin felt a stinging jolt in his shoulder. He knew he had to leave, and the weight of the robed man caused Sashin to panic. He attempted to run forward and tried shrugging him off, jumping to the floor backwards. A blinding light appeared before his eyes, and once again Sashin found himself experiencing flashing images. He was no longer on the mountaintop, but found himself at the bottom of some stairs alone. He felt relief at escaping but anxious to know where he was now.

He looked up to see the stairs were golden. On either side of the stairs stood two huge columns, each topped with a statue of a lion. The stairs led up to a large double gate. The gate was closed. Sashin felt himself levitate as he took in the whole expanse of the stairs and columns. The lion statues were sat on all fours as if guardians of the gate. Everything seemed to be made of gold.

As he gradually pulled away from the scene, a beeping sound brought him back into a semi-conscious state. Everything was blank in his mind. He opened his eyes to a misty haze that filled the room. He blinked and found his view to be clear. Sashin looked over at his phone and saw that he had received a message.

The message was from Reshma, which read, 'How did you find the meditation videos?'

'Not a good start,' Sashin thought to himself. He felt tired from his meditative sleep and wanted nothing else but to get to bed.

After completing his evening ritual of brushing his teeth, washing his face and changing into night clothes, Sashin retired for the night in the comfort of his bed. He picked up his phone that he normally left on the bedside cabinet and replied to Reshma's text message.

Sashin: The videos were pretty good, but I ended up falling asleep during the meditation and had a really weird nightmare. Not a great start, to be honest.

Reshma: It would help if you didn't fall asleep during the meditation, Sashin. Try it again.

Sashin switched off his bedside lamp and closed his eyes. After several minutes of thoughts dancing through his mind, he drifted off into a deep sleep.

Walking down his staircase, he sensed that he was in a lucid dream. He made his way into his living room, conscious that the house was his own, the surroundings familiar, the same layout of black sofas, wooden flooring and white paint on the walls. As he walked to the centre of his living room, heading towards the kitchen, he caught a glimpse out of the corner of his eye. He turned to see someone sitting on his sofa. Sashin stood frozen as he acknowledged that the person in his living room was the robed man.

Lifting up his head gave Sashin a full view of the robed man's face in daylight. His face was hard to look at, almost disfigured, with a grey skin that was weathered. Sashin began to walk slowly backwards, stopping in his tracks as the man spoke.

"I searched the planes, endured so many wretched places looking for you, and then just like that, you appeared again. I sensed your presence and heard that there was someone appearing on the plane with a childlike wonder but little mastery. What I want to know is, how are you here walking between the plane and the physical world? I have asked myself this question many times – how is this possible? It infuriates me. Tell me Ahmenemat, what do you believe in? A god, a higher self, a divine being? Is this how you exist here, or are you some freak of effect, a result that should never have been?"

"You're calling me a freak, but what does that make you?" retorted Sashin.

Suddenly, an electronic chiming noise could be heard in the background, and Sashin moved his gaze towards the window. He realised the unrelenting noise was his alarm. He opened his eyes and found himself looking up at the ceiling. He felt like he had hardly slept. He got out of bed and sat for a few minutes trying to remember as much as he could from his dream.

It was all very vague. Sashin could hardly remember anything apart from walking down his stairs and entering the living room. He got up to go to the bathroom, mulling over the fragmented memories of his dream. He could picture his living room again, and now he could recall the man in the room, macabre looking. The dream seemed bizarre, and Sashin struggled to relate the events to anything that could have been lurking in the annals of his subconscious.

He dismissed the dream as one of those peculiar ones he had been having and continued on with his morning ritual of getting ready for work.

Chapter Three

Sashin had formed his consultancy with a fellow student from university after offering services to local businesses to support their studies. Two days a week would be spent in the office if necessary with a small team of consultants. On these days, the consultants would visit clients and could be out for most of the day if the client needed a local presence.

On his drive into the office, Sashin felt slightly more fatigued than normal, yawning whilst looking out of the window. Once at the office, Sashin discovered that one of the business consultants was attending a trade fair at the ExCel London, canvassing for new opportunities. He checked his emails first thing to see what potential activity to deal with for the day. There was a meeting at half past ten with a new client, Suzanne D'Costa, who worked for an American company that had set up a head office in the city. Sashin recalled that he had organised a meeting two weeks ago, but it had never materialised due to a clash of events. There was a feeling of butterflies in his stomach, like he used to experience when he attended interviews soon after graduating. He liked the slight feeling of nervousness when meeting new clients, as he felt that it kept him on his toes.

Whilst enjoying his ten o'clock coffee, Sashin looked at the clock on his desk phone that read '10:10'. He started to prepare for his meeting.

With all his papers organised together and his meeting structure finalised, he made his way to one of the few meeting rooms in the building that was nearest to the entrance of the office.

At twenty past ten, Suzanne was escorted to the meeting room by Dev, one of Sashin's three fellow consultants.

"Hi!" said Sashin enthusiastically while extending out his hand.

"Hello, so nice to meet you finally," responded Suzanne, her grip firm. There was a subtle aroma of cinnamon and citrus. Suzanne's hair was long and dark brown with highlights. She was taller than Sashin and wore a beige skirt suit. As she smiled, Sashin noticed the dimples on Suzanne's cheeks; he felt slightly overwhelmed by her presence as she exuded a strong demeanour and confidence.

Suzanne was heading up the launch of a new head office in the city for a travel club that she worked for and sought Sashin's services to help with the set up of the office. The meeting between them went on for an hour with various trips to the whiteboard as they both drew numerous boxes and diagrams to emphasise their trains of thought.

"So your main point of contact will be a lady called Alexis. She's done really well and has recently been promoted to Head of Network Marketing. Could I ask that you visit the office in the city to meet her?" suggested Suzanne.

"Yeah, sure thing," replied Sashin intrigued.

Sashin looked at his watch as Suzanne was getting ready to leave.

"That's odd," he said out loud with a somewhat bewildered look.

"What?" responded Suzanne inquisitively.

"Oh, the time; it's eleven eleven," replied Sashin.

"What are the chances of that eh, double digits?" chuckled Suzanne.

'A sarcastic one,' thought Sashin.

The remainder of the day moved slowly. With all tasks completed, Sashin left the office and headed home early afternoon, one of the perks of working on his own terms.

Back at home and with a mug of tea in hand, Sashin reflected on the dream experiences he'd had, trying to make sense of the jumbled up memories. He looked back over the messages that Reshma had sent him containing the various web and YouTube links.

'I need to make sense of what this astral travel is – there is so much information here. Astral travel, astral projection, what's the difference?' Sashin thought to himself as his right hand slowly rubbed his forehead.

Chapter Four

After looking through a number of websites, Sashin came across the site of a lady who had written a book on the subject of astral travel named Lindsay Meyer. She was an American author who had experiences with the so-called astral since she was seven years old.

The two terms, astral projection and astral travel, were explained right there on the screen. Sashin felt like it was a lucky coincidence to find exactly what he was looking for. He read eagerly, more engaged with the information.

Astral projection seemed to suggest an out-of-body experience in which consciousness could be projected out, whereas astral travel was an out-of-body experience where the astral body would leave the physical body and be free to travel the astral planes. Both terms seemed very similar in Sashin's mind.

'How is this related to me, my dreams, and my experiences? Maybe I have to learn to do this to control it,' thought Sashin.

After having read the information on Lindsay Meyer's website, he decided to order her book, 'A Guide to Astral Travel.' He felt somewhat relieved at having taken a step further to understand and decipher his experiences.

Continuing to click on the links Reshma had sent him, Sashin came across a video on a guided astral meditation. He took off his slippers and positioned himself comfortably in his chair. The voice of a softly-spoken woman prepared him through deep breathing for meditation. The meditation was based on visualising a place and taking in all the sights and sounds of the location chosen. The voice instructed him to focus on smells, colours, and sensations.

Sashin felt himself beginning to loosen up and become immersed. He pictured a market square in a village, several stalls lined up in the square, a baker, a clothes stall, a sweet stall, a spice stall, and one stall, which he focused on more than the others, one that surprised even him as to how it came up in his visualisation. It was a stall of spiritual items. He saw a poster similar to the one he had seen at Reshma's of the seven chakras. There was incense burning, a sweet woody scent filled the air. He saw crystals of various shapes, sizes and colours, an ankh ornament in silver, and wooden staffs, like the ones used in martial arts, leaning against the stall in a wicker basket.

Over in the background, Sashin saw a small arch bridge over a stream. It was a quaint village, and there was an air of serenity about the place.

Next the voice said, "Now push your mind out to this place and explore around – listen to what people are saying."

Sashin ventured forward over the bridge, but his visualisation was beginning to wane, and as he went over, the road seemed to dissolve and everything became white. He saw colours of blue, purple, and green. He tried to reform the image of the road, but it was not working. Sashin's breathing became shallower and soon, the colours were completely gone. All that was left was blackness. He began to open his eyes. Sashin felt lighter, relaxed and still. He got up to make himself something to eat, after which he resumed looking through the various videos on YouTube. He came across an astral projection guided meditation, which had astral hypnosis in the description.

"Let's give this one a try," said Sashin out loud.

He started the video and realised the meditation was one and a half hours long, so he looked up the video on his phone and made his way over to his bedroom, where he lay on his bed. Leaning over to his left, he pressed play on his phone, which sat on his bedside cabinet. As another softly spoken voice began the guided meditation, Sashin looked up at the ceiling, staring at the silver light shade that sparkled as the light shone off the mock diamonds that lined the frame.

He thought back to when he received the light shade for his last birthday from his parents, then rebuked himself for letting his mind wander and focused in again on the voice. He closed his eyes and let the voice guide his thoughts. Sashin was not sure at what point he no longer heard the voice, but it was replaced by a static noise. The sound now became an aeroplane engine taking off. It was loud, and he could feel an energetic buzz. Suddenly, he felt as if he was coming out of his body, like there was a separation beginning to occur. The incessant sound and sensation felt weird to Sashin. His heart pounded, and he began to panic. He felt himself snap back into his body, and the noise dissipated. Sashin tried to get back to the sound and sensation, but he could not. He opened his eyes and took a deep breath. "Woah," he whispered.

There was a feeling of adrenaline pumping, so Sashin got up, his body tingling all over. It was his first attempt at something like this and even though he felt frustrated at his fear of the sound and the sensation that followed, he was glad he got as far as he had. After gulping down a glass of water, Sashin thought it best to take a break by watching some television and then calling it a night. The meditation had made him very relaxed, but he was also tired.

Falling asleep didn't take long after Sashin recalled the attempts he had made at the guided meditations. Then, something began to happen. He felt like something was pressing down on his chest. Sashin felt paralysed and the pressure got heavier and heavier, and a streak of panic came over him again. Suddenly, the buzzing sound returned that quickly morphed into the aeroplane engine taking off.

Determined not to be scared this time, Sashin did not fight the pressing sensation; he could feel separation taking place again, like he was coming out of himself. He lifted out of his body, seeing the ceiling as he rose up, with his nose right up against it. Sashin turned his head from side to side to see the walls of his room. The feeling was incredible, but he was unable to move, and this caused Sashin to panic again. Another sensation began. It was something pulling him, as he rose up through the ceiling with great force. Sashin could see a tunnel of light, and his panic was getting more intense. He suddenly felt himself snap back into his body. Opening his eyes, he saw that he was in bed. Looking over at his bedside cabinet, his alarm clock read 4:44 am.

The following day, Sashin questioned whether the rising up to his ceiling was a dream or if it was actually real. He grappled with the idea; it was unbelievable. Thoughts raced through his head – could he recreate the experience or was it a one-off? The idea of being able to do it again excited him.

The phone pinged. It was a message alert from Suzanne.

Suzanne: Alexis is available for most of the day today. Are you able to come to the office?

For Sashin, it was a work from home day, so he was able to go into the city. The office for Dream Ventures was in London Bridge, half an hour on the Northern Line from Hendon Central. Leaving London Bridge station, the office was a ten minute walk away. Once there, he saw that it was a modern, open plan space in Southwark Bridge. As Sashin walked in, he was impressed by the high arched ceiling, spaced out sofas in the middle of the floor, and the airy feel. He thought, 'I'm curious why they asked me to help with the floorplan, this office looks well designed already.' Alexis sat on one of the sofas and got up to greet Sashin. To his surprise, he recognised her from the tube on his way back from his reading with Doreen Dorell. He felt himself getting a little flushed as he went to shake her hand.

"Hey, I saw you on the tube the other day," said Alexis energetically.

"Yes, you did," replied Sashin.

"You were smiling nervously," responded Alexis cheekily.

"Nervous smile, hmm, didn't feel like I was smiling nervously, just smiling," replied Sashin coyly.

"Okay, we'll sit here to discuss the plans," chuckled Alexis, pointing to one of the sofas.

"That's fine. Looks good to me," said Sashin.

Alexis went on to discuss the plan she had for launching the network marketing contingent of the company and had an idea of using one of the meeting rooms for holding presentations. She showed Sashin the meeting room. He stood there with his hand on his chin, looking contemplative.

"What is it?" asked Alexis.

"Well, I've been approached by many different companies over the years, from lotions, pills and potions, broadband to utilities. What is so different about your company? Tell me about your product," challenged Sashin emphatically.

"Sure, follow me." Alexis walked back over to the sofas and picked up some A4 leaflets from the table and handed them to Sashin.

"We are a travel club that offers curated holidays – these are deals that can't be beaten on price. It's subscription based and all the money from your subscription is paid back in travel, so you never lose out. Plus, you get perks as part of the travel membership, such as included transfers and lounge access. We're currently working on special packages for Peru, India, and Egypt," explained Alexis.

There was a sudden twinkle in Sashin's eye when he heard Egypt. "Sounds great," he said.

"There's a few travel clubs out there, but they only offer curated holidays on set dates, and their booking sites are not very good. We have curated holidays and a booking engine to allow you to book hotels, flights, Airbnbs, excursions, and experiences. We have formed relationships across the industry, and we own our own airline and hotels, so we're able to offer competitive pricing," explained Alexis.

"That's impressive. Tell me about your special packages to say, Egypt?" replied Sashin.

Alexis wore a white silk shirt and navy jean trousers, with white open-toed block sandals. She brought her left leg under her right leg and sat back comfortably before she started to speak. Her black hair was curly. Sashin was attracted to her. He remembered looking at the company brief that contained pictures of the employees as part of his research, which was where he had seen her even before meeting her on the train.

"The Egypt package is specially curated; it would be ten days covering Cairo, Giza Plateau, Luxor, Abydos, Esna, Aswan, and Sakara. You get private visits with our specially procured guides, something you don't normally get through other excursions," responded Alexis excitedly.

"Wow, that sounds great," said Sashin. "What I would recommend is that you don't hold the presentations for guests in the meeting room. It's too claustrophobic and formal. Hold your presentations right here in the main open area, which feels more inviting. Offer tea and coffee with pastries and biscuits.

You could even have pizzas, a 'pizza and presentation' evening if you will. That way, at least you get a free slice of pizza just for turning up. Have someone to meet and greet and set up the session, but don't have someone present the material. Instead, use a video presentation, so you literally press play. That way people at the meeting will feel that they can do the same, as you want this to be duplicatable," he added.

"Some good ideas there, Sashin. Getting our money's worth out of you," said Alexis while smiling.

After further conversation and looking over some of the leaflets and the floor plan, Sashin got up to go and turned to Alexis.

"Let's keep in touch to finalise the floor plan and presentation structure."

"I'd like that. Also, it doesn't all have to be about work. I'm new to the area, so I wouldn't mind having a guide of my own," replied Alexis.

"I'll take you up on that offer!" said Sashin enthusiastically.

He left the office feeling good about the meeting, but he still had a pressing feeling in the back of his mind about the floating up to the ceiling experience. He had to give it another go.

Chapter Five

The sensation of something pressing down had started again during the night, despite Sashin not being successful during the guided meditation before he went to sleep. The loud sound had erupted, the whirring of an aeroplane engine. He felt himself separating, coming up and out of his body. He saw the ceiling, but this time he was able to spin to his side. He moved forward and straight through the wall into the open. Floating by his window, Sashin looked down his street, feeling liberated, and in awe, proceeded to fly down his street. He saw one of his neighbours leave their house; he was wearing a blue jacket and walking towards his red SEAT car.

The feeling of liberation came to an end when Sashin felt the pulling like he had before; he was jolted away and through a portal of black. Within seconds, he was in unfamiliar territory, and back on his feet. It was a barren landscape with some trees in the distance. It was dark, and the field beneath Sashin's feet had a grey hue. Something felt strange about this place; the air was denser. There were bodies scattered ahead on the ground, black, motionless, and unidentifiable. Some were beginning to dissolve and fade. Sashin could see the particles rise and wither away; his awareness seemed more acute as he could see the detail of the particles rising up. Sounds were coming from behind him. Sashin looked back to see a number of figures moving towards him, some looked like people but grey in complexion, others were black figures, some with unclear features. A feeling of foreboding began growing inside him.

He began to pick up his pace, going from a brisk walk to a jog, but then the ground changed form, and looking down, Sashin found himself in a large puddle of a black, viscous substance. He struggled to move. He exerted all his effort to move quickly while the entities behind him were closing in.

"Come on, move!" he shouted.

The entities had caught up – one had the clear appearance of a person, another was faceless, and there were more approaching in the distance. The figure that looked like a person had the appearance of a corpse. It grabbed onto Sashin who flung his arm out to push the entity off. At that point, the faceless figure had latched on, and Sashin felt a sting, like an electric shock. He looked over to see he had a visible aura like a luminous mist. The entity was feeding on the aura. Waves of light were being sucked in from Sashin's astral body, through the aura and into the entity's mouth.

"Get off!" screamed Sashin as he lunged forward. He trudged through the pool of black liquid and could see solid ground ahead to his relief. He moved forward, lifting his heavy legs, feeling his energy wavering. Finally making it out of the viscous ground, he began to run. He began to feel depleted, but he pushed through the fatigue. Looking back, he saw more shadow beings gathering.

"Oh no," he said. He feared what would follow, so he picked up the pace and ran on.

'What is this place and how do I get out of here?' he thought.

Running up a small hill, Sashin saw a lake on the other side. He made his way down and ran parallel to the lake, his pace slowing down as the fatigue continued to take hold. The shadow figures approached. He was surrounded, and as the entities moved in, he attempted to will himself away. He started to levitate, but the shadow began to latch on, and then there was a snap.

Slowly coming around, Sashin felt himself back in his bed. He soon fell back to sleep.

The following morning even after eating his breakfast, a daily bowl of cereal, followed by a cup of tea, Sashin did not feel like himself. He felt groggy and fatigued. 'Did I manage to astral travel or was it a nightmare?' he thought. He was not as excited at the prospect of projecting now and felt he had to be able to control it better. He pondered what to do and then remembered what Doreen had said about calling her if he needed help. That's exactly what he planned to do later.

The doorbell rang. It was the delivery of the book 'A Guide to Astral Travel'. Sashin took the book with him to the office; his intention was to start reading it in bits to break up the working day.

As Sashin drove towards the office, he saw the red SEAT car from his astral experience and stopped his car. He parked up on the side and got out. He walked up to the neighbouring house and rang the doorbell. Admiring the charcoal coloured door and shiny knocker, he wondered if anyone was in. As the door opened, he heard a sound and saw a man standing behind it.

"Can I help you?" asked the man.

"Hi, I live up the road. I was just wondering if you popped out early in the morning?" replied Sashin.

"Why? Who wants to know?" replied the neighbour grumpily.

"It's just part of the neighbourhood watch – I saw someone from a distance and was just checking," explained Sashin.

"Yes, it was me. I had an early shift – don't check on me again!" barked the neighbour closing the door emphatically.

With that, Sashin swiftly turned and left.

‘It was real. Wow, I was actually travelling,’ he thought.

At the office, the full team was in. A box of Krispy Kreme doughnuts adorned one of the worktops, alluring Sashin over with its sugary scent. ‘Maybe later,’ he thought as he settled down to work.

There were times when the team had a chance to talk a lot more in the office, but as the market had picked up, each of them had increasing portfolios of work which meant they did not get to converse as much on the more trivial elements which resulted in less office banter. Sashin thought it was time to organise a social event. He added this to his to-do list. As the day progressed, he felt a little burnt out and decided to go for a walk to get some fresh air. It was mild outside. Sashin unbuttoned his jacket and took out his mobile phone. He dialled Doreen Dorell’s number. After a few rings came a response.

“Hello,” she said.

“Hi Doreen; it’s Sashin here.”

“Oh, hello, Sashin. Nice to hear from you. How are things going?” replied Doreen.

“I have had more experiences. I think I might have had a nightmare last night, but I can't be sure. I was in a dark place and was attacked by these shadow people,” explained Sashin, concerned.

“I’ll tell you what. Video call me tonight and we can talk about it, free of charge. I have some client sessions this afternoon. Speak later, after five,” said Doreen.

“Speak later,” replied Sashin, wanting to get it all off his chest.

Back at the office, Sashin walked up to Dev and Krish, who sat near each other. Dev was Sashin’s university friend, with whom he started consulting part-time to fund their study. Krish was brought into the team soon after they formally set up the consultancy. With an excited look on his face, Sashin put his hands on the desk and addressed them both.

"Lads..." But before he could finish, Dev said, "What's up with you Sash? You're on a high today."

"I feel like crap actually, but look, we've all been busy lately, and I know there hasn't been a lot of banter in the office. How about a night out?" replied Sashin.

"Funny you should mention it. I was just saying to Dev how it's been ages since we went out. Partners or no partners?" asked Krish.

"I don't mind. We can either relive the nights out like we used to have or we can get everyone out. Either way is fine," replied Sashin cheekily.

"Let's get partners out – it would be nice for us all to be out," said Dev.

"Fine, that's settled then. When's good?" asked Sashin.

"Put something in for next Friday," replied Krish.

"Cool, I think I'll celebrate with a Krispy Kreme," said Sashin.

"You're welcome," replied Dev.

Sashin got home that evening at six-fifteen. He had messaged Doreen before he left the office to say he would call her when he got home.

He went through the parts of Lindsay Meyer's book, 'A Guide to Astral Travel,' that he had read and started to highlight sections. Keeping the information fresh in his mind made him feel a bit more prepared for the call with Doreen. So far the book had corroborated what Doreen had said about there being negative entities on the astral plane, and about overcoming fear and being prepared when projecting. The book also talked about different times to astral travel, saying that before sleep was a good time but that one could also travel during the day.

Emotional control was important when embarking on a projection, as fear could attract negative entities that fed on the vulnerable.

Unsure what type of mobile phone Doreen had, Sashin made a WhatsApp video call. Doreen answered and was sitting at her desk in what seemed like a home office.

"Hi Sashin – so, what's been happening?"

"As I briefly mentioned earlier today, I had a nightmare experience in which I was in a very eerie place and I was being chased by these things, some like people and some not so human. I also saw these shadow entities that I saw before when I encountered this hooded man with serious evil vibes. He called me by a name, 'Ahmenemat'. I also managed to project myself out of my body the other day and floated up to my ceiling," said Sashin, reeling off his thoughts.

Doreen paused and shared, "I mentioned to you before that there are good and bad entities out there when you astral travel. It seems like you have an entity that is drawn to you, some connection with a previous life maybe. That name the man called you by sounds Egyptian. I was certainly picking up on Egypt when I saw you, love. It's great that you managed to project, but I did say you had this ability. It was like you were born with this ability – it's a gift. The question is why this being is pulling you in when you travel. What does he want? Does he want to harm you or not? So you need to find out more. Also, there are different levels; it sounds like you were pulled to a lower astral plane where many negative entities reside, typically lost souls that are unable to move on. You want to aim to reach the higher levels. Don't be scared though, because if you travel in fear, then the experience will be a living hell. I don't mean to scare you, but it's important that you protect yourself."

"How do I do that?" said Sashin.

With a stern look on her face, Doreen answered, "By raising your frequency."

"My what? How would I go about doing that?" responded Sashin, confused.

"By meditating more, clearing your mind, and doing things like chakra balancing. You can find loads of stuff online like on YouTube for how to do this. If every time you astral travel you encounter this being, then you will need to face him at some point or another. And when you do, you will need to be prepared; otherwise, it could leave you drained. Raising your frequency, or some say vibration, will ensure you are better protected because the lower vibrational beings won't be able to get to you," said Doreen.

"I have a book called 'A Guide to Astral Travel' that I've started reading," said Sashin.

"Read the book, no harm in that. It will give you some answers, but it won't give you all of them," replied Doreen.

Sashin held up his hands in an 'I'm not sure what now' manner and put his hands behind his head.

"It looks like I'm going to have to look into my past life, as absurd as that sounds."

"Well, I hope it all works out for you, Sashin. Don't forget you can call for help you know. Ask the higher beings, angels, whoever you believe in for help, for protection," offered Doreen before she ended the call.

Sashin sat back and felt a little lost. The mystery was why the being he encountered was drawn to him. What was the connection? Why was he so intent on tracking him down, and what did he mean when he said, "I wondered what had become of you?"

An idea emerged in Sashin's mind, one that he had initially reacted negatively to when it was suggested to him:

past life regression. He thought it would be something that he would have to succumb to despite his reluctance. He would have to call Reshma and admit defeat as she gloated. She loved this kind of stuff.

Chapter Six

By the time he got ready for bed, Sashin felt burnt out and not his optimal self. He did not want to do any kind of guided meditation or astral projection, for that matter. A good rest is what he felt he needed to recharge.

Feeling a little restless, Sashin turned on his side and then on his back. He opened his eyes and looked over at his bedside alarm clock to see it was 2.45am. He closed his eyes again and tried to clear his mind so that he could fall back to sleep. Sashin suddenly felt a tingling sensation throughout his body, and he could see his room. Then came the high-pitched sound. Sashin felt himself slowly being pulled out of his body. He began to panic.

'No, no,' he thought.

The notion of travelling now terrified him as he was feeling slightly weak. He felt like he was choking, so he started to concentrate on his nose and started breathing through it, which caused the pulling sensation to intensify. Sashin resisted, and he then felt himself merging back. The tugging started again, something was pulling him out. For several minutes, a tug of war took place, and Sashin rolled onto his side to prevent separation. However, this caused him to fly out of his body instantly and off the side of the bed; it was like a sensation of free-falling, which invoked panic as his astral body fell through the floor.

Appearing in his living room, Sashin forced himself to stop as he did not find the idea of flying through the ground appealing. Now standing up, he flew out of his house and onto the street outside. He could sense something, a distant presence pulling at him, and he could not shake the sensation. He then had an idea. 'What if I could go to someone's house?'

He thought about Reshma's house and imagined the front door. With a sudden whoosh, he stood in front of Reshma's house.

'Woah, that's new,' he thought.

Looking at the white door, Sashin proceeded through it. Once inside, he made his way up the stairs and through the bedroom door. There asleep were Reshma and Ketan. Reshma's body was lit up as if a bright, shiny light was sitting inside her body. For Ketan, his body was very faint. Sashin was able to see Reshma's astral body; it was as if he had X-ray vision. Her astral body was wiggling inside her physical one, and it then turned and stared at Sashin. Surprised by this, he started to float around the room and he saw Reshma watching him. He then floated above her and reached out his hand to touch her astral body; there was a jolt of energy, and she shrank back from the touch. Sashin thought it best to leave her alone and floated out of the room and downstairs. Once downstairs, he went into the kitchen and saw on the fridge a small whiteboard that Reshma and Ketan used for reminders and as a to-do list. One of the reminders was for an MOT on Wednesday. He mentally made a note. As he made his way out of the kitchen, the pulling sensation had returned, and Sashin made his way outside. Once outside, he was pulled back like a jolt, and flew through a black tunnel and appeared on a city road. He looked around and could see shops on either side and people walking about.

Sashin walked along the road. It was busy, with many people passing by. Various shops, restaurants, and bars were strewn alongside the road. The road carried on into the distance and could be seen rising up into the sky. The sky in the distance flashed with colours and images, like a gigantic cinema screen.

Sashin stopped a man wearing a navy suit; he had glasses on and looked like he was in a hurry.

"Excuse me, do you know where this road leads?" asked Sashin.

"It takes you to the higher plane," replied the suited man, scurrying off.

Sashin noticed that objects looked different, more vibrant, and the colours were sharper. He looked at a restaurant, 'The Curious Parlour'; the door to which was a deep burgundy. Its glass window had a goldish aura. Looking at a lamppost, Sashin could see all the sides of it at once. It took a bit of getting used to, and he blinked several times to try to revert back to three-dimensional sight. He then shook his head rapidly from side to side. This seemed to work as his sight was back to normal, but if he concentrated hard enough on an object, he could see it in the fourth dimension.

Leading off from the pavement were side lanes, also with small shops and pubs. Sashin walked towards one to explore, and he spotted a lady who looked confused. A man leaned against the wall further down the lane, in between a pub and shop. Sashin faintly heard the lady say she was lost. The man ventured over to her, with a smirk on his face, and he put his arm around her. Next, the man proceeded to bite the lady on the neck, and light emanated from her neck as she screamed. Sashin was about to run over, but a hand grabbed his shoulder. He turned to see a large woman with a green jacket on and ginger, frilly hair.

"Energy vampires are very dangerous – you'd be wise to stay away. Britt's the name," she said.

"I'm Sashin. Nice to meet you. Is that lady going to be okay?"

"Not really, not here anyway. People like that who come here are easy prey," she replied.

"What is this place?" asked Sashin.

"These are intersections between the levels. This main road will lead up to the next level, so you get all sorts around here," explained Britt.

Pointing up towards the sky, Sashin asked, "What are those images?"

"Amazing yet bizarre, right? Images of things that have happened to people, like snippets of their lives," replied Britt.

"Where are they coming from?" asked Sashin.

"The Akasha, I think," replied Britt.

"I'm going to take a look," said Sashin.

"Enjoy," chuckled Britt.

Feeling apprehensive after having seen a predatory energy vampire, Sashin proceeded with caution, eyeing up all the people passing by. He walked further up the road until the line of shops and pubs stopped and there was just pavement. He briskly walked on until he was close to the flashing images above. The images of a family playing in a garden adorned the sky, a couple with a boy and a girl playing, and a close up of the mother's face showed some sorrow in her eyes. This image was quickly replaced by a man climbing a mountain with a look of determination on his face, at which point the image dissipated, leaving the night sky. He noticed this section of the road was not as busy, with few people journeying up to the next astral plane. Sashin made his way back to the hub of activity from where he came.

The notion of venturing down a side alley stuck in Sashin's head. The curiosity was burgeoning. 'As long as I don't look lost, I should be alright,' he thought. He stood on the spot, toying with the idea. Looking down the side lane, he could not see any predators waiting, leaning against a wall. He walked down, looking ahead and behind him. There were some quaint shops down the lanes, a sweet shop, and an antiques shop with various ornaments and objects of curiosity. These lanes reminded him of Brighton. He turned left and ventured further in. Ahead was a pub called 'The Lane Side.' Sashin had an urge to go in, curious what an astral beer would taste like.

Passing by the window, he saw that it was busy inside. Approaching the door, he saw a doorman standing on the other side. Sashin paused for a few seconds to see if the door would be opened, which it was not, so he pushed it open and walked in, looking at the doorman as he entered. The doorman wore a long black coat. His complexion was pale, he had short brown hair, and his stare was intense. Sashin noticed that both eyes did not look identical; one was static while the other moved. This led him to deduce that one was a glass eye.

Inside the pub, it was quite the spectacle, like a museum of the weird, wonderful, and bizarre. A gold pillar stood next to the door slightly shorter than Sashin, on top of which sat a Ganesh statue. In the corner to his right was an altar with a miniature totem pole in the middle and two Native American statues at either side. An antique French-style oval mirror hung on the wall to the left with an ornate gold frame. Further along to the left was another altar with a statue of Jesus on the right and a shaman on the left wearing Peruvian clothing and a headdress.

Following the room around in awe from left to right, Sashin saw the door to the toilets, which had serpents on either side facing each other and a dragon's head on top, like a gargoyle head statue. The colours of the walls were vivid with burgundy and gold. On one end of the pub sat an upper body statue of an angel with its hands in the air. To the right were three portraits on the wall. One was of an older lady with white hair and a rose in her hair, wearing clothes of the nineteen twenties era with a silver necklace and pearl earrings. She had a subtle smile. In the middle was the portrait of a man who looked like he was in his thirties wearing a dark brown jacket with dark brown hair and a sedate expression. His eyes gave a piercing stare. To the left of this portrait was that of a child, a young boy wearing a white shirt with green tipped collars and sleeves, smiling while holding a flute. The gaze was also piercing, and after looking at both paintings again, it was apparent that this was the boy that became the man to the right. Various shields also littered the walls with different insignias. In the far right corner sat the statue of a meditating monk with circles of colour along the front of his body. 'The chakras,' thought Sashin.

There was a selection of beers on tap, and Sashin immediately honed in on the 'Land Side Brew'. The bartender had just finished serving cocktails to a woman seated at the bar with her partner, who was sitting next to her. The bartender gave Sashin a glance, smiled and walked over.

"I'll try your Land Side Brew," he said.

"It's a good one," she replied, flicking her long black dreadlocked hair to the side as she pulled on the beer tap.

It was then that Sashin started to feel a little anxious. 'How do I pay for this?' he thought. He checked his pockets, but there was nothing in them. The bartender passed over the freshly poured pint and stood there staring.

"How do you pay here?" he asked.

With a look of amusement on her face, she replied. "Money or valuables. If you don't have money, you can leave something valuable behind to add to the collection," came her reply as she pointed around. "Or you can pay with your life." The bartender started to laugh. "The look on your face. This one's on the house handsome, but only this once."

Sashin breathed a sigh of relief, "Cheers."

He took a gulp and held up the pint to look at the liquid inside, which looked golden and bubbly, just like in the real world. The taste was peculiar at first, quite hoppy, but then settled to a familiar lager finish. By the window that Sashin had passed on the way in sat a young woman who was in conversation with a man. Two figures appeared, walking past and stopping outside the window looking in. They wore red gowns with yellow lapels and a yellow cloth belt. On their heads were red hats, like crowns with gold borders. They looked like Tibetan monks. One held a cream coloured mala with red tassels on either end. Both stared intently through the window. The woman sat by the window quickly got up and, grabbing the man's hand, ushered him out of the door rapidly. Whoever these people were, they had spooked the woman. The monk holding the mala lifted up his arm to point, and Sashin felt he was pointing directly at him.

An air of panic ensued in the pub as people started leaving after spotting the two figures outside. It dawned upon Sashin that he was drawn to this place, pulled to it. The last time that happened, he ended up in the dark, eerie field. This meant he had been tracked down, found, and brought here.

"Is there another way out?" Sashin asked the bartender.

"Fire exit at the back," replied the bartender, pointing.

Sashin raced over to the fire exit and pushed hard on the door. He was still weak from the previous encounter in the hellish landscape, and as much as he had found this astral plane intriguing, he was not keen on another encounter with negative beings.

Once outside, Sashin made his way to the right and saw a turning into another lane on his left. There was a sudden sound of a howling wind. Sashin turned around to see the doorman blown to the ground, sliding back by a gale force wind.

The two monk-looking figures appeared and walked over to the doorman and now faced Sashin. He swiftly made his way down the lane ahead, frantically looking into shop windows and through to the other side to see if there were further side exits. 'I have to get back to the main road,' he thought.

There was a lane exit ahead, but two more monks appeared walking in his direction, blocking the exit. Sashin looked around quickly, and he was startled to see the robed man in the air. Without thinking, he dashed into the bookshop on his left and ran through, causing people in the shop to flinch and look over.

"Is there another way out?!" he shouted. The girl behind the counter just nodded her head from side to side, indicating an emphatic "no."

Sashin quickly turned around to see a clothes store opposite. He could make out that a delivery was being brought in through double side doors, and he made the sprint.

Flying out of the bookstore, Sashin's momentum was halted by people walking into the clothes shop.

Descending from above, Sashin saw the robed man landing a few metres in front of him.

"Ahmenemat, you cannot keep evading me," he said.

"Who are you? What do you want? Why do you keep chasing me?" replied Sashin sternly.

"Maybe it is best if you do not remember. I am Bakenkhons; this name may not mean anything to you now? But it will," replied Bakenkhons.

Sashin went to open the door to the clothes shop quickly, but it was locked. The shop owner stood terrified behind the door, turning over the door sign to 'Closed.'

With nowhere to go, the monks stood ahead and behind Sashin. Bakenkhons launched his arm forward and into

Sashin's chest – it went straight through as if his body was more liquid than solid matter. The pain was excruciating, causing Sashin's whole nervous system to come alive.

"Cut his chord while he weakens!" yelled Bakenkhons.

A monk in front produced a dagger from under his robe, chanting while rubbing his mala over the blade. Sashin focused on the blade for a second and went into fourth dimensional vision – he could see the particles in the blade begin to fizz and grow tighter together, denser while the blade turned from silver to charcoal in colour.

Sashin grabbed onto Bakenkhons' arm tightly and pulled hard, but with the pain pulsating through his entire body, he struggled to sustain his grip. 'I can't take this,' he thought. He tightened his grip again and willed the arm of malevolence out. Sashin's arm began to heat up, which intensified, growing from a dull warmth to pulsating heat. His arm started to vibrate, Bakenkhons' eyes widened, and he withdrew his arm as if wounded.

Sashin flew up immediately but Bakenkhons grabbed hold of his leg. Sashin pulled himself up with the flailing strength he had left, taking Bakenkhons up with him. Bending over whilst in the air, he grabbed hold of Bakenkhons' wrist with his vibrating arm, which made him flinch and let go. Sashin flew off into the air and straight into the hanging sign for the clothes shop that slid off its hinge, crashing to the floor. Bakenkhons dropped down onto the two monks that stood in front. Trying to re-orient himself, Sashin flew straight ahead and saw the main road. He looked intently towards the fading flashing images in the sky and flew forward at speed.

"You cannot run!" snarled Bakenkhons, flying behind.

As Sashin grew closer to the ascending road, he was engulfed by a strong gust of wind. He spun round to see the monks in the background chanting while holding their mala; they stopped where they stood, and Bakenkhons too stayed stationary.

"They're not coming any further," murmured Sashin. He tried to fight the gale, but it was like flying in a storm. He persisted and tried to fly on, but his energy was rapidly depleting. It felt like adrenaline was the only thing keeping him in the air. His astral body was weakening as he began to fall back. Free falling through the air, the sensation caused Sashin's physical body to have a hypnagogic jerk, which snapped him back into his physical body.

Chapter Seven

It was Saturday morning. Sashin opened his eyes. His throat felt sore, and his body ached as if he had the onset of a cold. He felt down; the astral experiences had begun to take their toll on him. It seemed like Bakenkhons was intent on harming him in the astral realm and now he felt this in his physical body. He ruminated about his most recent encounter, feeling a little despair. 'How long could this go on? How can something that happens when I'm asleep affect me in the waking world? I can't live in fear every time I close my eyes,' he thought.

Being the optimist that he was, he was thankful that he managed to escape. Getting out of bed, he sat there for a few minutes with his eyes closed and began to breathe deeply, going into a short meditation. He had not told anyone about his experiences apart from Doreen, and he thought that it was time he told Reshma.

Whilst eating breakfast, Sashin continued to read through 'A Guide to Astral Travel', but he found it difficult as he felt depleted, and this took away the enjoyment of being fully engaged with the content. He had covered the basics, projecting was coming fairly easy without having to do too much preparation; it was more control over his emotions and over the astral environment. There was still a quarter of the one hundred and forty-six pages to finish. He would do that later, after he felt better.

Normally on a Saturday, Sashin would spend the latter part of the morning cleaning his two-bedroom house, hoovering and dusting, the pinnacle of his domesticity. Some afternoons would be spent pottering around Brent Cross shopping centre, and on other afternoons he would get unfinished work out of the way, logging on to his laptop for a few hours. This afternoon he did not feel up to doing anything apart from lying down and switching off. Sashin's parents had invited him over for dinner, he got the invite from his dad via WhatsApp during the week.

His mobile phone rang, he picked it up and looked at the screen with a look of despondency on his face. It was his mum. 'Better get this,' he thought.

"Hi Mum," he said.

"You don't sound at all well, Sashin. You got the invite for dinner, right, from your dad?" replied Sashin's mum.

"Yes Mum, six o'clock right?" responded Sashin.

"Come earlier, *beta*; if you don't feel well, I'll give you some Indian medicine," said Sashin's mum affectionately.

"Yes, I don't feel well. i'll come over in a couple of hours after I've had a lie down," replied Sashin.

"I will tell Reshma to come early too, okay," said Sashin's mum as she ended the call.

Still lying there, wondering how he was going to muster up the strength to make it over to his parents' house, he had a thought of trying a healing meditation from the various links that Reshma had sent him. Trawling through video after video, there was one that caught his eye, a chakra tune-up meditation. He pressed on play and followed it through to find it required him to chant sounds, these were "uh, ew, oh, ah, eye, aa" and "ee" while different frequencies played in the background.

Sashin felt a little self-conscious chanting the sounds but found it a powerful meditation during which he had a feeling of déjà vu. A vision of sitting in front of someone and chanting sounds of this nature came into his head, which felt familiar. The thought soon dissipated. Closing his eyes, Sashin took a light nap. He heard the sounds of the street outside, a passing car, the sounds of people walking past, a child shouting, and then it all went quiet.

There was a trail. Looking down, Sashin could see a grey path leading all the way into the distance. He turned to look behind and saw some people on the trail. On either side of the trail were barren grasslands, and a mountain range could be seen in the distance. The sky was blue with few clouds. It was pleasant, the air fresh but thin, and it felt like this was high ground.

A few minutes of walking led to a line of different coloured flags on the floor, tied to rope that was fixed to the ground with metal poles that had rusted. The flags wavered in the wind. There in the distance stood a large majestic mountain covered in snow. Continuing on the trail, rocks could now be seen littered ahead. Sashin started to feel dizzy and sat on a large rock nearby. After taking some deep breaths as he still felt weak, he took in the surroundings.

'Is this a dream or am I actually astral travelling? I've never projected during the day before,' he thought.

Feeling drowsy as he sat relaxed, his eyes began to close. The sound of a car honking outside brought him back to a waking state. Sashin looked at his watch, which read three twenty-five. He got up slowly, feeling marginally better. His phone rang; it was Reshma.

"What time are you going to Mum and Dad's?" she asked.

"Leaving in a bit, just about to freshen up and head out. I haven't been feeling well, so I took a nap," replied Sashin.

"Oh no, what's up?" said Reshma.

"I'll tell you about it when I see you later," responded Sashin.

"Okay, hope you're alright," said Reshma, concerned.

Whilst getting changed out of lounge wear and into a pair of jeans and a sweatshirt, Sashin remembered that the night out he suggested with his team and their partners was less than a week away, and even though everyone had agreed on a date, nothing was actually planned as to where they were going or what they were going to do. This echoed in the back of his mind as he left the house.

Driving through London on a Saturday afternoon was busy to say the least. The journey should have taken ten to fifteen minutes, but not today. It felt as though a collective of drivers had conspired against Sashin, as if a public post had gone out on social media declaring 'Make sure Sashin does not reach his parents' house on time.'

'Can this traffic go any slower?' thought Sashin frustrated.

By the time Sashin arrived at Holders Hill Drive, it was just past four-thirty. After ringing the doorbell, it was opened by Sashin's mum, Ushma. She had a black bob hairstyle and was slightly shorter than Sashin.

"Hello *beta*. How are you feeling?" she asked.

"Not well at all Mum," replied Sashin, taking off his trainers.

"Come and rest, I'll give you something to help you," said Ushma.

Sashin paused for a moment as he stood by the stairs, looking down the hallway. He smiled, he had many memories of this house growing up.

In the living room, Reshma was already sitting down watching television. She looked up.

"What's up with you? You look a state," she remarked.

"Not well," replied Sashin as he crashed down on a long black sofa, landing on his back.

"Dad is out getting some bits, I asked him to get garlic naan on the way. Anyway, what happened?" asked Reshma.

"Oh good. But first of all, have you got an MOT on Wednesday?" asked Sashin.

"Yes, how do you know?" replied Reshma.

"I saw it on your fridge," responded Sashin.

"What d'ya mean you saw it on my fridge?" asked Reshma.

"Well, I was in your house, I travelled there astrally," replied Sashin.

"What?!" yelled Reshma.

Sashin continued, "Keep it down. I don't want Mum to know as she'll only get worried – just keep this between us. The only other person I've told is that psychic, Doreen."

"What's it like?" asked Reshma.

"Actually getting the hang of it, it has been an amazing experience. I flew over to your house, and I saw you and Ketan sleeping. I saw your astral body, which was glowing inside you," explained Sashin.

"That's incredible!" replied Reshma.

"It's funny you should say, because a few days ago I had a weird sensation when I was sleeping."

"That was me," said Sashin.

"Mind blowing!" gasped Reshma.

"There's this person I saw in what I thought was a dream a while back, a robed man. He calls himself Bakenkhons. I think he may have some kind of history with me, some connection. He's a negative entity. He's been pulling me out towards him when I go astral, and he's set on harming me," explained Sashin.

"Oh no," replied Reshma.

"Last night I was pulled into this place, which was like here, like our normal world. It was a city like Brighton, but it had a road passing through that led to a higher astral plane. People pass through it, and there's shops and places to eat and drink. He was there with these Tibetan looking monks, evil ones, and he stuck his arm in me. It was really painful. Then he said something about cutting my cord. I woke up feeling really ill, and I think he did something to me," shared Sashin.

"This sounds very serious, Sash. I mean, if he can affect you when you're asleep dreaming."

"When I'm astral," interrupted Sashin.

Looking at Sashin sarcastically, Reshma continued.

"When you're astral, then this is dangerous."

"Do me a favour? I left a book in the car on the passenger seat. Bring it in – I've been reading it to get some info," asked Sashin, pulling out his car keys from his jeans pocket.

Taking them, Reshma looked at Sashin sympathetically.

"You relax," she said with residual sarcasm.

Returning with the book, Reshma flung the car keys to Sashin. She eyed the pages.

"I've read most of it. I just got about a quarter left," said Sashin.

The door opened and in walked their dad, Satish.

"Hi guys, I got your naan."

"Thanks Dad," responded Reshma without turning to acknowledge him, engrossed in the book.

"A Guide to Astral Travel" by Lindsay Meyer. Well done on doing your own research!" said Reshma excitedly.

Ushma walked over with a mug in her hand, which she gave to Sashin.

"Drink this – it will help you. Then we can eat."

"What is it?" asked Sashin.

"Just drink it – it's *Jivan Sanjivani*, the best Indian medicine for a cold," replied his mum.

Sashin took a sip.

"Ew, it's vile!" he complained.

Reshma started giggling. "Drink it! It's proper Indian medicine. Hurry up so we can eat."

Reshma then lowered her voice and continued, "After that we can continue this conversation because this is serious shit!"

Sashin looked shocked, he rarely heard Reshma swear.

It felt good to be sharing this with someone else, especially a loved one. He had felt alone when he had woken up in the morning but opening up to Reshma felt cathartic.

Chapter Eight

At the dinner table, his father Satish gave them an update on the Polish convenience store he had sold, one of several that he had once owned and run.

"Ambrozy, the manager moved everything around. Can you believe it? I told him I spent a long time working out the best way to organise the products for the shopping experience. He just changed it, bloody idiot!" he snapped.

"Dad, you don't own the store anymore. Let Ambrozy do what he wants," replied Reshma.

"Sashin, you don't look well. Eat, man," said Satish.

"Yeah, I'm not feeling great and am not that hungry," replied Sashin.

"Eat what you can, especially the naan, as I got it for you. Then you can sleep here, and just lie on the sofa and rest," said Satish.

"Yeah Sash, get some rest; it's not like you have anyone to go back to," said Reshma with her head to one side, eyes wide open, smiling.

"Sashin, don't you think it's time you settled down? I want a nice daughter-in-law," said Ushma.

Reshma looked down, giggling.

"Not now guys. I haven't got the energy," replied Sashin.

"Have a whisky after your meal," said Satish.

"Actually, I'll make a hot toddy. It'll taste better than *Sanjivani*," said Sashin.

"Oi, but *Sanjivani* is the best medicine," scolded Ushma.

"What whisky have you got, Dad?" asked Sashin.

"I have run out of Balvenie, but I have Chivas," replied Satish.

"Chivas is fine for a hot toddy," remarked Sashin.

After dinner, Sashin made himself a hot toddy. He asked his mum for a lemon slice, some cloves, and a cinnamon stick, which he topped off with a spoon of honey, drizzling it over the whisky. Finally adding the hot water, he stirred and took a sip.

"Mmm, nice."

"I'm having a private conversation with Sash. You two stay in the kitchen and put the TV on," said Reshma.

"I hope you're talking about a girl," replied Ushma.

Back on the sofa, Sashin pulled out the blanket that was stored under the side storage seat, the same blanket that had been there for years. He made himself comfortable as he lay down.

Reshma sat on a recliner, scanning through the book. She spoke aloud as she flicked through the pages.

"The astral planes."

"I've been to the lower plane and a higher one, which is like the real World. Bakenkhons pulled me to the lower plane, not a nice place," replied Sashin.

"Oh, there's a bit here about the astral cord. There's two reasons you wouldn't get back into your body. If something severs your cord, only something really powerful can do this and is able to get past your spirit guides. The other is if something kills your physical body," said Reshma.

"Well, I would consider Bakenkhons really powerful, with a major grudge," replied Sashin.

Reshma continued. "Let's see, there's a section here on protecting yourself, right near the end. Listen. You can call for help when you are in trouble, astral guardians like archangels or spirit guides."

"Doreen said something similar," responded Sashin.

"You can't be scared every time you go to sleep. Otherwise it's going to be a nightmare on astral street," said Reshma.

"I know I need to control it better. I've found out things I can do randomly, but I just need a better understanding," replied Sashin.

"You're going to have to face this negative being and face your fears. Seeing you like this worries me," said Reshma.

"I will once I'm better. I don't think I would make it if I faced him in this state," said Sashin wearily as he began to close his eyes.

"Don't say that! Stay positive," replied Reshma.

Reshma put the book on the coffee table near Sashin and picked up the empty tumbler, she could smell the whisky and cinnamon from the glass. She walked into the kitchen, where her mum and dad sat watching television.

"You can go inside now if you want – Sash is asleep," she said.

"It's fine, let him sleep," replied Ushma.

"Right, I'm gonna go. Thanks for dinner. I'll phone you during the week," said Reshma.

With her arms open, Ushma gave Reshma a hug. "Okay thanks for coming, see you soon."

"See you soon, love," said Satish, giving Reshma a hug too.

Walking past the living room on her way out, she glanced over at Sashin with a concerned look on her face. She would do what she could to help him with all that she had learnt over the years, in whatever small way.

Checking to see Reshma had gone, he closed his eyes, relieved to be getting some rest. There was darkness and then some ambient light as Sashin began to open his eyes, squinting to see as his vision was blurry. The sight of familiar trees made him anxious. He lifted up his head and saw the barren landscape, dark and desolate. He got up by pushing his right arm against the ground. He felt heavy but began to walk. There was the familiar grey hue on the ground. Sashin lifted up his hand and looked at it, but his aura was not glowing or as bright as before. It was a dark grey mist.

'I can will myself out of here like I did last time outside my house and teleport myself away. I don't need to be here,' he thought. So he closed his eyes and thought of his parents' living room. He thought hard, even clenching his fists.

'Come on. Go back, go back,' he chanted in his mind.

He opened his eyes. He was still there. He closed his eyes again and tried once more, but still nothing. He opened his eyes, looking ahead, knowing he was desperate.

'Help!' he thought.

Chapter Nine

Walking became difficult as Sashin breathed in the dense air, and his legs felt heavy. In the distance, he could see figures. Two hovering figures came into clearer view; it was the shadow wraiths. Behind them was the robed Bakenkhons, with a monk on either side of him.

Sashin turned around and saw the entities approaching, the grey and the black faceless beings. It was an ambush.

"You are too weak Ahmenemat; there is nowhere to run!" shouted Bakenkhons.

Sashin attempted to run, turning to his right and pushing himself to move as fast as he could. It felt like he was in the throes of a marathon as he began to pant, his legs aching.

The sound of a horn filled the air; it made Sashin stand still and look around to see where it was coming from. Bakenkhons and his entourage stopped in their tracks. Sashin tried to work out where he had heard that sound before. The horn sounded again, but this time, a curtain of fire raged across in front of him. And with a crackle, flames shot up and across behind him. A path of fire was created.

Sashin looked over to see Bakenkhons with his arms up, covering his face from the heat. The monks did the same, and the shadow wraiths fled.

Ahead, Sashin could see colour. There, at the end of the path of fire he saw an opening, a portal. He made his way towards it, turning around and walking backwards at one point to see what Bakenkhons was doing. The fire kept him and his monks at bay, as well as the dead beings on the other side. The warmth from the fire felt somewhat soothing, and he took this sensation and used it to push forward. At the entrance to the portal, Sashin saw an archway on the other side with lines of flags on ropes all connecting up to the archway. These were like the flags Sashin had seen earlier in the day.

Sashin stepped through, into the light of day out of the darkness. A green carpet with many flags on either side, all tied to ropes, was laid out on the path. There must have been twenty-two ropes, all adorned with flags. The air was light and the sky blue, a refreshing change of environment. He quickly turned around to see that the portal had vanished; it was gone in an instant.

The archway had a small base with steps. Two white stone pillars supported a slab of red stone, topped with smaller white stone slabs, upon which stood a red cylindrical stone crowned with a gold spire. Walking through the arch, Sashin brushed against some hanging bunting tied to a wooden handle, which rang the bell it was attached to. As he stepped out, he saw a snow-covered mountain a few hundred metres in front of him.

The ground ascended up on his right, covered in very short grass, and on the left, the ground was flat. The path rose up to a gradient, and Sashin took deep breaths as he walked up. The path was now dusty and rocky. A herd of yaks could be seen up ahead on the flat ground grazing.

Approaching the mountain, Sashin stood for a moment and took in the view. Looking up, he saw snow glistening at its peak. He walked around the base and saw a smaller path leading down; he followed it and saw an opening. The opening led to an inner sanctum within the mountain, which was huge, and there were steps ahead of brown stone. At the top of the stairs, the light from a fire created a giant shadow on the wall. Sashin proceeded cautiously, slowing down his pace as he neared the top.

A fire burned and a man sat near it cross-legged in meditation. Looking around, he saw it was a huge inner cave structure. Behind the meditating man was a massive black ornament, with a round base and flat middle protruding outwards. On top of it was an oval stone. The stone had three short white lines across it. Sashin approached the fire. The meditating man's eyes opened, and he spoke in an Indian accent.

"Come and sit near the fire."

Sashin sat cross-legged by the fire, opposite the man who was wearing a red Nehru top with a red scarf and red bottoms. He sat barefoot. Around his neck were brown beads, and the buttons on his collar were gold.

"What is this place?" asked Sashin.

"This is Mount Kailash; you cannot get to this very place in the physical world, only on the astral plane. This is an astral cave temple, an astral *mountain* cave temple... an astral *inner mountain* cave temple," replied the man.

"Astral temple's good enough," said Sashin.

"Okay. I am Rajarshi."

"I am..." Sashin was about to say but was interrupted.

"This is your current incarnation... nice to meet your current incarnation," said Rajarshi.

"Was it you that caused the fire?" asked Sashin.

"You asked for help didn't you? So this is why you are here," responded Rajarshi.

"Where was that place I was in, a lower astral plane?" asked Sashin.

"Yes, that is correct. There are different planes in order of materiality that go from dense to fine. These are physical, astral, devachanic, sushuptic, and nirvanic. There are actually two higher ones beyond this, which are beyond conception. As for the astral plane, this has a further seven sub-divisions. The difference between the sub-divisions would be like the difference between solid and liquid. Divisions four to six are like your physical world. The seventh is the lowest," answered Rajarshi.

"What about levels one to three?" responded Sashin curiously.

"Those are the higher planes on the astral level, where the causal plane is. You were pulled onto the lower plane by the negative being," replied Rajarshi.

"He calls himself Bakenkhons," said Sashin.

"Well, this Bakenkhons' existence is unnatural on the astral plane. He should have touched the devachanic plane and been swept into the line of normal evolution. Instead, he defied the natural order of evolution by keeping himself on the lowest astral plane with the use of magical arts," remarked Rajarshi.

"Magical arts?" questioned Sashin.

"He has an alliance with the black magicians, former members of the Nyingma Pa, also known as the Red Hat sect. They are adepts, except their development has been used for evil instead of good, and the powers they acquired are for purely selfish purposes rather than the benefit of humanity," replied Rajarshi.

"Yes, I've met them. With their help, Bakenkhons has been trying to harm me," Sashin said.

"I can see from your aura that your astral body has been affected. In fact, I wouldn't normally help, but because your astral body was damaged, I decided to give you some guidance," replied Rajarshi.

Sashin looked a little puzzled. "What do you mean?"

"You are an adept like me. I am only supposed to help those who are less spiritually evolved. Your forced reincarnation had some side effects because you don't remember that you are an adept," replied Rajarshi.

"An adept?" said Sashin.

"Yes, one who is spiritually evolved," remarked Rajarshi.

"But I got hurt. Well, my astral body did. I don't remember being an adept," said Sashin, clearly saddened.

"This is in fact two questions. You know, in the physical world there is talk of manifesting. You want a car, a house, a partner, and you manifest these things, right? This may take days, weeks, months, or years. Here on the astral plane, you can manifest instantly. You can manifest weapons, a sword, a shield, any armour you so choose," explained Rajarshi.

"I see," replied Sashin.

"As for your damaged astral body, I want you to look down at your stomach," said Rajarshi.

Sashin looked down and was horrified to see an octopus-like creature attached to the stomach region of his body; it was grey and its tentacles were attached, and the head was long and thin and embedded in his stomach like a spike. Sashin held up his arms in shock.

"Get it off me!"

"This is affecting both your *svadhisthana* and *muladhara* chakras. Only you can remove this parasite," replied Rajarshi.

"How? How do I do it?!" yelled Sashin, clearly in distress.

"By your will – you must want to remove it," said Rajarshi.

Sashin grabbed the parasite and started to pull. The parasite began to pull harder on Sashin's stomach, and there was a jolt of pain that caused Sashin to yell.

"Ahhhh! It really hurts!"

Sashin pulled hard with both hands and the parasite came free.

"Throw it into the fire," said Rajarshi urgently.

Sashin threw the parasite into the fire and watched as it burned with a dark flame, eventually turning to blue.

"Take some deep breaths and relax. This is why you have been brought here, to heal," said Rajarshi.

Sashin closed his eyes for a few seconds while taking in some deep breaths.

"Are you okay?" asked Rajarshi.

"Yes, I'm feeling much better, thanks," replied Sashin.

"Now, the key for you is in remembering," said Rajarshi.

"But how do I do that?" asked Sashin.

"You can meditate. Go inside yourself and search your mind. This may take some time, days, months, or maybe seven lifetimes," responded Rajarshi.

"Seven lifetimes? I don't have seven lifetimes!" exclaimed Sashin.

"Let me see," Rajarshi contemplated. "There is a way, a shortcut."

"Which is?" replied Sashin.

"The Akasha. The records of all that has happened are there. But it is not easy to get to, even for you. It is possible if your will and focus is strong enough," said Rajarshi.

"How do I get to the Akasha?" asked Sashin.

"The Akasha is on the causal plane. However, the unnatural Bakenkhons follows you when you are on the astral planes, so going to the Akasha would be like putting a pinpoint on a map. He may be able to find you with the help of the Nyingma Pa exiles," explained Rajarshi.

"I guess I'll have to take that chance. But you're right – I need to find out what happened in my past life," replied Sashin.

"There is also one other thing. Moving through time, again, is not easy and requires extreme focus and intent. Don't be surprised if it doesn't work. The more personal and psychological connections you have with an event, the more likely you will be able to travel there in time. You can also move forward in time, but that is an entirely different conversation. I remember when I was on my own evolving spiritual journey. I practised moving through time and went to the future," explained Rajarshi

"What did you see?" asked Sashin fascinated.

"I saw *Satya yuga*, the cycle after *Kali yuga*, which we are in at the moment. I saw a Golden Age of peace, but this is a possible future of many outcomes," replied Rajarshi.

"Well, thank you for your help even though you weren't meant to help," said Sashin, getting up off the floor. He stretched out his legs by squatting down on each one to the side.

"I guess I could go the way I came down the stairs and out. Will that take me back home?"

"Once you leave the temple, you can go wherever you want to go. This mountain is of very high energy – there will be no lower vibrational entities here as they couldn't get near. I hope we don't meet again, in a nice way. Take care," replied Rajarshi.

Sashin proceeded down the stone stairs, feeling much better. Before he descended, Rajarshi spoke.

"Remember, you don't have to astral travel if you don't want to; you can always close the door."

Sashin nodded his head in approval. When he got to the bottom of the stairs, he turned and looked up. Rajarshi stood watching, holding up his arm to wave goodbye.

Sashin waved back and then turned and walked out of the mountain's opening onto the small path. Walking back along the path and onto the trail that led around Mount Kailash, he proceeded back down towards the archway. He took one last look at the mountain and thought, 'What an amazing place and experience.'

When Sashin entered the archway, he rang the bell intentionally this time. He looked up to see the bell and felt the resonance of the sound. Everything went blurry, and he snapped back into his body on the sofa at his parents' house. He awoke to the sound of a ringing bell. Ushma was doing her morning prayers.

Chapter Ten

Sashin slept through the whole night on the sofa. He got up and stretched while yawning.

"Morning! Are you feeling better?" asked Ushma.

"Yes Mum, much better," replied Sashin.

"All you needed was a good rest. There's a spare toothbrush in the bathroom cabinet. Help yourself to breakfast," said Ushma.

During breakfast, Sashin asked his dad, "What do you know about Mount Kailash?"

"I have seen several documentaries about the mountain. It is smaller than Everest, but no one is allowed to climb it because the Chinese government has banned it."

"How come?" replied Sashin.

"It is a sacred mountain, the abode of Lord Shiva. There are many theories about the mountain. I saw on one episode of 'Ancient Aliens' that said it is actually a pyramid. Some consider it the spiritual centre of the universe," explained Satish.

"Interesting," replied Sashin.

"Why do you ask?" questioned Satish.

"I had a dream that I was there," responded Sashin.

"That is very auspicious!" said Ushma.

"You can do a walking trail around the mountain; it's a whole day event for someone who is fit. Otherwise it takes two or three days. There are stations along the way where you can stop to get food and rest. I was thinking of doing it myself with your mum," said Satish.

"Oh wow, that sounds great!" replied Sashin.

After breakfast, Sashin said his goodbyes and headed home. The roads were less busy on Sunday morning. He showered when he got home, despite Ushma being adamant that he should shower before he left.

Sashin was determined to finish 'A Guide to Astral Travel'. He had a notebook at the ready and felt back to his optimal self again. The last section of the book covered travelling safely, protection, low vibrational beings, and closing the door on astral projection all together.

The shadow beings that Sashin had encountered were mentioned in the book, which he found fascinating. The author shared how she would sometimes travel to the lower plane to build up confidence and strength to overcome lower vibrational entities. Finally, the book ended on avoiding astral projection by closing the door, staying grounded, and resisting separation if sleep paralysis occurred along with the high-pitched whining sound.

Sashin needed a break from projecting for a few days to get his thoughts together. The next time he astral projected, he did not want to be at the mercy of Bakenkhons. He wanted to be the one seeking him out, ready to stand his ground.

Sashin put on his jogging bottoms and long-sleeved training top. Sifting through his jackets hanging behind his bedroom door, he found his sports jacket. He was going to spend Sunday afternoon going for a walk. He made his way over to Hendon Park which was roughly a fifteen minute walk away. On the way, he messaged Reshma:

Sashin: Hi – I think it's time to see that lady about the past life regression.

Reshma: Yay! Her name is Sarah Mark. She's based in Croydon.

Sashin: Should I contact her?

Reshma: Leave it with me. I'll sort it out.

Sashin: Okay.

Once at the park, Sashin looked up at the sky, which was overcast but mild. It was sunny in the morning with a clear sky. There were a few people out in the park, some walking the path around the park. Sashin joined the path and started to walk around briskly. He started to think about the night out next Friday with his team, going through places and things to do in his mind. He was also thinking about being the only one without a partner there, which caused him anxiety as he felt his stomach knot up. He was not keen on being the fifth wheel. That's when the thought crossed his mind, 'What if I ask Alexis?'. He had to see her during the week for the first networking presentation; maybe he could ask her after the event. He contemplated messaging her as he completed one lap of the park and walked round for the second time. 'I'll leave it until I see her,' he thought.

Sashin's phone pinged – it was Reshma:

Reshma: I spoke to Sarah, and she's arranged the session for Saturday afternoon at 2pm.

Sashin rolled his eyes as he began to type a response:

Sashin: I'm going out on Friday night. Can't you do it for another time?

Reshma: She's going on holiday on Sunday and won't be back for two weeks. I thought you wanted to get this done quickly.

Sashin: Bugger, okay. It'll have to be Saturday.

Reshma: Just take it easy on Friday night.

Sashin: Er, easier said than done.

Reshma: See you on Saturday.

Still thinking about where to go on Friday night, another thought crossed his mind: the London Bridge area. It was near all of the team and Alexis' office, so all the more reason for her to say yes to the invitation.

'I feel like doing something a bit spontaneous,' thought Sashin as he walked straight out of the park and towards Hendon Central. It literally only took him five minutes to get to the station. Once there, he touched the screen on one of the ticket machines to bring it to life and purchased a ticket to London Bridge. It was time for some intelligence and reconnaissance in order to gain some good ideas for the night out. He wanted to impress Alexis. That is, if she was willing to come out.

It was busy at the station, and tourists scurried towards the underground platform. Sashin caught the Northern Line, which took forty minutes to get to London Bridge. It was warm on the train. The weather had been mild for September, and the train was packed. Sashin stood up and held onto a grab handle. At Euston, droves of people exited the train freeing up some seats, and Sashin sat down, relieved not to be squashed up against a stranger.

The train pulled into London Bridge. Exiting the station, Sashin stood outside and looked left and right, pondering which direction to go in. Wondering if this was such a good idea, he shrugged off the doubting thought and went from a brisk walk into a jog, heading to his left. He whizzed past shops, fast food outlets, banks, and a few pubs scattered in between.

It was becoming apparent that walking around on a Friday evening to find a drink or a bite to eat would not be much fun for the group, so Sashin crossed over to the other side of the road and ran back in the direction he came from. He passed various shops, restaurants, and the odd bar, eventually stopping at the opening to Borough Market.

'Of course!' Sashin thought to himself.

Sashin walked in. There was an array of food stalls from artisan foods to cheese, coffee, Persian, Arabian, a bakery, wine, Indian food, ice cream, a grocer, and sweets all under one roof. This would be a perfect start to the evening where everyone could get something to eat. There were even a few pubs inside. Sashin walked around, eyeing all areas of the market. Leaving the market, he took a moment to survey the surroundings. There were a number of bars and pubs, but something niggled him. He wanted to organise something different rather than just a pub crawl.

For the first time since arriving at London Bridge, Sashin pulled out his mobile phone. He Googled things to do in the area. Looking up, he conveniently saw a Starbucks and went in for a caramel macchiato. He sat down and started to scroll through the options. One particular venue caught his eye called 'Belushi's'. It was a sports bar that hosted various activities. Sashin looked up the location on Google maps and took a last sip of his coffee before heading out.

Belushi's was only five minutes away, so Sashin briskly walked rather than jogged there. From the outside, the venue looked like an American bar. The typography for the sign was a bright orange, modern, and informal font that screamed fun. Three wooden signs were attached to a metal frame at the front of the venue. One read 'Games', another 'Happy Hour', and the last 'Book Now'. Sashin walked in and was met with a very long bar, with a sign on the wall behind it reading '2-4-1 Cocktails 4-7pm Mon-Fri' and 'Beer Pong'.

"Can I help you?" asked a petite Asian lady.

"Just looking around, thinking of coming here next Friday with some friends," replied Sashin.

Sashin had a look around the venue. There was a viewing area for watching live sports on television, and there was a games area in a separate room for beer pong. The Asian bar lady came over.

"I can make a booking for you if you like. It gets really busy on weekends," she said.

"Yeah, why not? It's for six people. I'm interested in beer pong," responded Sashin.

"Sure thing, I'll book you a table. What time do you want the booking for?" asked the bar lady.

"We're going to Borough Market first and will come over after, so say seven-thirty," replied Sashin.

"Give me a minute. Can I take your name and number please?"

Sashin gave his name and number.

"All done for you. If you ask on the night, then one of us will set you up for the game and explain the rules to those who haven't played before," said the bar lady.

"Brilliant, thanks," replied Sashin.

Sashin left Belushi's feeling good. 'That's one worry taken care of,' he thought.

On his way back, he passed Borough Market for one last glance over. He then proceeded back to London Bridge underground station, but as he approached the station, he saw something that made him stop in his tracks. It was a bookshop, 'Ancient Egyptian Books'. An elongated statue of a leopard stood outside the shop, painted in gold. Sashin had to look twice to make certain that it was a leopard. On the other side of the shop front sat a sphinx statue, the size of a large dog. It was an ornate statue also painted in gold. The head had blue streaks and the chest plate had been painted in red, blue, and green. It was a beautiful piece and Sashin spent a moment admiring the statues. He felt compelled to go in.

Inside was no-frills, a mixture of antiquities and books crammed into bookshelves and piles strewn about the floor. A Tutankhamun sarcophagus stood tall next to a bookshelf. Sashin walked around and over piles of books. The owner was busy organising books into further piles, deeply engrossed in the activity. He ignored Sashin.

Despite the chaos within the bookshop, the selection of books was impressive. Sashin picked up a book, 'The Mummy In Ancient Egypt', had a flick through and then moved on to another, 'The Egyptian Book Of The Dead'. Over on another pile sat a book called 'The Secret Order Of Amun', whose front cover was a picture of a man wearing Egyptian headgear and an ornate chest plate. Sashin went over to pick up the book and wondered whether the picture was that of a pharaoh.

The owner shouted across, "I haven't sorted that pile out yet!"

"Oh okay – I was just wondering who this is on the front cover of this book?" asked Sashin, holding up the book to show the owner.

"That is Amun who became the God Amun-Ra by joining with the sun god Ra," replied the owner.

"Right. Okay. Well, I'll leave you to it," said Sashin returning the book to its pile.

"Oh no, I won't be long," replied the owner, nearly falling backwards as he got up off the floor.

"Don't worry, I'll come back another time," said Sashin.

Sashin caught the tube back to Hendon Central and from there jogged back home.

Chapter Eleven

Sashin was in the office on Tuesday and it was a full day ahead. He messaged Alexis to ask if she was free Friday evening.

Alexis: Why do you ask? I might be. I'll need to double check. Let's discuss it when I see you for the launch prep.

Sashin: Sounds good!

This left the prospect of a definite yes or no open. However, Sashin was optimistic. Sashin sat near Dev and Krish in the office.

"All set for Friday guys?" asked Sashin.

"Yep, but what exactly are we doing?" replied Dev.

"Going out to London Bridge," responded Sashin.

"How come London Bridge?" said Krish.

"Well, it's easy to get to for all of us and you know my client's contact is based there. I'm going to ask her out," replied Sashin.

"What? You're asking someone out and they're your client?" remarked Dev.

"I'm still getting past the fact he's asking someone out," chuckled Krish.

"In all fairness, Alexis works for my client," replied Sashin.

"Ooh Alexis," said Dev, making a shocked look, opening his mouth wide while looking directly at Krish.

Krish reciprocated and puckered up his lips, opening his eyes wide to give an exaggerated look of surprise.

"What's she like?" asked Krish.

"I've only met her once. She seems nice – she's new to the area and looking for company," said Sashin.

"Smooth operator," replied Dev grinning.

"Cool, look forward to meeting her," said Krish.

Sashin gave a cheeky smile and said, "Play nice when you meet her."

Dev held up his arms while smiling.

"It's us!" he said while glancing over at Krish who was nodding his head.

"Ha ha," replied Sashin.

With that, Sashin got down to work. He had preparation to do for the presentation launch for Dream Ventures in the evening. There were a number of calls to make, including to the Direct Selling Association. This was a key area of Sashin's checklist as it covered the legal aspects of the Dream Ventures networking business and ensured everything was above board. With time going quickly Sashin began to feel the pressure. His last call was to a prominent network marketer, whom he discovered through his cousin Manish, who had shared how he was once in business with this rock star network marketer. This rock star had reached the upper echelons of the ranks within the business he was in and had become a part of the core management team, giving valuable input and influencing decisions. The name of the legendary networker was Eddie Mann, and Sashin had a magazine open with an article on Eddie as part of the main feature. The magazine was from Eddie's networking company. Manish had lent it to Sashin to prove he was not telling tales.

The conversation with Eddie went well, and he agreed to attend the presentation in the evening on short notice to give feedback, but under the condition that Eddie was able to prospect anyone that was not showing any interest in the Dream Ventures opportunity. Sashin thought this would be hard to ascertain and ended up trying to negotiate with Eddie, explaining that just because someone didn't sign up then and there, it didn't mean they were not interested. They eventually came to a compromise whereby Eddie would talk to guests during the post-presentation mingle and ask what they thought of the presentation. Sashin also mentioned that there would be free pizza, which seemed to help with the persuasion.

The day had felt long by the time Sashin was able to take a break and make himself a cup of tea. Dev was working with a pharmaceutical company, helping with the marketing and branding of a new range of supplements through various media, especially social media. Krish was dealing with a manufacturing business based in Wembley where the staff were experiencing low morale due to archaic management. Krish had been brought in to recommend modern techniques for managing and motivating. Both Krish and Dev had left the office by four-thirty, leaving Sashin on his own. He stood staring out of the window, sipping on his tea.

Sashin fell into a mini-trance as he stared out of the window, watching the cars go by and people walking past. His thoughts turned back to the Egyptian bookshop he'd come across by chance in London Bridge. The book he found with Amun's picture on the front reverberated in his mind.

"The Order of Amun," he thought.

The phone pinged.

Alexis: Sashin, are you able to come an hour early?

Sashin gulped down the last bit of tea and frantically packed his laptop up. His plan was to drop his car off at home and catch the tube to London Bridge, but it was five o'clock, the dreaded rush hour. The tube would be packed. Sashin responded in a panic.

Sashin: Just leaving the office now.

He freshened up at home, changing into a long-sleeved polo top and spraying on some eau de toilette, before he swiftly made his way over to Hendon Central. He slowed his pace down midway so as to not break into a sweat.

As expected, the station was chaotic and Sashin made it to the platform, after navigating through the groups of people all moving at different paces. The tube was packed from one end to the next with commuters making their way home from work. Sashin was barely able to look around – he was squashed up against the door, holding onto the handrail tightly. One person was reading a book, another had their headphones on, while another stared into space nonchalantly. Sashin moved his head down to a diagonal position to avoid the passenger at his side breathing all over him.

Exiting the train from the madness of 'rush hour', Sashin quickly made his way to the Dream Ventures office. He looked at his watch. It was six o'clock. He was going to make it with no time to spare.

Delivery men were bringing in posters and stands through the front door. There was a buzz about the office as a long table was being arranged with tea, coffee and soft drinks. The stands were being assembled, and various posters were being put up by the Dream Ventures travel club. Faraway places and exotic locations could be seen all around. Just then, the pizza girl arrived balancing a whole stack of boxes. Alexis ran over and instructed her to put them on the end of the table. The pizza girl said there were more boxes to come, and she went off to get them.

"Hi Sashin! What do you think?" said Alexis.

"It's looking great. Get some chairs out and arrange them in lines over there by the television," replied Sashin.

"Yes, yes, I know," responded Alexis, sounding somewhat stressed.

"Don't stress; it's all looking good. What are you playing on that massive TV?" asked Sashin.

"Oh you'll see; it took a lot of time and effort to put the presentation together. We took your advice about the push-play method," replied Alexis.

"Good, looking forward to it. How did you promote the event?" asked Sashin.

"Social media, radio and billboards, but we are looking to only focus on word-of-mouth and social media eventually," answered Alexis.

"Yeah, I was going to say, you don't want to be spending too much before you've even started," said Sashin.

Guests started to arrive, and Alexis greeted them and showed them over to the long table for refreshments. Sashin joined in to offer moral support. Four members of Alexis' team arrived and began greeting people as well, just as more people started to turn up. Soon, the room was alive with guests eating pizza and sipping on drinks. Some opted for tea or coffee with a biscuit instead.

Alexis spoke into a wireless microphone in hand.

"Welcome everyone to this inaugural Dream Ventures presentation evening. Yay!"

Guests started to clap and whoop.

She continued. "Please make your way over to the seating area."

At that point, a commotion was heard from behind. Sashin turned around to see Eddie Mann had arrived with an entourage of three people. Some of the guests had clearly recognised him and went over to say hello excitedly.

Eddie stood six feet tall and towered above the excited guests, including Sashin who was five feet nine inches. Eddie wore a black wax jacket with blue jeans and black suede Chelsea boots. He had short black hair and a dark brown complexion. His teeth were bright white and when he smiled, he had the expression of a Cheshire cat. Sashin went over and extended out his arm.

"Nice to meet you Eddie; glad you could make it."

"Sashin, right? Nice to meet you. Nice setup, and not a bad turnout," replied Eddie.

"Get comfortable – the presentation is about to start," replied Sashin pointing over to the seating area.

Alexis stood watching with a bemused look on her face. Sashin gave a soft smile and made his way over to a chair. Alexis vigorously ushered him over to sit in a designated seat. She then continued on the microphone.

"After the presentation, come and talk to either my team or me, as we would love to hear what you think." Alexis pushed play on the remote and sat next to Sashin.

The presentation started by introducing the concept and then showing the type of trips and holidays on offer as well as the benefits. This was followed by a business presentation that explained the compensation plan for those who wanted to become not only members of the club but to market the business. Sashin was very impressed with the whole presentation. He turned over to Alexis and gave a nod of approval, and she gleamed with delight.

"Well done," he whispered.

Following the presentation, guests made their way back over to the refreshments table and began to mix and talk. Alexis and her team made their way around the guests. Some of her team had iPads in hand. Sashin shadowed some of the conversations to see what guests were saying. Some found the presentation exciting, while others were fairly expressionless, and some were not impressed and shortly left after airing their opinions. A few, however, were very impressed, and team members signed them up for the membership as well as the business.

A blonde-haired lady stood next to Sashin.

"Hi, my name is Katja."

"Hi, I'm Sashin. How did you find the presentation?"

"It was really interesting. I really like this concept and the prices for the trips are so great," replied Katja.

"Fantastic. Would you be interested in becoming a member and getting involved in the business?" asked Sashin.

"I just don't have the money," replied Katja.

"All the more reason why you should get involved, to try and change that. And remember, the upfront cost and subscription you get back as travel," said Sashin.

"Yeah, I guess so," responded Katja.

"Here. Why don't you talk to one of the team," replied Sashin as he ushered over one of Alexis' team members.

Sashin felt someone touch his shoulder and he turned to see Eddie Mann.

"Well handled. Are you in the business?"

"Oh, no. I'm helping with the launch and kick off," replied Sashin.

"I like the idea of this product and the opportunity," said Eddie.

"That's great. I'd like to introduce you to that lady there, Alexis," responded Sashin.

Sashin waved to Alexis and called her over. She held up her hand as she was listening in on a conversation between one of her team members and a guest. She uttered something, which Sashin lip-read as two minutes, so he continued talking to Eddie.

"How's it going with Vista Life? I read your article in your company magazine."

"All good, but you know with lotions and potions, it's getting tougher. This is a sexy concept that you have here. Plus, I've had a lot of attrition within the team," said Eddie.

"Attrition?" asked Alexis who was now standing next to Sashin listening.

"I'll explain later." Sashin continued.

"This is Eddie Mann, the top distributor for Vista Life."

"Nice to meet you Eddie – I'm Alexis. My fellow colleagues and I," putting her arm around Sashin, "have been successful in launching the Dream Ventures network."

"I was just saying to Sashin, the lotions and potions industry is losing a bit of traction at the moment. What you have here is a good concept – travel is sexy. I'm very interested in getting involved," said Eddie.

"Why don't you go over there with Alexis and get signed up?" said Sashin looking wide-eyed at Alexis.

Alexis was stunned and stood there processing, not expecting this. Sashin held her arm and spoke softly.

"You're part of the networking business, right?"

Alexis nodded her head.

"Then sign up Eddie," Sashin replied.

Alexis's eyes widened with excitement.

"Follow me Eddie! Right this way," said Alexis as she led him over to the end of the long table.

"Grab a slice of pizza. I'm just going to get an iPad."

Eddie helped himself to some pizza.

"Are you interested in the business as well as becoming a member?" asked Alexis.

"Yes – sign me up for both," replied Eddie, chewing on the pizza. After gulping down the slice, he continued.

"And my team will also join. I'll sign up first, and then can you sign them up as my team."

"No problem," replied Alexis.

Eddie looked over and pointed at each of his three team members, ordering them over with a 'come hither' signal with his finger. They huddled around him like a team with their coach on a football field. Eddie explained that he was going to join and that they would then join as part of his team. Seeing some hesitation from the team members, Eddie gave a pep talk.

"Look, this is a great opportunity. Get in now and be at the forefront of something really exciting!"

The team started to nod their heads and then gave their approval.

Alexis registered them on the iPad.

"Sashin, you sure you don't want to be part of my team?" asked Eddie.

"No, I'm good. I've got enough going on at the moment," replied Sashin.

Alexis looked over with an inquisitive look.

"Look forward to working together," said Eddie as he left.

"Bye everyone," said the team members, grabbing a slice of pizza each before following Eddie out.

Alexis walked over to Sashin, and she ecstatically gave him a hug.

"Thanks so much for bringing in Eddie as part of my team."

She gave him a kiss on the cheek.

"No worries. Just helping to kick things off," replied Sashin. He continued after Alexis stopped hugging him.

"I messaged you on Monday, and you said you wanted to talk after the presentation today. Are you free Friday evening?"

"Ah yes. I am free on Friday evening, why? Are you asking me out?" responded Alexis.

"I don't mean to be forward, but well yes, I guess. I've arranged a night out with my team of consultants and their partners," answered Sashin.

"Ooh, team night out, nice. Yes, I would like to come. It would be nice to hang out with you and meet your teammates," said Alexis.

"Cool! Kickoff is at five-thirty right near here in Borough Market. Should I meet you there, or do you want me to pick you up?" asked Sashin.

"No, it's fine, I'll meet you there. I will try and finish early so I can get home and get ready. Here, take a pizza home," replied Alexis.

"You got any veggie pizza?" said Sashin.

"Yes! I got a veggie hot. Here you go. You're a veggie then?" asked Alexis, handing over the pizza box.

"Yep," replied Sashin.

"I prefer meat," said Alexis smirking.

"What about hot and spicy?" responded Sashin cheekily.

Chapter Twelve

Just before bed, Sashin smiled, reflecting on Alexis saying yes to his invitation. But soon after, the pressing on his chest started again, along with the high-pitched sound. The first time this happened, Sashin resisted as hard as he could. This caused the pressing to subside and the sound to dissipate. The second time, detachment had started, and Sashin felt himself rising up and out of his physical body. He immediately snapped himself back successfully. He knew he could only do this so many times before the one time he let his resistance slip and he was out and astral, vulnerable to being pulled.

Sashin had thought long and hard about his projection experiences so far. He felt it was time to take control and stop running. The onset of sleep paralysis had started; he rose up out of his body. He was ready. If he started to feel a pull, he would embrace it and go with it rather than panic.

Sashin hovered through his window out into the street, where he began to fly. He flew down the street. And as he did, he felt himself getting faster. It was time to see just how fast he could go. With full intent, Sashin flew immensely fast, so fast in fact that everything became a blur. He flew through houses and buildings in seconds, over fields, forests, and towns. There was no longer anything in his way. He slowed down and realised he was flying over the ocean.

Turning around, he saw the coast. He flew back towards land and descended. There was a signpost that Sashin walked up to. It read 'Land's End'. 'Woah, I'm about two hundred and sixty miles from London,' he thought. He rose up in the air and flew back the way he came, again at great speed. This time, he started to slow down slightly so that he could gauge where he was going. His street was in sight and, while flying closer to his house, he noticed a lady approaching from his side. Looking over, he saw that it was Jyoti whom he had seen in his earlier astral projections, which he thought were bizarre dreams.

She held out her arm and touched him, causing his aura to tingle, which triggered something energetically. He found himself being pulled through a vortex. Looking from side to side, Sashin saw time moving backwards, as if moving back through a video clip. He was taken to Jyoti's house a year prior. He was led in and saw Jyoti in her bed, surrounded by her husband, two children, and a nurse. This scene was being replayed, forwards and backwards, which Sashin found disorientating. And then all of a sudden, the scene just played out, showing Jyoti's last minutes before she passed. Her family grieved inconsolably. Jyoti looked confused. Sashin spoke to her, "Are you okay?"

"I couldn't let go. My family was so upset, and I couldn't go," replied Jyoti.

"You've been stuck here, haven't you?" asked Sashin.

"Yes, I ended up in some dark place where I saw you last time, remember?" said Jyoti.

"The lower plane," responded Sashin.

"What?" asked Jyoti.

"It's okay," replied Sashin.

"Wherever I was, I was trying to get away from the robed man and his shadow ghosts. He was terrorising us," said Jyoti.

"He's been terrorising many people on the astral planes," remarked Sashin.

"It took a long time to get back home. It was through the help of some of those people I was with," said Jyoti.

Sashin put his hand on Jyoti's shoulder and consolingly spoke to her.

"Jyoti, you do realise that you have passed, right? You're showing me this because your family's grief kept you on the astral plane," explained Sashin.

"I've been stuck," said Jyoti.

"You need to pass over to move on," replied Sashin.

"How do I do that? Can you help me?" asked a concerned Jyoti.

Sashin took a moment to think.

"Come with me," he said.

He took Jyoti by the hand and flew out of her house and then up into the air. Closing his eyes, he focused intently and then in a flash, they appeared at the astral intersection. Descending with Jyoti onto the road, amid the bustle of people walking by who were looking at them as they levitated down, he introduced her to the place.

"This is a place where people can travel up to the higher plane. See? Look over there."

Sashin pointed over to show her in the distance the road rising up with the flashes of light and distorted images fading in the sky, and he continued.

"Follow the road and keep going. This will take you to the higher plane and you will pass over. Don't be afraid."

Jyoti looked around and was pleasantly surprised.

"What is all this?" she asked.

"On your way to the next plane, you come across these places where you can shop, eat, and drink, much like passing through a city centre or like a massive motorway service," replied Sashin smiling.

Jyoti looked amused. It was the first time Sashin had seen her smiling and about to break into a laugh which was reassuring.

"Being stuck on the astral planes like this makes you a lost soul and vulnerable to negative beings who will take advantage of your confusion, like the robed man did. But you have nothing to worry about now. Just move on up. You can have a look around if you want to before you move on, but avoid going down the side lanes over there," explained Sashin pointing.

"Why?" asked Jyoti.

"Trust me, it's nothing you need to worry about," replied Sashin.

Jyoti thanked Sashin and gave him a hug before she started to walk off towards the road leading up to the next plane. He stood like a watchful guardian, oblivious to the people walking by who had to walk around Sashin. She ventured further into the distance until she was hardly visible. Sashin breathed a sigh of relief. He was glad he was able to help Jyoti, which brought his thoughts to all the other lost astral souls that resided on the planes.

"Hello Sashin, I'm glad you're okay."

Sashin turned to see who it was. It was Britt.

"Hi Britt. I'm okay, thanks," replied Sashin.

"I thought you were a goner after your run in with the black magicians," said Britt.

"You know about those guys?" asked Sashin.

"Oh yes, they hardly come around these parts, but when they do, you know there's trouble," responded Britt. She continued. "And you were smack bang in the middle of it."

"Yes, well, I intend to do something about that," replied Sashin.

"Like what?" asked Britt.

"I'm going to find them," said Sashin.

"You must be crazy," remarked Britt.

Sashin began to experience a tugging, as if someone was pinching the back of his top. This soon turned into a pulling.

"It looks like they've found..."

Sashin fell through the ground, through the earth. He saw particles as he slid through rapidly. Like a lead weight was tied to his legs, he sank down further and further. He appeared in a lower plane and straight down again through the ground. Eventually, he descended into the dark, barren landscape. Landing with a thud, Sashin was slightly dazed. He quickly got to his senses. The thought suddenly crossed his mind – he was able to travel through time, albeit because of Jyoti, who caused him to go back, but he had managed to do it nonetheless. 'Could I do it again?' he wondered.

Faint groans emerged in the distance. Sashin rose up into the air and flew towards the sound – it was the faceless dead. He landed only to become the centre of attention as the dead beings headed straight for him. Sashin focused on his hand and willed a sword to appear, but nothing happened. He turned, ran a short distance and then stopped to try again. He visualised a sword and willed it to manifest.

A tingling sensation started in Sashin's hand, and he felt it begin to vibrate. A sword of light started to appear. He held up the sword to admire it as it glowed effervescently with bright white light. As the faceless being approached, Sashin took a swing with the light sword at the dark being's body as it howled and dissipated.

More entities approached. Sashin willed the sword away and then focused on manifesting a shield. A shield of light appeared. He charged towards a dead being that was closing in and had the clear features of a person. Hitting the entity with the shield, it fell back to the ground. On his right a faceless being appeared and grabbed onto him. Sashin spun round and hit the being with his shield, releasing its grip. He then slashed it with the side of the light shield, causing it to dissolve into the ground. The grounded being began to get up off the floor. Materialising the light sword, Sashin lunged forward and stabbed it, and with a squeal, the being vanished.

Turning, Sashin ran across the dark barren field, light sword and shield in hand. As he encountered dead beings, he stabbed and sliced them with his sword, watching them disappear. Sashin tried something else. He focused and willed a bow. The bow appeared and glowed just like the sword, but it appeared to have no string. When Sashin put his hand through it, he felt a string of light. He pulled it and then released it, which fired an arrow of light.

He saw a faceless being ahead and lined up the bow. He pulled back on the string and shot an arrow at the entity, which caused it to dissipate instantly.

Rising up, Sashin flew at great speed until he came to a hilly area where he slowed down and descended. There stood Bakenkhons with the shadow wraiths.

"No longer the coward Ahmenemat?!" shouted Bakenkhons.

"I'm tired of running, and I just want answers," replied Sashin.

Sashin held up his shield at the ready. Bakenkhons hit the shield with his palm releasing a surge of energy that caused the shield to fade. Taking a swing with his light sword, it was immediately blocked by Bakenkhons who had an astral sword of his own except his glowed with a dark hue. A smirk came across Bakenkhon's face; he smashed his sword against Sashin's with force, which caused Sashin to jolt back.

Sashin's light sword began to fade in and out and then completely dematerialised. Bakenkhons took a strike with his sword, and Sashin leapt to the ground, rolling over as he landed. Getting back up on his feet, he composed himself and focused on producing the light shield again. As Bakenkhons took another strike, Sashin blocked it with his shield. Bakenkhons sent another surge of energy through Sashin's shield, causing it to fade. He knocked Sashin with force as he slid back.

Bakenkhons leapt up and over Sashin, and grabbed him round the neck. He then attempted to stick his hand into Sashin's astral body. However, Sashin willed a chest plate that appeared on his body glowing. It looked just like the chest plate he had seen Amun wearing on the cover of the book 'The Secret Order of Amun'. The plate prevented Bakenkhons from entering.

"You're trying to kill me aren't you? Why?" groaned Sashin.

"To finish what I started," replied Bakenkhons.

Sashin was confused by Bakenkhons' answer. He struggled to get free from the chokehold and was beginning to feel fatigue. He tried with all his might to materialise something, anything. Thoughts flashed through his mind on what to will into existence. He felt something appear in his hand, and he lifted it up to see a taser. Lifting his arm around, he quickly pushed the taser into Bakenkhons' neck and activated it, causing Bakenkhons to yell and let go.

"You fool!" he cried.

Clearly irritated, Bakenkhons produced a mace and took a strike. Sashin created the light shield and blocked the hit which sent him flying back, but before he hit the floor, he stopped and levitated inches above the ground. Dropping onto the ground, Sashin rolled over and got up.

"When I have cut your cord I will attempt to enter your mortal body and walk the Earth plane again. I will then go after the people that you love."

"Never!" yelled Sashin.

"Maybe with their help I can," said Bakenkhons smugly as he looked over to his side.

It was the black magicians of the Nyingma Pa. One of them walked over to the other side of Bakenkhons, slid his hand under his shawl, and pulled out a dagger. There was no time to hesitate. Sashin held up his arm and focused. He willed a boomerang, which materialised. Holding the boomerang up, he threw it towards the black magician with the dagger. The boomerang knocked the dagger out of his hand. Keeping his focus on the boomerang, it spun around the back of Bakenkhons and hit the other black magician, knocking the mala out of his hand. It seemed that Sashin was able to control the boomerang in mid-flight. Turning his attention to Bakenkhons, the boomerang whirled back around and hit Bakenkhons in the face, he yelled.

"Enough of these games!"

Bakenkhons produced a spear and threw it angrily. Sashin attempted to materialise the light shield, but it faded in and out and then appeared, but the spearhead had already pierced his astral body. The rest of the spear had broken off after the shield appeared. Sashin felt a sharp pain in his shoulder. He immediately pulled the spear head out, reeling from the pain.

A wave of anger came over Sashin. He held up his arm and focused, materialising a grappling hook, which he began to spin round over his head and threw towards Bakenkhon's leg. The hook spun around his leg, at which point Sashin pulled hard with both hands bringing Bakenkhons to the ground. Rising back up, Bakenkhons cut the grapple rope with his astral sword and then flew towards Sashin. Sashin produced his light sword, and the two locked in a duel with their astral swords clashing, sparks of dark and white light shooting off their weapons.

The whooshing sound of a strong wind could be heard, followed by a strong gale that pushed Sashin back. He looked over to see both black magicians chanting with their malas. Attempting to escape the astral wind, Sashin ran over to the side and willed his light bow to appear. Pulling back on the light string, he fired an arrow, but the gale swept it far away from his target.

He then fired off one arrow after another in various directions, and one hit the black magician in the chest causing him to drop his mala and fall to the ground. The other black magician looked over at his fallen accomplice and then at Sashin in disgust. Sashin held up his bow and fired an arrow straight at the black magician's arm, causing him to drop his mala. The black magician held his arm to alleviate the pain. Sashin ran towards Bakenkhons and whilst doing so, he materialised the light boomerang.

Sashin threw the boomerang, but it also flew off in another direction. He pushed forward against the conjured blast of air. He grew more weary as he fought against the gale until he was close enough to Bakenkhons.

"You're not so powerful without the Nyingma Pa black magicians," said Sashin as he looked Bakenkhons firmly in the eyes. He continued.

"I am going to find out the truth."

Bakenkhons stopped smiling.

Sashin closed his eyes and visualised his street and quickly teleported there. Appearing in his street, he hovered over to his house and through the wall into his room, where he lay down in his body and remerged.

Chapter Thirteen

Thursday morning felt like a drag. Sashin was tired, but not depleted or feeling ill like last time after his encounter with Bakenkhons on the astral intersection. He was mildly sore, like he was experiencing the after-effects of weight training. Thankfully, it was a work from home day. Taking a break from the laptop, Sashin stood up and stretched his arms and legs. Then he laid on the floor, put one leg over the other, twisted from one side, and did the same on the other side. He felt better in himself that he had been able to face Bakenkhons, but the idea of him taking over his body was unthinkable. Sashin was determined to understand why Bakenkhons would want to do this.

The feedback from the Dream Ventures presentation launch was mostly positive. Alexis now had a new team of networkers who were keen to expand the business, including Eddie Mann. She had tasked Sashin with helping to compile training for new networkers. The brief was to create training for new starters to fast-track their progress, and subsequent training for networkers as they became more experienced. Sashin got to work running ideas through his head and putting these down on paper as a mind map. From the many conversations Sashin had with his cousin Manish, he had learned that there was one person who had extensive knowledge of this type of training for networkers: Eddie Mann.

After making the final tweaks to his mind map, Sashin scanned the paper and pulled up Eddie's number on his phone. He dialled the number, and after four rings, Sashin suspected Eddie was not going to pick up. There was a beep and then a pre-recorded female voice asking to leave a message.

"Hi Eddie. It's Sashin, I wanted to talk to you about training. I know you have a lot of experience with regards to training in the industry. I have some ideas that I've captured on paper. Give me a call back when you're free."

'Did that sound okay?' thought Sashin.

It had turned eleven o'clock, and while Sashin sat at his desk staring into space, Jyoti crossed his mind. He dialled his parents' house. Three rings in, and Sashin thought it was a day of nobody picking up the phone. Finally, his mum answered.

"Hello."

"Hi Mum. I'm going to swing by for lunch and then pop over to see Ajay, and the kids too if they're in," replied Sashin.

"Okay, no problem. Why are you going over to Jyoti's?" asked Ushma.

"When was the last time you went to visit, Mum?" said Sashin.

"It's been months. They didn't want people visiting. They even changed their home phone number, so I can't ring them," replied Ushma.

"Well, I want you and Dad to come – it will mean a lot to them."

"Why all of a sudden, *beta*?" asked Ushma.

"Trust me, I just got a feeling it would be a good time to," responded Sashin.

"Okay, we will quickly have lunch and then go over. I know you will be on lunch break," said Ushma.

On his way, Sashin stopped off at the nearest supermarket. It was busy with a flurry of people around the fridge near the entrance. It was the lunchtime frenzy for a meal deal. He navigated around the lunchtime marauders and looked from side to side. The clock was ticking, and he did not want to spend his break walking around the aisles. Stopping a worker in uniform walking by, he paused midway through his sentence.

"I'm looking for..."

He spotted what he wanted and lifted up his hand with an apologetic gesture. It was flowers that he was looking for. He walked over and stood by the selection and had a quick look over each, growing more confused. 'Which one would be most appropriate?' he thought. A bouquet of white lilies caught his eye. Sashin found the flowers to possess simple beauty and serenity. He picked up the bouquet and made his way over to the self-service counter, finding nothing but mayhem. Looking at his watch, he knew he had to make a move. There was only one person at the magazine and tobacco counter, so he quickly headed over and managed to be second in the queue. With flowers in hand, Sashin dashed out of the supermarket and on to his parents' house.

Opening the door, his father Satish remarked, "We've been waiting for you."

"I know, I know. I had to go to the supermarket to get these," responded Sashin, holding up the flowers.

"Oh, very nice," said Satish.

They all sat down to eat.

"I made your favourite, *mag ni dal*," said Ushma.

"Ooh yes," replied Sashin.

Sashin was what some would consider a fast eater. It was a habit from when he was young, and he would occasionally race against Reshma to finish a meal, much to the chagrin of his mum.

"Stop eating so fast! Take your time. Even after all these years you are still in a hurry. Chew your food properly. Enjoy it," scolded Ushma.

"I *am* enjoying it!" responded Sashin.

"Right, let's get going," said Satish. He continued. "I don't want to miss the cricket."

"Cricket can wait," replied Ushma.

It had been aeons since Sashin had visited anyone's house with his parents. It used to be a regular thing to do when he was living with them, especially going for a walk a few doors down for a social visit to Jyoti's. He thought about how a person's presence can make an impact on other people's lives, and how their energy can bring warmth and unity.

Outside the front door, Sashin stood behind his mum and dad. Ushma turned and grabbed Sashin by the arm and led him forward.

"Ring the bell," said Sashin.

"You do it, it was your idea," replied Ushma.

Sashin rang the bell and waited. The sound of someone approaching the white UPVC door could be heard with a figure behind the frosted glass. The door opened to reveal Ajay looking nonplussed. After a short pause that felt like a minute of silence, Ajay spoke.

"What a surprise! Come in."

Walking in, the porch gave way to a small hallway that led into the living room. The living room was open and airy with neutral colours of light brown walls, a cream sofa with recliners, and wooden flooring. There was a subtle smell of lavender, which invoked memories of sitting and listening to Jyoti talk about her trip to the lavender fields in Banstead. Sashin handed the bouquet of lilies over to Ajay, who received them with a thankful yet sombre look.

"A little something for remembrance as it's been just over a year," said Sashin.

"Thanks. I'll put these in some water. Jyoti would've loved this," replied Ajay.

Putting the lilies in a vase, Ajay then placed the vase on the fireplace. He looked at Sashin.

"Take a seat."

Sashin saw that his mum and dad had already made themselves comfortable with Ushma sitting on one end of the sofa, and his dad on the recliner. Ajay came over and sat in between Sashin and Ushma.

"I'll call Karishma down. She is upstairs revising – she had a morning lesson at college and has finished for the day," said Ajay.

"Oh no, it's no worry," replied Ushma.

"No, it's okay," responded Ajay.

A few minutes after Ajay had gone upstairs, he returned with Karishma, his seventeen-year old daughter. She was slightly taller than Ajay and had long black hair with dark brown highlights. She looked a little bit like Jyoti but mainly looked like her dad. With a smile on her face, she greeted Ushma and Satish, giving them a hug. Sashin got up and gave Karishma a hug.

"It's been ages," he said.

"I know. Last time I saw you was at the funeral," replied Karishma.

"I know it was really tough. How are you guys holding up?" asked Sashin.

"Coping, just getting on with it. It's been hard," responded Karishma solemnly.

"She's in a better place now," said Sashin.

Karishma nodded her head. Sashin continued.

"Tell me all about college."

"Yeah, it's going fine. I had a lesson this morning, which was the only one for the day, and I came home early. I'm studying business and finance," replied Karishma.

"Oh right, good subjects," said Sashin.

Ajay got up and offered everyone tea. Satish agreed emphatically, Ushma said 'yes', and Sashin looked at his watch and reluctantly accepted the offer. Ajay went off to the kitchen and Karishma followed to help. Ushma offered to help but was told to sit and relax.

Ajay and Karishma came out with freshly made masala chai along with Indian savoury snacks.

"We have just had lunch," said Ushma.

"Don't worry – you can have some Indian snacks with your tea," replied Ajay.

"Okay, a little bit," said Ushma relenting.

It did not take much persuasion for Satish, who had already started helping himself. Sashin took a sip of his chai. He did not normally drink Indian tea, but on the odd occasion he would have a cup. The chai was nice, and he tried some of the *farsi puri* so as not to offend the hosts.

"You wouldn't happen to have the sports channel for cricket, would you?" asked Satish.

Ushma rolled her eyes.

"Yes I do. I'll put it on," replied Ajay.

Satish's face lit up like a child's about to watch their favourite cartoon.

Soon the conversation turned nostalgic as they recalled stories about Jyoti. There were outbreaks of laughter. Ajay, Karishma, and Ushma chuckled while Satish joined in the conversation while watching the cricket. He went from shouting at the television to laughing and then instantly turning back to an intense frown. This amused Sashin. Drinking the last bit of chai, Sashin looked again at his watch to see it had been well over an hour. He felt apprehensive about spending too much time on his lunch break.

"Thanks so much for the tea and snacks. It was really nice to see you both. Give my regards to Raj."

Raj was Ajay's youngest child, and was still at school.

"Thanks for coming, and the flowers are really nice," replied Ajay.

"Anytime. I would love to stay but I have to get back to work," said Sashin.

Karishma stood up and gave Sashin a hug. Ajay went to show Sashin out but he stopped him.

"Sit and chat. I'll see myself out."

As Sashin was leaving, he stopped at the living room door and turned to look over at everyone talking, smiling, and reminiscing. He then looked over at the fireplace. There was a headshot picture of Jyoti smiling on the mantelpiece. Next to the picture was the vase containing the lilies. Sashin smiled and gave a subtle nod, and then he made his way into the mini hallway, where he put on his shoes and left.

In the car on the way back, he thought about Jyoti. She had crossed over and was now free. It would have been difficult to sit there and drink chai and eat snacks knowing Jyoti was still lost on the astral plane. Sashin was glad he had been able to help her. Then the thought emerged that if he was able to help Jyoti, maybe he was able to help others. Arriving home, he felt the buzz of his mobile phone in his jacket pocket, and the name 'Eddie Mann' flashed on the screen.

Chapter Fourteen

"Thanks for calling back Eddie. I wanted to talk to you about training," said Sashin.

"I got your message. What exactly do you want to know? How to do the training, how to deliver the training, or what to train on?" replied Eddie.

"All of the above. I'm looking at how to train new networkers. The next step would be training for the more experienced networkers like yourself," said Sashin as he walked into his house holding his mobile phone to his ear.

"For new team members, the first thing you want to do is get them started right. That means showing them how to reach out to people in their own circles who might be interested in a business or the product or both, and then inviting those people to a presentation. Further down the line, it's all about more detailed training on techniques and methods of duplication," continued Eddie.

"Sounds good. I put together a mind map of ideas. What's your email address?" asked Sashin.

"I'll message you. There's some things that have worked well with Vista Life, like incentives to fast track new members. I'll talk you through them," replied Eddie.

"Let's do that in the office with Alexis," suggested Sashin.

"Yeah okay, send me what you have and I'll take a look," responded Eddie.

"Will do, thanks for your suggestions," replied Sashin ending the call.

That evening, Sashin sat down to meditate. He decided not to follow any particular meditations that had been sent to him but rather to just sit still in silence and turn inward. As he sat trying to clear his mind, the image of the book appeared that he saw in London Bridge. He was unable to shake the image. This was the second time the book had crossed his mind. 'The Order of Amun' he thought. It was becoming an annoyance. He was unable to clear his head.

Sashin leapt up and walked over to his computer. He typed in a search for 'the Order of Amun'. Nothing actually came up apart from a few sites, one of which was a Wiki on the Theban High Priests of Amun. Information on the subject was scarce. Delving into the information, it became apparent that the high priests had such power that they ruled Egypt for more than two thousand years. They clearly wielded influence during their reign. 'Maybe the book contains more information,' he thought. He clicked on various other links that led Sashin down a rabbit hole that he would rather not have ventured down. There was one particular site that was related to esotericism and Egyptology. Reading through the material, Sashin found it a heavy read, as it was a thesis written by a professor five years previously. There was a link to the professor's website that Sashin clicked on. On the site, an option was available to request further information by submitting personal details, including an email address. Sashin's eyes grew heavy as he attempted to digest the information on the screen. He thought it best to call it a night after submitting his details and research another time when he was feeling more awake and engaged.

That night in bed, Sashin woke up and felt an intense tingling throughout his whole body. It was like electricity was coursing through him. The sensation was intense and uncomfortable. Sashin could see his room but was aware that his eyes were closed. The high-pitched whining began, and then there was a feeling of being pulled. Something had grabbed hold of Sashin's astral body and was pulling him out. Sashin resisted and attempted to stay merged, but the sensation only grew stronger. Suddenly the pulling got faster, and Sashin was out and astral.

He could sense the presence of two beings in the room. One was near the ceiling on the left, and the other was on the right, near the bed. The being on the right jumped onto Sashin and started to push him down. They both went through the floor into the living room, and as the being attempted to push even further into the ground, Sashin fought back and pushed up, causing them both to be at a deadlock in the living room. Breaking free, Sashin then flew back up to his bedroom.

In his bedroom, he hovered over to his physical body, but the other being stood in between. It was one of the black magicians.

"Are you sure you want to go back into your body?"

"Yes, so get out of my way!" replied Sashin.

"Why don't you join us?" snarled the monk.

"And why would I do that?" asked Sashin.

"For knowledge, for power," responded the being.

"No! And don't ever come to my house again!" barked Sashin.

Sashin hovered around the black magician and went to climb back into his physical body but was unable to merge. 'What?' he thought as he began to feel anxious. Laughter could be heard behind him.

Sashin turned and said, "You already have a disciple. Where is he, could he not come himself?

"Oh, he will," responded the monk.

Sashin looked directly at the black magician.

"Leave now and don't ever come back."

The other being emerged from the floor. It was not a black magician but similar to the astral vampire Sashin had seen at the astral intersection. Sashin produced his light sword and flew forward. The black magician disappeared through the floor, leaving the vampire in the room. Sashin turned and saw him next to his physical body.

"Get away from me!" shouted Sashin.

Flying forward with his light sword, Sashin took a swing, and the vampire moved out of the way and out through the wall. Sashin followed out into the street. Hovering outside, the vampire could be seen flying off. Sashin produced his light spear and threw it. The vampire turned and jerked out of the way to avoid the spear which caught the being on the shoulder, causing it to wince.

"Don't come back here again!" yelled Sashin.

Holding its shoulder, the vampire replied.

"I'll be seeing you around."

The vampire flew off into the distance. This invasion of his personal space was unnerving for Sashin. He returned to his physical body and merged successfully.

Chapter Fifteen

The day had finally come for the big night out. In the office, Dev and Krish were upbeat. There was an air of levity with it being a Friday and the social evening to look forward to. Sashin had bought a box of Krispy Kreme doughnuts on his way in and placed them on top of the stationery cupboard.

"Good lad," said Dev.

"I've got an assortment box," replied Sashin.

"Ooh go on then," said Krish getting up. He took a doughnut, sat down and continued.

"I've got a lot on today."

"I don't want any of us working late, so try and finish by four. That should give you enough time to get home, get ready and out," replied Sashin.

Checking his messages, he saw Eddie had sent his email details. Sashin compiled an email and attached his mind map, which he copied Alexis in on as well.

Dev looked stressed, as he had been working on a marketing and social media campaign for a large pharmaceutical company, 'Star Group', who had launched a new range of supplements.

"What's wrong?" asked Sashin.

"It's this social media campaign. It's driving me nuts. I need to come up with an idea for this new line of supplements, but I'm running out of ideas," replied Dev.

"What's so good about these supplements?" questioned Krish.

"Yes, good question," remarked Sashin.

"They're natural, no synthetics, and purely organic. I've thought about a series of sexy ads, some glitz and glamour," responded Dev.

"But why glitz, glamour and sexy advertising? That's what the majority of companies do – they just throw money at the ads," said Krish.

"You want to keep it grounded. If the products are purely natural then that's what you want to get across in your campaign," added Sashin.

"What I want to know are the benefits of the supplements – what do they do? I want to be told a story about how these products changed lives," said Krish.

"You could have the inventor or someone who uses the supplements talk about the product and give consumers the ability to follow how it has affected them," suggested Sashin.

"That's actually not a bad idea. That would be the advertising, with the user talking about their experience with the supplements," replied Dev.

"I see on Instagram people doing lives. You could do the same with this person, doing a number of live streams just talking about the supplements. Whoever does this must know the product inside out and actually be taking the supplements," said Krish.

"Well guys, great idea. I'm gonna demolish a doughnut," replied Dev excitedly.

"How's your project going, Krish?" asked Sashin.

"It's okay. I mean, the management is so old-fashioned that any modern techniques are having immediate effects. I'm already seeing an improvement in morale. They just need a lot of handholding," responded Krish.

"I bet you're loving that," chuckled Dev.

Krish just smiled while holding up his middle finger.

Alexis had emailed back regarding Sashin's mind map, and she thought it was a good start. Eddie Mann also subsequently emailed quite a lengthy message. He talked about incentivising new networkers through the training. The incentives would help fast track new members to get started quickly. Eddie had seen these types of incentives in Vista Life, and this had been successful in helping networkers build teams quickly. Eddie's email went on to say that if a networker managed to build a team of, say, four people then they could potentially receive a fast track bonus.

Sashin sat back and thought about the concept. He went online and started to look up compensation plans in network marketing. A number of interesting sites came up that explained the different types of plans, but this did not concern Sashin so much. Dream Ventures already had a robust compensation plan in place; it was more the role of incentives to enhance it. He then came across an idea that was mentioned on one particular site around subscription-based memberships.

'That's it,' he thought. The concept was related to the subscription. If a new member built a small team initially, then the subscription would be waived for as long as the team was maintained. This seemed like an excellent idea to Sashin because no one wants to pay a subscription. Obtaining a free membership would really excite members, new and existing. Just then, Sashin's phone pinged. It was Alexis:

Alexis: Thanks for the email and for reaching out to Eddie. There's some good ideas there. What time are you heading out tonight?

Sashin: No problem, Eddie has loads of experience and his ideas about incentives are really good. In fact, I have a really good idea for incentivising members. I'll head out at around 4.30pm to try and avoid the rush hour on a Friday.

Alexis: Tell me about your idea then.

Sashin: It's a surprise. I'll tell you later.

Alexis: Okay, I'll see you tonight x

Sashin: See you later x

Krish started packing up by three-thirty.

"I've done everything I needed to do. So I'm heading home. I will see you both in a bit."

"No worries, see you later," replied Sashin.

"See you in a bit," said Dev.

Krish grabbed a Krispy Kreme as he left.

"One for the road."

Dev had pitched the idea of having a face for the social media campaign to his team at the Star Group. They had already responded. The feedback on the concept was positive, and the team had proposed that the inventor of the supplement be the face and for Dev to manage the whole campaign.

"The idea for the social media campaign went down really well. I've got a guy who will be the face of social media, the dude who came up with the idea for the supplements. I'm in charge of the whole campaign."

"That's brilliant!" replied Sashin.

"Yep, good chat earlier, bouncing ideas around. It reminded me of the uni days when we would think about how we were going to change the world," said Dev.

"Ah yes, the good old days of thinking big," replied Sashin laughing.

Dev swiftly packed his laptop away into his rucksack and made his way out.

"I've got to drop the kids off at my parents. They will stay the night there."

"Cool, proper date night for you then," remarked Sashin grinning.

Sashin began to pack up his things; he took the box of remaining doughnuts. He felt uneasy about the black magician being in his house with the energy vampire. It was one thing being pulled to the lower astral plane, but to be pulled out of his body in his house crossed the line.

Sashin locked up the office on his way out; it was a small office unit that they rented to give them a base to work from and look professional to clients who wanted to visit.

At home, Sashin got changed and walked to Hendon Central station. It looked like his plan of getting to the station before five o'clock had paid off. It was not very busy, and Sashin managed to get a ticket and make his way to the platform quickly.

Krish lived with his parents, and was the youngest of three children. He chose to stay at home, feeling a cultural obligation as the youngest son, expected to care for his parents. They were getting older, and with Krish being around, it was reassuring for them to have him there to help. Krish picked up his partner Sabrina from her house, and they both made their way over to the station.

On the tube, Sashin managed to get a seat. The train started to get busy at Hampstead. At Euston, instead of people getting off, a horde of passengers were waiting to get on. The carriage was now packed, and Sashin's view was obscured by people standing in front of him. He was starting to feel a little claustrophobic.

Two carriages ahead, Krish stood up with his partner Sabrina, holding onto a grab rail. Sabrina had one arm around his waist whilst holding onto a rail with the other.

Dev and his wife Hema were running late and arrived at Hendon Central just after five o'clock. The station was packed, and they were unable to get on the tube due to a wave of people in front of them. They waited for the next tube, which was due in fifteen minutes. Dev looked at Hema.

"This always happens when we go out. I told you we have to leave at least an hour before," replied Hema.

"It's alright, they'll survive without us for ten minutes," said Dev.

"Twenty more like it," responded Hema, rolling her eyes.

Alexis had already arrived at Borough Market and stood near the entrance.

The tube had arrived at London Bridge station. Sashin got up and fought his way through the crowd. His phone pinged with a message from Alexis saying she had arrived. Sashin began to pick up his pace, as he did not want to come across as laissez-faire on his first date. Taking the escalator, he looked up to see Krish right at the top.

'Great,' he thought. "I'm going to be the last one there."

Now walking up the escalator past the people who preferred to stand still and enjoy the ride up, Sashin attempted to catch up with Krish. It was no use; he was unable to see him in the crowds ahead.

Borough Market was minutes away. Sashin passed the Egyptian bookshop and paused for a moment to look over; it was closed. He continued on and saw Alexis in the distance, waiting by the entrance. Getting closer, he saw she was wearing a khaki coat with a brown skirt and black top. She had wedge sandals on. Her hair was frizzy and curly, and she had hoop earrings on. Sashin felt himself getting warm as he drew closer, feeling turned on. Alexis stood smirking.

"What time do you call this Mr.?"

"I'm only a few minutes late, right?" replied Sashin, smiling.

Alexis leant over and gave Sashin a hug, she smelled citrusy.

"One of my team members, Krish, is already here," said Sashin.

"Oh great," replied Alexis.

They both walked through into the market.

"You look nice," remarked Sashin.

"You don't look too bad yourself," joked Alexis as she touched Sashin's shoulder. She continued.

"I've walked past here a few times but never actually been in. Some of my friends have mentioned it."

"All positive I hope," replied Sashin.

"Oh yes," said Alexis.

Over at one of the stalls, he saw Krish and Sabrina talking to a vendor. It looked like Krish was deep in conversation, pointing at what looked like a sack of brown beans. Upon closer inspection, it turned out to be a coffee stall. The vendor was explaining the different types of coffee beans; Krish asked further questions, which spurred on the vendor. Holding out some beans in his hand, he asked Krish to smell them. Krish wafted in the aroma with much melodrama. Sashin turned to Alexis and gave a look of amusement. Sabrina looked less enthused by the experience and turned around. With her eyes widening, she yelled.

"Sashin!"

She came running over and gave him a hug. She then held her arms out towards Alexis.

"You must be Alexis. So nice to meet you."

Chapter Sixteen

The air was alive with a blend of aromas. Wherever you walked, there was a different combination of smells, from smoked fish to cheese, Mexican food, coffee, Indian street food, and an artisan baker. Sashin scanned around for potential stalls to eat at. There were so many choices. His mind processed the different foods, and whilst he was trying to mentally interrogate one type of cuisine, Alexis touched him on the arm, breaking his line of thought.

"There's so much here! Loads of food places."

"Too many," mumbled Sashin.

Krish came over and greeted Sashin. He then spoke to Alexis.

"Is a handshake or hug acceptable?"

"A hug is fine. I'm a hugger," replied Alexis.

"Nice to meet you," said Krish, hugging Alexis.

"Where's Dev?" asked Sashin.

"I haven't seen him and we were the first to get here," replied Krish.

"He must be running late," remarked Sashin.

They all walked on a bit further. Krish spotted a speciality beer bar and pointed over.

"Let's grab a drink and sit over there so we can keep a lookout."

"Sounds like a plan," responded Sashin.

The small beer bar sign read 'Corner Pop' and celebrated all things in popular culture, from movies to music and cult classics. Posters adorned the walls. There was a large one on the wall above the entrance to the beer garden at the back, that was a clever take on the Lord Kitchener poster that read, 'Your Bar Needs You'. Eighties pop music played on the speakers. Looking around, Sashin took in the various nods to the evolution of pop culture, which made him feel nostalgic.

However, one particular poster looked completely out of place; it had symbols on it. Sashin felt a hand on his shoulder as he stared. He turned to see Alexis coming closer to his face.

"That's the Egyptian eye of Horus with an ankh."

"It looks out of place, don't you think?" remarked Sashin.

"Well, the Ujat is a powerful symbol of protection, also known as the 'Eye of Horus' and the 'all seeing eye'. In ancient mythology, there was a battle between Horus and Seth. Horus lost his eye, and it was magically restored by Thoth," explained Alexis.

"Horus? I can't say I've heard of him," replied Sashin.

"He's also known as Ra," said Alexis.

Sashin's expression changed from complete bewilderment to one of interest.

"The ankh represents eternal life, immortality, death, and reincarnation. Now *that* I got from studying up on Egyptian culture for the trips we're putting together, so that they are authentic," continued Alexis, smiling.

Sashin half talked and half whispered.

"It's all really fascinating and familiar."

"What's that?" asked Alexis.

"Oh, just that it's intriguing. Isn't it the eye on the dollar bill?" asked Sashin.

"That's the 'eye of providence', another 'all seeing eye'. It symbolises the eye of God," replied Alexis.

Krish caught their attention by waving his hand.

"What are you drinking? There's a menu up there above the bar," he pointed out.

"What do you fancy?" asked Sashin.

"A beer will be fine," replied Alexis.

"Two beers!" shouted Sashin across the bar.

"Dude, they do loads of beers. Which one? A blonde, bitter, IPA, or lager?" asked Krish, looking irritated.

"Lager for now. You choose," said Sashin.

Sashin leant over to Alexis and spoke in her ear.

"Are you okay with lager?"

"That's fine," replied Alexis.

"What would you like hun?" Krish asked Sabrina.

"A nice exotic cocktail," she replied, clapping her hands together.

"They don't do cocktails," responded Krish.

"Oh. Pink gin and lemonade then," replied Sabrina less enthusiastically.

With drinks in hand, the group made their way out of the entrance and sat at a couple of round tables outside the front. No sooner had Sashin taken his first sip than Dev turned up with Hema.

"Don't panic. We're here now," said Dev with his arms out wide.

Pointing, he yelled, "You must be Alexis! I've heard so much about you. Get up and come over here."

Alexis gave Sashin a bemused look and got up, walking over to Dev apprehensively.

Dev gave her a tight hug, and she gasped at the bear hug of an embrace.

Hema waited and excitedly added, "I can't believe Sashin brought a partner."

"Um, it's just the first time out," replied Alexis whilst being hugged by Hema.

Alexis sat back down with wide eyes looking over at Sashin.

"I just bought a round," said Krish.

"We'll get ours," replied Dev.

Hema and Dev walked into 'Corner Pop' and shortly came out with drinks in hand. Both of them joined the rest after Sashin had pulled another round table closer.

"Sorry we're late. Blame him," said Hema pointing at Dev.

"I slightly miscalculated the timings with dropping off the kids and getting to the station," replied Dev nonchalantly.

"Well, you're here now. Cheers everyone!" said Krish, raising his pint glass.

Everyone raised their drinks and yelled, "Cheers!"

Soon the group was immersed in conversation. Sashin checked the time; it was a quarter past six.

"Let's get a bite to eat as I have a surprise venue in store for seven-thirty," said Sashin.

"Oh yeah, is there now? Trying to make an impression," remarked Hema amusingly.

Sashin just gave a dry smile and got up. He held out his hand to Alexis.

"What do you want to eat?"

After sipping her beer, she put her glass down and spoke.

"Let's do Greek food."

"Greek?" asked Sashin.

"I'm Greek. Couldn't you tell? Mind you – my grandmother is Egyptian," replied Alexis.

"Oh right, I was thinking Mediterranean. Greek cuisine it is," said Sashin.

Alexis grabbed hold of Sashin's hand.

"You guys get something. We'll go in a bit, I only just got drinks. We'll look after your drinks," said Dev.

Alexis pulled Sashin over to a stall she clearly had her sights set on. Sashin liked this side of Alexis, he found it alluring. She had brought him to a stall called 'Colossus'.

"I'm going to have chicken souvlaki. What would you like?" asked Alexis.

"Is there a vegetarian option?" asked Sashin.

"Yes there is, it's made with vegetables and halloumi," replied Alexis. She continued.

"Oh and it comes with fries too."

"Sold," responded Sashin chuckling.

"I'll get these," said Alexis.

Returning to join the others after being served, Dev and Hema were the only ones there. Krish and Sabrina had gone to get something to eat too. They shortly came back with shawarma.

"You should get something guys; the clock is ticking. I mean, you will be able to get something to eat at the next venue, but you might as well get a bite here," said Sashin.

"Okay!" said Dev, smiling.

"Look after our drinks or what's left of them," he added.

"I'll get another round. Do you want the same?" asked Sashin.

"Yeah, that's fine," replied Dev.

Sashin took a bite of his souvlaki and nodded a sign of approval to Alexis before he rushed in to get another round of drinks. He returned walking slowly with a tray, carefully negotiating his way around people walking in and making it to the round tables.

Dev and Hema had returned with their food.

Krish remarked.

"Don't you get tired of Indian food?"

“We saw the Gujarati Kitchen stall and had to try, to see what it's like,” replied Dev.

“Yeah, to see whether it’s worthy of our seal of approval,” added Hema.

Engrossed in their food, there was a moment of quiet. Sashin began to feel the effects of the alcohol as he thought about tomorrow and the past life session. He wanted to know more about his past, but at the same time felt afraid. But, he needed to find out as much as he could. Dev noticed Sashin deep in concentration.

“Why are you looking down, Sashin?”

“Just thinking about tomorrow. I have to be up early as I have an appointment. I can’t get too crazy tonight,” replied Sashin.

“For one thing, I’m not going to be up early tomorrow,” said Krish.

“Appointment for what?” asked Dev. A look of hesitation crossed Sashin’s face as he debated internally whether to disclose any information about his situation.

“I started having these weird dreams and tomorrow I’m having a past life regression done.”

Dev nearly spat out his beer, Sabrina started to do her mini clapping, Krish was wide-eyed as was Hema, and Alexis looked at Sashin intrigued.

Sashin continued.

“In fact, let me rewind. I went to see a psychic a while back, as recommended by Reshma. She mentioned that I had a past life connection and I want to explore this to find out more.”

Looking at Alexis he shared, “Reshma is my sister.”

Alexis nodded silently.

“Yay! That’s so cool,” said Sabrina.

“I’ve always wanted to have something like that done,” she continued.

“Past life regression, what is that?” asked Dev.

“It’s where you recall your past lives through a practitioner who takes you back,” replied Sabrina.

“Are you sure your dreams aren’t psychosomatic? I don’t believe in psychics, sorry. I think they’re fake. They ask broad questions and give very generalised information,” added Hema.

“I don’t think dreams are a result of any particular condition. And as for psychics, I was very sceptical like yourself, but I found what she said really interesting and now, I’m more open minded,” replied Sashin.

Alexis put her hand on Sashin’s and spoke softly.

“If it’s what you want to do, go for it and see what you find out.”

“I love all this stuff,” said Sabrina excitedly. Krish’s eyes widened again.

“I just think you should be cautious with seeing all these people. Make sure you don’t get conned out of your money,” said Hema sternly.

“I had no idea you were into all of this stuff,” said Dev who turned his head to look at Krish.

“Well, it’s something I want to explore,” responded Sashin.

“Are any of these dreams nightmares?” asked Alexis.

“Some are, yes,” replied Sashin.

With a concerned look, Alexis said, “Right. Well, I hope you work it out.”

“Me too,” replied Sashin.

“Have you thought about therapy?” asked Hema.

Dev’s eyes widened and he stared at Hema in disbelief.

"I'm just putting it out there," she replied.

"I haven't lost it!" responded Sashin, shaking his head.

Just then Sashin's phone rang.

'Good timing,' he thought.

It was the lady from Belushi's.

"Hi, I just wanted to confirm that we will be seeing you at seven-thirty?"

"Yes, we are just on our way," replied Sashin, gesturing to the rest of them to drink up.

"Great, we'll see you shortly," replied the lady.

"Right. Time to eat up and drink up everyone – we're moving onto our next venue," said Sashin, rubbing his hands together.

Chapter Seventeen

The group exited the market and stood by the entrance. Sashin held his elbow out to Alexis, hoping she would put her arm through, which she did to his relief.

"So where are you taking us?" asked Alexis.

"It's a surprise. Where could this madman be taking you?" answered Sashin, smirking.

"I don't think you're mad. If you think this regression thing will help with your nightmares, then maybe it's the right thing to do," said Alexis.

"It's a start to try and work things out. Thanks," responded Sashin.

"For what?" asked Alexis.

"For not accusing me of being crazy," replied Sashin as he broke into laughter.

"Is this place far away?" asked Krish.

"Nope, just down the road," answered Sashin.

It was a busy evening and Southwark Street was alive with people.

"Turn right here," ordered Sashin.

They soon approached Belushi's. Sashin turned around and addressed the rest of the group.

"I would like to welcome you all to 'Belushi's" for a night of fun and games."

They all stood and looked at the front of the venue.

"Look, it's happy hour; we've still got some time to make it," remarked Dev.

Once inside, the Asian bar lady spotted Sashin and walked over to greet him.

"Hello. If you want to get together by the bar, I will set you up in the games room," she said.

"Sure," replied Sashin.

"Just to let you know, you get a jug of beer included," added the bar lady.

"What's everyone having?" asked Dev.

"Cocktail for me," said Sabrina.

"I'll have a cocktail as well," spoke Alexis.

"You're not switching yet lads, are you?" asked Dev.

"No, not yet. I'll have another beer," replied Krish.

"You get a jug of beer included with the game," said Sashin.

"Result," replied Dev.

"I'll have red wine. I'll give you a hand," said Hema.

After receiving their drinks, the bar lady came over to the group and introduced herself.

"Hi, my name is Selina and I will be your host for the evening. If you want to follow me to the games room, I will explain the rules."

Dev turned to Sashin and spoke with pleasant surprise.

"Games room!"

Selina led the group through some double doors into a large room with a blue ping pong table in the centre. The net had been taken off. On either end of the table were six white plastic cups arranged in a triangle. Selina stood by the table and began to speak.

"This is beer pong for those of you who have not played before. The rules are simple – you normally get into teams of two. You take the ping pong ball and throw it with the aim of getting it into one of the cups on the opposite end. If you get the ball in the cup, then one of the team members on the other end has to drink the contents of the cup and the cup is taken away. If you don't wish to drink from the cup but drink from your own drink, then that is okay. In that case, you would fill the cups on the table with water, and there's a jug of water over there. You continue until there are no cups left on one end, and that would be the losing side. Have fun. Just to let you know, from eight to ten, it's bottomless cocktails for twenty-five pounds per person."

"Do you want to drink from the cups?" asked Krish.

"I'm not drinking beer from the cups, especially after that ping pong ball has been in there," replied Hema.

"Fine, use your own drinks but not little sips okay?" prodded Dev.

"What about the teams?" asked Krish.

"Stick with your partners. You and Sabrina play Sash and Alexis. We'll play the winner," responded Dev.

"Here guys. Take your cups of beer," said Sashin.

Krish and Sabrina took their positions at the end of the ping pong table. Sashin removed his jacket and stood ready with Alexis, who looked very relaxed. Sabrina took the first throw and missed the cups completely. Krish covered his face. Next it was Sashin's turn. He lined up his hand with one of the cups and slowly moved his arm back and forwards as if playing darts. He threw the ball, which hit the rim of the cup and bounced off.

"Oooh!!!" cried Sashin.

Krish took his go, throwing the ball into the air; the ball descended. It hit the rim of a cup and landed in the cup next to it.

"Yes!" yelled Krish.

"I'll take one for the team," said Alexis as she took a sip from her cocktail.

Putting her drink down, Alexis took the ball, squinted her left eye and threw the ball directly into the cup nearest to her.

"Wow! Good shot," said Sashin.

The game continued on with Sabrina getting the ball into a cup on her next go. Sashin too managed to get a ball in.

Krish missed and Alexis got the ball in another cup.

"You've played this before," commented Sashin.

"I did a bit of travelling in the States where I played lots of beer pong," said Alexis winking.

Dev yelled, "I reckon in my former life I was a dictator like Caesar or Mussolini!"

"I can believe that," replied Krish.

"So can I," remarked Hema.

"Who do you think you were in your past life, Sash?" asked Dev.

"The psychic mentioned an Egyptian connection," responded Sashin.

"Oh, like Tutankhamun," said Sabrina.

Alexis giggled.

"Psychics will say anything," replied Hema dryly.

"I think I was a witch in my past life," said Sabrina.

Krish stared with wide eyes again.

Dev chuckled. "What if you were a mummy?"

"Now you're just taking the piss," replied Sashin.

Sashin felt irked by the insouciant attitude towards him bringing up past lives, but he thought about it for a moment. He had not told them everything, just part of the whole situation. If he was considered crazy for what he had already mentioned, disclosing the whole story would make him look completely bonkers.

There was now only one cup left for Krish and Sabrina and two left for Alexis and Sashin.

Alexis had her first miss. Both Sabrina and Krish missed on their go. It was now back round to Sashin, who lined up his hand again, took a deep breath, and threw the ball, which landed directly in the remaining cup.

Sashin leapt up with joy and put his arms around Alexis as they both jumped up and down.

"Right, prepare to lose to us!" said Dev, jumping up.

"Wait, before you play the next round, who's up for bottomless cocktails? It works out cheaper," remarked Krish.

"Pay by your teams," said Dev.

They all went up to the bar. Sashin offered to pay but Alexis stopped him and spoke.

"You don't have to pay for us both. I'll pay for mine; it's fine."

"Okay, fine by me," replied Sashin.

Everyone returned to the table with cocktails. Dev arranged all the cups and took position. He took the first throw and missed.

"Ah, damn it!" he cried.

Sashin threw his ball towards the cups and it hit the rim of the cup in the middle and ricocheted into another one.

"You are jammy. Drink up, Hema," said Dev.

Hema screwed up her face and took a sip of her cocktail.

Hema threw the ball hard, causing it to bounce off a cup and off to the side. Alexis flicked her wrist when throwing the ball, making it literally drop into the cup at the back.

"You're incredible at this," said Sashin.

Alexis smiled and danced her eyebrows.

Two cocktails in, and the group began to feel tipsy.

"I'll be interested to know what you find out from your past life thingy tomorrow," said Dev.

"Me too," replied Sashin.

"How did you guys meet?" asked Alexis.

"I met Dev at uni. We started consulting part-time for income to help with uni," said Sashin.

"And I was a mutual friend. If it wasn't for these two guys, I probably would've ended up in a very different situation, or worst case, jail," said Krish.

"Really?" replied Alexis.

"Yes. He bummed about after sixth form, dabbled in college, but never really finished. He lazed around for a couple of years, in and out of various jobs. A few years ago, his parents practically begged us to take him on," said Dev.

"Not quite *begging*," replied Krish.

"Once these guys gave me a chance, I invested heavily in personal development and completed some Open University courses."

"And you have me to keep you grounded, babe," remarked Sabrina.

"Yes, hun," replied Krish unconvincingly.

Krish looked over at Sashin and Dev.

"I love these guys!" said Krish.

"The cocktails have kicked in!" responded Sashin, laughing.

"That's a great story. I'm glad you turned things around," said Alexis.

Dev got his ball in, and that left both teams with one cup each. Sashin took his turn.

"C'mon, you've got this," said Alexis.

Sashin took the shot but the ball narrowly missed.

It was Hema's turn. She eyed up the remaining cup in front of her and with her tongue partially out, took her throw. The ball hit the rim of the cup and bounced off.

"Hema, come on!" yelled Dev.

"What? It's a bit blurry!" cried Hema.

Alexis picked up the ping pong ball and gave it a wipe with a tissue. She lined it up with the last cup on the opposite side and threw the ball ever so lightly. The ball flew through the air in a descending curve and hit the rim of the cup. There was a moment of tense silence as Dev put his knuckles to his mouth. Krish and Sabrina stood up, and Sashin stared with eyes wide open. The ball hit the rim, bounced up and landed straight down into the cup. Alexis jumped up and down in joy. Sashin put his arms around her and gave her a kiss on the cheek. Dev covered his face and then put his hands down, devastated.

"You were lucky," he said.

Finishing off their remaining cocktails, Sashin looked at his watch, which read ten forty-five. He felt a little tipsy and was aware that he had to be up relatively early the next day. He addressed the group.

"Right, I'm going to make a move."

"I'll join you," said Alexis.

Everyone made their way to the bar area. Sashin thanked Selina, and the group headed outside.

"It's been a good night out Sash, well organised," said Dev.

"Yeah, nice one Sash," added Krish.

"Yay!" said Sabrina, clapping her hands. She gave Sashin a hug.

Hema walked over to Sashin and gave him and Alexis a hug.

The group exchanged farewells with Alexis and Sashin.

"We're going to stay out for a couple more drinks," said Krish.

"We'll join you," said Dev.

"Okay, see you guys next week," replied Sashin.

"Nice to meet you all," added Alexis.

As Krish, Sabrina, Dev, and Hema walked off, Alexis turned to Sashin and spoke.

"I'm going to get an Uber."

"Okay, I'll wait with you until it comes," replied Sashin. He continued. "I hope you had a good time."

"Yes I did; it was nice. We should do it again soon," replied Alexis.

She looked at her phone to check the status of the Uber.

"It's only a couple of minutes away. I hope it all goes well tomorrow."

Sashin lunged forwards and gave Alexis a kiss on the lips. She was taken aback.

"Oh," she said, pulling back. She then moved her head forward and reciprocated. Her lips felt soft, and he savoured the moment until the sound of a car pulling up near them caused Alexis to break away.

"Okay, see you later," said Alexis.

Sashin stood with his hand up as Alexis got into the Uber.

At home, Sashin drank two glasses of water before heading up to bed.

He felt mildly intoxicated and hoped that he would not go astral during the night. If he did, he would not have any control over the projection or possibly even remember what happened.

Chapter Eighteen

Luckily, the effects of the alcohol had dulled Sashin's senses, which meant he did not have an episode of the pressing down on his chest with the high-pitched sound. His mobile phone alarm sounded. It was nine o'clock. Looking at his phone, he noticed a message from Reshma:

Reshma: Be ready for 11.45am. I'll pick you up. I want to allow an hour and a half to two hours for travel.

Sashin: Thanks for driving.

Reshma: You owe me.

Sashin got up and was feeling somewhat hazy. He showered, taking longer than normal to let the water soak in to freshen him up. Feeling marginally clearer, he made himself avocado toast with tomatoes and a large mug of tea. During breakfast, his phone pinged. *Alexis*.

Alexis: Hi, thanks for a lovely evening. I just wanted to say, let's move steadily and take things slowly and only until you're finished with the project. I'm just a bit uncomfortable mixing work with pleasure. I hope you understand x. Speak later.

Sashin: Hey, I understand. I have some things to sort out anyway, what with the dreams and the past life stuff. There are only a few meetings left. After that, I think the network is pretty much good to go, and your team is already taking off.

Alexis: Yes, it is going really well. I appreciate everything you've done and there are only a couple of months left now.

Then you're a free man, onto your next project. All the best for today.

Sashin: Speak soon x

Still feeling a little groggy, Sashin looked at the time, it was 10.30am. He decided to go for a walk around the block to get some fresh air and clear his head. Grabbing a bottle of water from the kitchen, he headed outside. The sun was shining and the warmth on his cheek felt soothing. He partly closed his eyes, tilted his head back a little and took in a deep breath.

Walking down the street, he wondered if he had spooked Alexis with his kiss. He felt in his gut it was the right thing to do, so he went with it. He understood the hesitations about having a relationship with someone he worked with, and he did not want things to be awkward or uncomfortable. At the same time, the thought crossed his mind that he might not even be around to see the relationship through.

He needed to know more about why Bakenkhons was so intent on ending him. Worse still, why was he trying to take control of his body if that was even possible? From what he had read in the book 'A Guide to Astral Travel' it did not seem so. Sashin was not keen on finding out if this was true or not.

Almost as if in a daze, he walked from his street and all the way to the bottom, further than he wanted to. He spun back to turn right, back to his house. Approaching his street, he realised he had been walking for nearly an hour and picked up the pace to get home. Just before he got to his door, a white Audi Q5 turned up on his drive. The passenger side window whirred down, and Reshma spoke through it.

"Look at the state of you! I said to take it easy."

"I'm alright, I'm alright," replied Sashin.

"There's traffic – I checked the navigation app," said Reshma.

"Just give me a minute", responded Sashin.

After quickly freshening up and using the toilet, Sashin grabbed two bottles of water, set his house security alarm and locked up.

"Right, all set. Here you go," he said, handing Reshma a bottle of water.

"Ta," she replied. "We should hopefully have about fifteen minutes to spare if we make it on time," she added.

They encountered traffic as soon as they neared Brent Cross shopping centre.

"How was your night?" asked Reshma.

"It was a nice, fun evening. The girl that is working for my client, Alexis? I took her out with the team," replied Sashin.

"Whaaat? Tell me everything," demanded Reshma.

"There's not much to tell. I've been working on a project with her on the launch of a network for her travel company. I asked her out and it was our first date, kinda," responded Sashin.

"Alexis, eh? And did it go okay?" questioned Reshma.

"Yeah, it was fine. She wants to keep things slow as we're currently working together. After I finish the project, then we can move things along. Plus, I have all of this stuff going on with the astral. I mentioned to my friends that I was going for the past life regression today. The reason I gave them was that I was having weird dreams," answered Sashin.

"And how did that go down?"

"Not quite as I expected. I was made out to be crazy," replied Sashin.

"Don't get me wrong, your friends are nice, but this is what you get when you deal with closed-minded people," explained Reshma. She continued.

"It's great that you've met someone, but I think the timing isn't great for you. I mean that's if she's able to understand what you're going through."

"Yes, too heavy for a first date," replied Sashin.

The congestion seemed to be coming to an end further up.

"Finally, we can break free from this traffic," said Reshma. She escaped from the traffic jam and sped off.

"It is a Saturday, and you know the traffic gets manic on the weekends," replied Sashin.

"We'll get there on time. The main thing is, are you alright and ready for this regression?" asked Reshma sternly.

"I guess so. I mean, yeah," responded Sashin.

"Good, just be open and relaxed," added Reshma.

The traffic eased off until they arrived in Tooting, where Reshma navigated through pockets of congestion.

Eventually entering Croydon unscathed, they grew closer to their destination.

"It should be off Shirley Road just coming up ahead," said Reshma, eyeing the navigation on her dashboard screen.

"What's the name of her road?" asked Sashin.

"Hang on a minute," replied Reshma, concentrating.

The car slowed down to a standstill held up by a queue of vehicles ahead.

"It's coming up on the right, Peacock Close," Reshma pointed out.

The cars in front started to move, and Reshma turned right into the close and drove down until coming to a dead end. She parked the car next to a long fence that had brown panels and ones that were green where the paint had weathered and faded. On the other side of the fence was a large field.

They both got out of the car. Reshma turned to Sashin.

"It's number thirty-one. I think it might be the house on the corner over there."

Sashin walked over to a white PVC panelled front door that had the numbers three and one on the top of the door and on a small square on the bottom right, on the bricks. Lifting the gold knocker on the door, he gave it two hard knocks.

Chapter Nineteen

The door opened and a lady about the same height as Sashin stood before them. She had light brown hair with dark brown highlights. Her eyes were dark brown, and her nose was long and thin. Her white teeth could be seen as she smiled. The purple V-neck T-shirt she was wearing revealed a blue amulet around her neck. She wore tight-fitting light blue jeans and was barefoot.

"You must be Sashin," she said.

"I'm Sarah, nice to meet you." She held out her hand, which he shook.

"Hi Reshma. So nice to finally put a face to the voice," added Sarah giving her a hug.

'Where was my hug?' thought Sashin.

"Can you please take your shoes off?" asked Sarah.

Taking off his trainers, Sashin looked up. He saw a staircase ahead to his left and a kitchen further down the landing. A man stood in the kitchen. He was taller than Sarah, wearing a psychedelic T-shirt with an array of colours on it that looked like the effects of a drug-induced trip. He had whitish grey long hair. Two kids ran around playing. The man seemed to be lighting something with a match.

"Sky! Aaron! Stop running around in the kitchen!" yelled Sarah.

The kids stopped, paralysed, and looked down towards them before running down the hall into the living room. An earthy aroma wafted into the hallway with the hint of a sweet fragrance. The man came towards them holding what looked like a white bunch of herbs tied together that were lit and gave off smoke.

"This is Jerry," shared Sarah.

“Hi Jerry,” said Reshma and Sashin at the same time.

“We burn sage before every session to cleanse the house and make it a clean space,” explained Sarah.

Sashin nodded his head intrigued. Jerry walked into the living room followed by Sarah who addressed the kids.

“Can you please leave the living room? Mummy has to work.”

Jerry circulated the burning sage around the living room. While he did the cleansing, Sashin noticed a picture hanging on the wall to the right. He approached it to take a closer look. It was a painting of a Native American chief. The chief wore a majestic headdress with a blue and gold headband, from which protruded stems that housed the many feathers that made up the headpiece. The feathers were white with black and red tips. He wore a light brown top with a white and red decorated collar and two bands of red and orange on either shoulder coming down to the outer chest. The chief had an endearing look. He also wore a blue amulet, similar to the one Sarah had on. In the background, a white wolf stood staring. Sashin stood transfixed by the beautiful and captivating painting. He followed Reshma into the living room.

“Jerry, can you take the kids out into the garden?” snapped Sarah.

“Okaay luv,” replied Jerry, placing the sage on an ashtray by the window sill. It continued to burn as clouds of smoke lingered in the air and he ushered the children out of the living room.

Sashin noticed a wall unit by the wall at the end of the room. He wandered over and saw small framed paintings of Native American women behind the glass cabinet doors. In one picture, the lady wore a striking headdress with a metallic band and red and white feathers, and red and black paint on her cheeks. The woman looked contemplatively to the side. She stood in the woods. He moved closer to inspect the background; it looked very similar to the woods from the lower astral plane.

'Fascinating,' he thought.

Another painting depicted a Native American woman in a vivid array of colours, from pink, blue, orange, red, and purple to black and white. The style of the picture was like pop art. The lady looked like a fierce warrior with a striking gaze.

On another shelf in the cabinet were various crystals. There was a line of small purple, blue, green, red, orange, and black stones, followed by a greyish one. In the corner to the left stood a very large light purple crystal; the inside, which could be seen through its translucent surface, was a crystalline structure that twinkled in the light. Sashin put his hand out near the crystal and could feel a strange sensation around it, like something pushing ever so gently back against his hand. He continued to move his hand over the crystal, but his concentration was abruptly broken.

"Sashin, can you come to the centre of the room please?" asked Sarah.

Sashin turned around to see a chair had been placed in the centre of the living room. Reshma sat on an armchair behind and to the left of the chair. Sashin walked over and sat on the chair, wondering what was to come next. Sarah went over to the wall unit, opened one of the bottom drawers and pulled out a large feather. It was unlike anything Sashin had seen before. Around the stem of the feather was a black lace that had been wrapped around a red lace. The feather itself was light brown with a black and white tip. Jerry returned with the sage, letting the smoke linger around him before leaving the room. Sarah walked over to Sashin and stood in front of him.

"I'm going to clean your auras. I'll start with you, Sashin, just in case you have picked up anything during the day. So, I will be doing a cleansing ceremony with this eagle feather. This is normally done standing up, but I put the chair there in case you preferred to sit."

"I'm okay to stand," replied Sashin, rising up from the chair.

With smoke still lingering, Sarah started near Sashin's head and shook the feather furiously, followed by quick, long flicks. Sashin heard the snap of the feather and tensed up to avoid flinching.

"Just relax your body," encouraged Sarah.

She worked her way down Sashin's body, shaking and then flicking the feather with long strokes close to his body. Jerry returned with the burning sage in a clay bowl with a handle, which he gave to Sarah. She let the smoke surround Sashin and worked her way down his legs. Sarah then did the same thing on the other side of Sashin's body. After her final strokes down his legs, Sarah spoke.

"Right, you're done."

Sashin opened his eyes. Sarah gave a small bow, and Sashin reciprocated with his hands together.

"Okay Reshma, come over," said Sarah.

After Reshma got up, Sashin went to sit in the armchair.

"Sit on the couch," said Sarah.

"This looks really interesting," said Reshma excitedly.

"I'm studying to be a shaman. Getting there," replied Sarah.

Reshma stood in front of the chair. Jerry had left the room and was in the garden with the children. Sarah let the smoke from the sage linger around Reshma. She then began the cleansing ritual and shook and flicked the feather around Reshma's body from her head all the way down to her feet.

"Right, you're both cleansed now so we can begin preparing for the regression," said Sarah.

Reshma returned to the armchair.

"I ask you both to put your mobile phones to one side there on the side table," instructed Sarah.

Whilst putting their mobile phones on the table, Sarah put on some music and turned to face them.

"I will play some meditation music for five minutes to relax you and bring your brain waves down to alpha and then the theta level. After that, we can begin," said Sarah.

The music went from raindrops with ambient sound to a harmonious flute with the sound of rain in the background. It reminded Sashin of Native American flute music.

Sarah handed an A4 pad to Reshma along with a pen and whispered to her.

"You take notes once we begin the regression as I'm not recording."

"Okay," responded Reshma, nodding.

Sashin found the flute music to be soothing and just what he needed for the brain fog from his mild hangover. He started to feel more relaxed and was conscious of his breathing that became deeper.

In a comforting voice Sarah began to speak.

"Sashin, please lie down. Use a cushion under your head and get comfortable."

Growing more relaxed, Sashin felt himself falling asleep, but was brought back into lucidity by Sarah's voice.

"In a moment, I'm going to stop the music, as we've reached five minutes. I will then proceed."

Sarah brought the chair closer to the couch and sat down, continuing.

"You're going to start to feel a sense of relaxation. Let this spread throughout your body. It will feel amazing. It will then hit your mind and your mind will relax completely. You will then feel that you can tune in deeply to yourself. I will then ask to speak to your higher consciousness, and that will feel easy because the answers will pop into your mind. So it might feel like you're hearing something, sensing it, or feeling it. Just say whatever it is. I will ask a question, and something will pop into your mind, so just say it. Are you ready? Just get yourself comfortable."

"Okay," replied Sashin in his relaxed state.

Sarah continued.

"So the communication will be clear when your higher self talks to you, like a very strong thought. This is why I am relaxing your conscious mind so that all the thoughts can be placed into your mind by your higher self. So just start by focusing in on your breath, breathing in deeply. As you exhale, release any tension stored in your body, let everything go, breathing in deeply and fully, exhaling any tensions, any worries, let it flow right out."

Sashin began to find Sarah's voice hypnotic. She carried on speaking.

"In a moment, I'm going to count down from ten to one. When I get to one you will be at the top of a staircase. I will walk you down that staircase slowly. Are you with me so far?"

"Yes," responded Sashin.

"Okay, let's begin," said Sarah.

"Take deep breaths and exhale, let your tensions and worries flow out. The countdown will now start. Ten, nine, eight, seven, six, five, four, three, two, one... You are now at the top of a staircase. Look down and see the steps. The steps will lead you down, and at the bottom you will see three doors. Take your first step, feel your foot on that step. Now take the second step with your other foot. Feel the sensation of your foot touching the step. Can you feel the step?"

"Yes, I can," replied Sashin.

"Good. Now continue walking down the steps, one step at a time. Continue to feel the steps. Onto the third step, now the fourth one, keep going."

Sashin could feel himself walking down the steps. It was dark, and there was a glow coming from the bottom of the stairs that offered ambient light. As he got further to the bottom and was on step twelve, he heard a buzzing sound, not dissimilar to the high frequency pitch but somewhat different. The sound began to fade and as it did, Sashin blacked out.

Sarah carried on speaking.

"And now, do I have permission to speak with Sashin's higher self?"

"Okay," replied Sashin.

Reshma looked fascinated with the pen at the ready to take notes.

"I respect the power of the higher self, and I know you take care of Sashin's body. I also know you have the memories of everything, and I always ask permission to speak to you and ask questions. Do I have permission to ask questions?"

"Yes," said Sashin in a monotone voice.

"Where is Sashin now?" asked Sarah.

"At the bottom of the staircase," replied Sashin.

Chapter Twenty

A bamboo torch hung on the wall, lit and burning. This was the source of light that gave ambient illumination seen from the top of the stairs. Sashin looked down to see a light-brown stone floor and stone wall ahead, with three doors. They were large, dark-brown oak oval doors.

"What do you see?" asked Sarah.

"Three large, brown doors," replied Sashin, his voice slow and almost slurred.

"I want you to go through the first door and tell me when you have gone through," instructed Sarah.

"I opened the door and walked through," said Sashin.

"Tell me, what do you see?" questioned Sarah.

"I'm on a battlefield. There are lifeless bodies on the ground. I am wearing what looks like cotton bottoms, like a *lungi*. I have a golden chest plate on, with a red piece of cloth around my neck. I have gold-coloured pointed shoes on. Around my waist is a band that holds a sword in a scabbard. There are horse-drawn chariots around me. I hear an explosion in the background and screaming. Bodies are flying up in the air in the near distance. I cover my face to protect myself from flying shrapnel," explained Sashin.

Reshma looked amazed and started writing furiously. Sashin continued.

"I start to run to avoid arrows falling from the sky. There is another explosion nearby, and the blast knocks me down. I get up, but I feel a little dizzy. Over in the distance is a golden chariot with large wheels and a roof with a red flag on top. A man is sitting down. He wears a golden helmet and chest plate with a quiver on his back full of arrows. He is talking to another man who is standing up in the chariot. The man standing up also wears a golden helmet with a peacock feather in it. He wears an ornate outfit of gold with a white and red garland around his neck. The man sitting down looks shocked all of a sudden. He is in awe and bows his head. A bright light is coming from the chariot. It's so bright that I cover my eyes with my arm and fall to my knees. Other soldiers on the battlefield do not see the light. The light is so bright and intense; it's overwhelming. I am now outside in front of the doors."

The scribbling sound of a pen could be heard as Reshma captured the last of Sashin's description.

Sarah asked, "Can you now go through the second door and tell me what you see?"

"Okay, I am opening the door. I walk through. I'm standing on a beach. I have a light red dress on. I am barefoot. The sand feels nice. I am looking out to the ocean. There is a ship in the background sailing away," explained Sashin.

"And what does the ship look like?" asked Sarah.

"It's like the old type of ship with masts and cannons protruding from the sides. It reminds me of a ship from the fifteenth century like Columbus' 'Santa Maria'," responded Sashin.

"Is there anyone else on the beach?" asked Sarah.

"There is a man walking past. He carries many items with him. I think he is a travelling tradesman. He is looking at me and holding a bottle of wine. He shakes the bottle at me as if to say he's selling it. I nod my head and raise my hand to say 'no'. The man walks off, but the items he carries weigh him down, and his posture is arched. I feel a strange sensation," said Sashin.

"How would you describe this sensation?" asked Sarah.

"A feeling of sadness; there is a person on that ship leaving that is very dear to me. I feel abandoned and alone," added Sashin. He continued to speak.

"I am now outside the doors again."

"Proceed through the third door and tell me what you see," said Sarah.

Sashin began to speak more clearly.

"When I walk through the third door, I am in a monastery. I am wearing a brown habit. I think I'm a monk. I walk into a great hall and see other monks going about their daily duties. Ahead is an altar, and on the altar is a book. I walk to the altar and look at the book. It's large and bound in dark brown leather. When I open the book, the pages seem to be written in Latin. There are symbols and drawings. I hear someone shouting and turn to see a monk wearing a black habit looking angry. He starts to run over. I think he is angry about me looking at the book. I start to run away through the door I came in from. I am outside the doors again. However, now there is a fourth door."

Sarah looked shocked and with eyes wide open looked over at Reshma.

"A fourth door?" she mumbled to herself.

"Is that supposed to happen?" whispered Reshma.

"No it isn't. This is a first," Sarah whispered back.

"Can you go through the fourth door, Sashin? But proceed cautiously."

"Okay," responded Sashin. He then continued on.

"I open the fourth door and walk through. The sun is shining bright. The sky is clear blue. It is very hot. On both sides of me is a line of sphinxes. There is a massive opening ahead, and I walk through it. I am part of a group of four. I am wearing a white robe and have sandals on. I have a headpiece on. I touch it and it feels fairly heavy. I recognise one member of the group. He looks familiar. I can see a row of large columns ahead. The columns are white with paintings on them. The tops of the columns are green. There are two metal bowls on stands. Smoke is coming out of the bowls that give off a scented aroma. We walk past the row of columns into a large courtyard. We carry on into what looks like the majestic area of a temple. There are huge statues of pharaohs on either side. Walking out of this main area, we go into another courtyard. Standing tall is a statue. I know who this is. It is a statue of Amun-Ra. I stand looking, and the person I recognise from the group calls me by the name 'Ahmenemat'. This person... I can remember his name. It's Bakenkhons."

Reshma perked up in the armchair writing as fast as she could, trying to keep her writing legible. Sashin carried on.

"We turn right and walk through several smaller temples before arriving at a corridor. There are guards waiting at the entrance with spears. We walk down the corridor – it is very long. We get to the end of the corridor, which leads to a chamber. Outside the chamber are more guards walking towards us. In the chamber are what look like two stone altars, made from a dark grey stone. We all sit on the floor. Bakenkhons and I face the other two people. We seem to be meditating. We stand up. I get on the stone altar and lie on my back, and so does Bakenkhons. I close my eyes, and everything goes black. I can see vivid colours."

"And what do you see after the colours?" asked Sarah.

"I don't know. I can't see anything, like I'm drifting away. I'm now in front of the doors again," replied Sashin.

"Can I ask you to turn around and walk towards the stairs? Let me know once you are at the bottom," said Sarah.

"Okay, I am at the bottom of the stairs," replied Sashin.

"Take the first step and then continue back up until you reach the top," instructed Sarah.

"I am now at the top of the stairs," said Sashin.

"You will now wake up," responded Sarah.

Sashin awoke to Sarah ringing a small bell.

"You're bringing me back out so soon," said Sashin.

"You've been under for one and half hours," replied Reshma.

"Really? I only remember going through one door and seeing Egypt. It felt like a few minutes," said Sashin.

"Okay, get up slowly. I'll get you a glass of water," said Sarah.

Sashin sat up, turning to Reshma as he spoke.

"It feels like I was hypnotised."

"You were and you don't seem to remember most of what you said," replied Reshma.

"I don't," replied Sashin.

"It's a good thing I took notes, plenty of them," responded Reshma holding up the pages.

Sarah returned with a glass of water.

"Here you go. Take your time; it's okay. That was a long session. I normally record the regressions but my recorder is away for repair," said Sarah.

"That's okay – I took plenty of notes," replied Reshma.

"Good. I hope you find them useful," said Sarah.

"As long as he can read my handwriting," joked Reshma.

"So to recap, through the first door you were a soldier on a battlefield, from what you were describing, and it seemed like centuries ago. You witnessed some kind of event. Through the second door, you were a woman who lost a loved one and felt intense feelings of sadness and abandonment. Through the third door, you were a monk in a monastery where you were looking through a book. It sounds like it was an ancient esoteric book, and the head monk didn't like you learning what was in it. That says to me that you were a seeker of the truth. And then, for the first time in my experience of doing regression, you saw a fourth door through which you had an Egyptian past. You might have been a high priest from what you explained. I'm not sure. And you were practising some kind of ritual. One thing I can say is that spirituality has been at the heart of some of your past lives," noted Sarah.

Sashin looked intrigued and then began to speak.

"I remember the last part in Egypt. What was that temple? There was a statue of Amun-Ra."

"It's something you will have to explore," replied Sarah.

Jerry returned with the kids, who were now running out of steam as they both sat on the floor playing with their toys, oblivious to their new guests.

"Did everything go okay?" asked Jerry.

"Yes, it was a long session. Sashin saw a fourth door!" exclaimed Sarah.

"A fourth door! Wow, that's a first," responded Jerry.

Sashin got up with the empty glass, which Jerry took off him.

"Right, we best be on our way. Thank you so much for this regression," said Sashin.

"You're very welcome. It's normally fifty pounds but as I know Reshma I will do it for forty pounds," said Sarah.

After paying, Sashin waved goodbye to the kids, shook Jerry's hand and went into the hallway to put his trainers back on. On the way out, Sarah gave him a hug. Reshma stopped for a moment and talked to Sarah.

"That was really interesting; thanks so much."

"Anytime, Reshma. I hope to see you soon," replied Sarah.

In the car, Reshma handed her notes over to Sashin.

"Have a good read of these. I took everything down as best I could. It blew my mind what you were saying. Do you seriously not remember?" asked Reshma.

"Seriously I don't. I only thought a few minutes had passed," replied Sashin.

"That's nuts! I didn't think you of all people could be hypnotised," said Reshma.

"You know what? In my recollection of Egypt, I was part of a brotherhood. That's what it felt like. Bakenkhons was my friend. We were a part of something in that temple. The question is, what happened. What went wrong?" asked Sashin.

"I don't know, but something went very wrong between you," replied Reshma.

"I need to find out what that temple was... where it is. And once I know, I need to get there. I need to get to Egypt," said Sashin.

"Hold on. You need to really think this through. Why do you want to go out there? What will you do once you're there?" replied Reshma while driving.

"I'm hoping that being out there will jog some more memories. There might be answers out there," remarked Sashin.

Chapter Twenty-One

It was five-thirty by the time Reshma had pulled up outside Sashin's house.

"Why don't you come in? I can get a take away," said Sashin.

"No, I have to get back. Ketan will be waiting," replied Reshma.

"Okay, no worries," responded Sashin.

"Why don't you come over to my place, and we can get take out there? You can go over your notes and work out what you plan to do next. You could stay over if you wanted and have a few drinks," suggested Reshma.

"Okay, I'll get my overnight bag ready and I'll drive over a bit later. Take out is on me since you drove," replied Sashin.

"Sounds good. See you later," said Reshma.

Sashin packed his small overnight bag with night clothes, a toothbrush, face cream, deodorant, and a sweatshirt, boxers, and a pair of socks for the next day. He left shortly afterwards, as it was an hour's drive to Kingston.

Arriving in Kingston, Sashin called Reshma.

"I can pick up food on the way as I'm already in Kingston. What do you guys fancy?"

"Pizza is fine. Pop into Go Go. Get a large veggie and a pepperoni pizza for Ketan," replied Reshma.

"No worries, will do," responded Sashin.

It was busy at Go Go with a line of people queuing out of the door due to the shop being small. Fortunately, five of the people in the queue were in the same group, and it was not long before Sashin was at the counter, ready to order.

Parking up near Reshma's, Sashin threw his overnight bag strap over his neck and grabbed the two boxes of pizza.

Ketan opened the door and greeted Sashin animatedly.

"Hey Sash, how are you doing? How did it go? Here, let me grab the pizza."

"I'm okay. Today went well, really interesting, but more questions," replied Sashin.

"Isn't that always the way with these things?" said Ketan.

Sashin could see Reshma through the open living room door, nodding her head from side to side and putting a finger to her lip. Sashin gave a bemused look back. She ushered him into the room.

"What?" whispered Sashin.

"Don't say too much yet – I'll tell him properly," replied Reshma.

"I can't tell Mum and Dad, and now I can't say anything to Ketan? Who can I tell?!" exclaimed Sashin.

"Er, me! Look, he takes a little time to warm up, but once he does, he's a bit more open-minded," responded Reshma.

"Well it feels like a very small circle of people that I can talk to," said Sashin looking glum.

Reshma hit her hand on Sashin's shoulder and consoled him.

"Look little brother, one day you'll be able to tell the whole world your story. But before you do, you have to work out what you're going to do next."

Ketan appeared at the door.

"Beer, Sash?"

"Yes," replied Sashin.

Ketan shortly returned with two cans of beer. Handing one over to Sashin he spoke.

"I've put the oven on so let me know when you want to eat and I'll heat the pizza up a bit."

"Great, I'm in no rush to eat just yet," replied Sashin looking over at Reshma.

"Have a drink first, relax. You've had a long day," said Reshma.

"Just be aware that the footie is on in forty minutes, okay," remarked Ketan.

Reshma rolled her eyes.

"Do you want to watch the footie, Sash?" asked Reshma.

"I'm not too fussed. Who's playing?" replied Sashin.

"Man U of course," said Ketan looking shocked.

"We can talk over your notes from today while Ketan watches the game," suggested Reshma looking at Sashin wide-eyed.

"I'll sort out the pizzas, don't want to be messing about during kick-off," said Ketan.

"I'll give you a hand," added Reshma, disappearing into the kitchen.

Sashin followed to wash his hands.

Ketan handed over a plate with piping hot vegetarian pizza slices.

"There's garlic sauce there, help yourself," he said.

They all sat comfortably in the living room enjoying pizza. Ketan looked over at Sashin and began to talk.

"So what was it like? The past life...?" Ketan struggled, rotating his hand, trying to finish his sentence.

"Regression," added Sashin.

"Yes, that's it," replied Ketan.

"It was more like being hypnotised to be honest. Some of it I don't really remember as the lady, Sarah, was talking to my higher self," explained Sashin.

"But what's the point if you can't remember?" asked Ketan.

"Well Reshma made notes. The lady usually records the sessions but her device is off for repairs," replied Sashin.

"Right," said Ketan expressionless.

Just then, the football had started, and Ketan jumped up and down in his seat like a rowdy supporter.

"There's loads of pizza left. Come and get a few more slices, Sash, and grab your notes. We'll be in the kitchen," said Reshma.

"Yeah, yeah, fine," responded Ketan, glued to the television.

In the kitchen, Reshma sat at a white breakfast table in the centre and Sashin came in with the notes and joined her. Chomping down on a slice of pizza, he scanned the pages. Holding up the last page, he finished chewing the last bit of pizza.

"I came across a bookshop in London Bridge, and I saw a book in there that might help in finding out more about what I saw in the regression. The book is called 'The Secret Order of Amun'."

"You should get the book," replied Reshma.

"I've got a meeting at London Bridge on Monday. I'll go to the bookshop on my way there," replied Sashin.

"But like I said to you before, you plan to find out more information, right? Then, what are you going to do with it? What will you do if you go to Egypt?" asked Reshma.

"Alexis is putting together curated trips for Egypt. These are special VIP type trips that give you private access to areas at popular sites. It's a ten to twelve day tour, but that's too long. I'm thinking of talking to her about going on one of these trips, but a streamlined version," replied Sashin.

"Ooh Alexis, pulling out favours already? If she can help, that's great," said Reshma.

"I think it could benefit the both of us to be honest," added Sashin.

"I don't think it would be wise to go out there by yourself," remarked Reshma.

"I'm not," replied Sashin.

"Oh, are you going with Alexis?" questioned Reshma.

"No. *You're* coming with me," answered Sashin.

With her jaw dropping and eyes widening, Reshma spoke.

"I don't know."

"Well, think about it. You've always wanted to go back to Egypt since your holiday in Sharm. And what with all your study in spirituality, you might pick up on something," replied Sashin with hands up, palms showing by his head as if surrendering.

"Okay, okay," whispered Reshma, nodding her head in approval.

"How are you going to get it by..." Sashin said, pointing his thumb across towards the living room.

"Leave that to me," responded Reshma.

"Right, let's get back to the living room," said Sashin, getting up.

"Yeah, let's see if he's in a good mood or bad mood. Do you want another beer?" asked Reshma

"Just one more, as I'm still a bit tender from last night," responded Sashin.

Man United had won the game one–nil, so Ketan was in a good mood for the remainder of the evening.

It was coming up to ten-thirty. Ketan went into the kitchen and returned with a bottle in his hand.

"Do you fancy a whisky?" he said.

"Which one is it?" asked Sashin.

"It's the 'Balvenie Double Cask'," replied Ketan, showing him the bottle.

"That's a nice one," remarked Sashin.

"I got it from my work as a gift. I don't drink whisky, so you might as well try it," urged Ketan.

"Go on then; I'll have a nightcap. You should try it too," suggested Sashin.

"Okay, just to try. Any ice?" asked Ketan.

"One please, a small one," replied Sashin.

Ketan came back with two tumblers, both containing one ice cube and a decent measure of whisky, which he ascertained to be more than a double. Sashin took a sip and savoured the taste, showing his approval by raising his glass.

"Cheers," he said.

Ketan took a sip and scrunched up his face.

"More ice I think," he said, scurrying off into the kitchen.

Feeling the toll of a long day, a mixture of a mild hangover and the hypnotic regression, Sashin started feeling drowsy. He took the last sip of whisky, and his eyes began to weigh down. He was semi-conscious watching the movie on television.

"He's nodding off," exclaimed Reshma, pointing.

"Yeah, I'm off to sleep," replied Sashin.

Ketan took his tumbler and bid Sashin good night.

Chapter Twenty-Two

In the early hours of the morning, Sashin was awakened by the sound of a barking dog. He lay there, opening his eyes and staring up at the ceiling. Slowly getting up, he went over to the window and pulled the curtains to one side to look out of the window. There was a full moon. Everything was still and eerily silent outside, and soon the barking stopped.

Sashin crept downstairs and filled a glass of water from the filter jug on the kitchen worktop. After quenching his thirst, he put the glass in the sink and suddenly felt a strange sensation that drew him to the double doors that led to the garden. He stopped there for a moment and peered through the double-glazed doors. There was a glare from the light, so he switched off the light and looked again. He could sense something was outside looking in. Squinting his eyes, he narrowed his focus and, for a moment, thought he saw a shadow move.

Feeling a shiver through his body, he stopped himself and shrugged it off as an optical illusion caused by the moonlight. He returned back up to bed and whilst trying to fall asleep, the thought appeared in his mind to go astral. He remembered a technique from the book, 'A Guide to Astral Travel,' and started to relax his body from his head all the way down to his feet. He attempted to stretch out by lifting his astral arm. Slowly, his arm parted away from his body. He then tried to lift his other arm, which came free, but there was a strong magnetic pull on both arms that felt like they were being forced back in. He fought the pull and stretched his astral arms out even further, which created a momentum that began to pull the rest of his astral body free from his physical one.

With a final stretch forward, his astral form was completely free from his physical body. He floated out and away. Now standing by the bed, Sashin could see his body asleep. He walked downstairs and into the kitchen. Looking out of the double doors again this time, he saw a shadow being in the garden. Something was different about this entity. It was not like a shadow wraith but rather a shadow person. It banged its hand against the window, causing Sashin to flinch back, startled. Several other shadow people appeared in the garden. One shadow being ran towards the door and, upon attempting to crash through, was repelled back as yellow sparks bounced off the double-glazed window. Sashin was bewildered by what was happening.

Several of the shadow people tried to break through into the house but were being stopped by some kind of unseen barrier. Each time a being collided with the house, a cloud of sparks erupted like a firework.

Sashin materialised his astral sword, which glowed through the windowed door, and the shadow beings stopped and moved back. The moonlight was momentarily blocked by a figure descending from the sky. It was a robed man. It was Bakenkhons.

Bakenkhons walked towards the door. Sashin withdrew his light sword.

"I told you I would come for you and the people close to you," shouted Bakenkhons.

'No, not here,' thought Sashin. He looked and attempted to speak.

Bakenkhons lunged forward and was catapulted back by the force of repulsion.

"What magic is this?" he cried.

"I know we were once friends in Egypt and that we were a part of something," said Sashin.

Bakenkhons paused and stood frozen.

"I can't hear you. Why don't you come outside?!" he yelled.

"No!" replied Sashin.

Bakenkhons ordered the shadow people to run towards the house. A flurry of shadows ran and collided with the barrier, causing sparks to fly everywhere. A shock wave could be felt that pulsed through Sashin's astral body. Bakenkhons produced a mace and violently struck the door. The waves continued to be felt.

"This magic is weakening; keep trying to break through!" cried Bakenkhons.

Sashin had a sudden bout of panic. The last thing he wanted was a showdown at his sister's house. He suddenly thought about Bakenkhons and the shadow people entering the house and attempting to pull Reshma and Ketan's astral bodies out while they were asleep. He acted quickly and ran out of the kitchen and up the stairs.

Once upstairs, he glided through Reshma's bedroom door. A silhouette appeared outside the window. Sashin floated over and peeked his head through to see that Bakenkhons had flown around the house and hovered outside the bedroom window. He quickly retreated back into the room. Looking around, he saw various objects, toiletries, a picture frame, and an alarm clock with bells on top.

He flew over to the clock and attempted to touch the bell on top of it. But his hand went straight through it, and as it did, he felt the energy in his astral hand merge with that of the alarm clock; it was a strange sensation. He willed the alarm clock to move, saying it like a mantra in his mind, 'move, move!' But there was no movement. Sashin then willed his hand to vibrate fast and brought it closer to the clock, feeling his energy beginning to merge. He wrapped his energy around the clock and tried to use the melded energy to move the clock. There was a slight movement.

Sparks illuminated the darkness outside the window as Bakenkhons tried to break through. Sashin made another attempt. He took a deep breath and quickly focused. He brought his hand closer to the alarm clock as the energy began to merge. He willed the alarm clock on the floor. He visualised the clock on the floor. He then began to vibrate his hand, which in turn caused the energy to oscillate. The clock started to move more and as Sashin put all his might into vibrating his energy, the clock toppled over.

With a thud, the alarm clock hit the ground, causing the bells to chime. Reshma jerked awake and quickly rose up in bed. She leant over and shook Ketan.

"Ketan? Ketan, did you hear that? Something fell."

Rubbing his eyes, Ketan looked over.

"What? What is it?"

"Something fell, didn't you hear it?!" yelled Reshma.

"Yes," replied Ketan.

Ketan got out of bed and walked over to the high dressing table. He switched on the lamp and saw the alarm clock on the floor. Picking it up, he looked over at Reshma.

"Keep this away from the edge."

"I always do," remarked Reshma, unimpressed.

"It's a quarter to five, go back to sleep," responded Ketan.

Sashin's mind was alive with computations, working out when sunrise would be. 'For September, it is around six-fifteen,' he thought. He hoped that one and a half hours would be enough for whatever force was keeping Bakenkhons and the shadow people at bay to last until then. 'It would take at least an hour for these guys to fall back to sleep,' he thought.

Sashin took another peek through the window, and as he did, he saw a hand swiftly come towards his head. It was Bakenkhons who narrowly missed him as he jerked back into the room. Gliding through the wall, Sashin was in the spare room, where he walked over to the window and hesitated for a moment contemplating whether to look out. He decided against it and flew over to his body asleep, where he floated down and merged back into his physical body.

Opening his eyes, he got up and out of bed and went over to the window, where he peeled back the curtain. It was deadly silent. He walked back down to the kitchen and poured himself another glass of water. He felt somewhat drained from trying to move the alarm clock, which took a great deal of effort. However, it was another ability Sashin had gained to add to his repertoire of burgeoning astral skills. Gulping down the water, he walked over to the double-glazed door and could not sense any presence or negative energy. He walked upstairs and went back to bed with mixed emotions: anxiety, relief, and anger. He knew he had bought himself only a little bit of time.

Chapter Twenty-Three

It was a late start to Sunday morning. Sashin woke up at ten and made his way downstairs for breakfast. In the kitchen, Reshma sat on a chair by the double doors, meditating with a mala in her hand. Incense burned on the breakfast tabletop. He walked in slowly.

"What time do you call this, sleepyhead?" said Reshma without opening her eyes.

"Aren't you supposed to be meditating? You can't do that and talk at the same time," replied Sashin.

"I can," said Reshma with a dry smile. She continued talking.

"I've finished now anyway."

Opening her eyes, she got up and took the incense out into the garden.

"I'll put toast on. Help yourself to cereal. I've put some out on the breakfast bar. Do you want tea?" asked Reshma.

"Yes ta," replied Sashin.

"Ketan popped out to do some shopping. Did you sleep okay?" asked Reshma.

"Did you?" replied Sashin.

"We woke up in the middle of the night because the alarm clock fell. Ketan accused me of leaving it near the edge of the dressing table, which I didn't," responded Reshma.

"That was me," said Sashin.

"What? What are you talking about?" snapped Reshma.

"I woke up in the night and came downstairs for water. I sensed something in the garden and got a strange feeling. To investigate, I went astral and came down again. There were shadow people in the garden, and then Bakenkhons turned up. I didn't want to risk them coming into the house and trying to pull you guys out of your bodies," explained Sashin.

"Are you kidding me? You brought him here?" said Reshma.

"I didn't bring anything here, not intentionally. Bakenkhons said he wanted to cut my cord, take possession of my body, and then come after the ones I love. He tracked me down here. Don't forget, he's always astral and could be watching us when we least expect it," remarked Sashin.

"Well, he won't be getting in this house, hopefully," replied Reshma.

"Yes, that's right. The shadow beings couldn't get in the house. Every time they tried to break through, it was like a force field was stopping them. Same with Bakenkhons. Even he couldn't break through. I mean, he was beginning to weaken whatever the barrier was. Why couldn't they get in?" wondered Sashin aloud.

"I had this house blessed when we bought it. I meditate in the spare room and here in the kitchen. And I've used a protection spell on the house," answered Reshma.

"A spell? Wow, what kind?" asked Sashin with surprise.

"It's the 'lesser ritual of the pentagram,' which I performed in the kitchen. I started right here," said Reshma, standing beside the double-glazed doors.

"Right," responded Sashin.

"It involves all four directions, drawing the pentagram from east to all other directions and calling upon the Higher Self, God, or the Divine at each point. I learnt about it when I was studying High Magik," stipulated Reshma.

"Well, whatever you did worked. It stopped the shadow people and Bakenkhons. I've never seen those shadow people before. I've seen shadow beings, yes, but not shadow people.

And as far as this spell goes, you even stopped Bakenkhons and he's not an easy person to hold back. I know!" remarked Sashin.

"It takes long enough to do, so I'm glad it did," added Reshma.

"Now, tell me about this magic," said Sashin.

"You never asked. Do you want me to protect your house?" asked Reshma.

"No, it's fine. I need to get on Alexis's Egypt trip and get as much out of it as I can," replied Sashin.

"Okay, get yourself some breakfast. Grab some toast. There's chopped avocado in the fridge, or you can have peanut butter," said Reshma.

"What about tomatoes?" asked Sashin.

"In the fridge too," replied Reshma.

They ate breakfast in silence, reflecting. And soon after, Reshma offered him some masala tea. He rarely drank masala chai, but on this occasion, he did.

Yes, thanks," replied Sashin.

Sashin got up and took his plate and mug over to the sink to wash and dry them.

"I'm going to get ready," he said.

"Hey, not everyone knows what you're going through. I know it's tough. It's like you're living two lives. But whether you die on the astral plane, which of course you won't, or whether this continues, then you're going to be numb, so you kind of die inside anyway. Either way, it feels like the end," said Reshma.

"That's probably the most profound thing you've said to me," replied Sashin, smiling.

"No, not the only thing. You just haven't been listening," responded Reshma, smirking.

"Well, it's not the end – it's just the beginning I guess," added Sashin.

Ketan returned from shopping and, struggling to open the door with one shopping bag in hand, placed the other on the floor to free up a hand.

"Here, I'll give you a hand," said Sashin.

Walking over, he grabbed the shopping bag Ketan was holding and took it into the kitchen.

"Did you sleep okay, Sash?" asked Ketan.

"Yes. How about you?" replied Sashin.

"The damn alarm clock fell and woke us up in the middle of the night," said Ketan.

"So I heard," responded Sashin.

Reshma came into the hallway and pulled Sashin into the living room. Ketan made his way into the kitchen and began to unpack the shopping bags.

"How did you move the clock?" asked Reshma, whispering.

"It wasn't easy. It's like I merged my hand. Let me rephrase that – I merged the energy of my hand with the alarm clock and then willed it to move. Like... I visualised it to be on the floor. So I had to vibrate my hand so that the energy was activated," explained Sashin, holding up his hands. He continued. "Does that make sense?"

"That's amazing!" replied Reshma.

Chapter Twenty-Four

Sashin had a meeting with Alexis and Eddie Mann at one-thirty in the afternoon, which would most likely last two hours at most. He worked from home on Monday morning and prepared his notes for the meeting ahead. The plan would be to get to London Bridge an hour or so early, around lunch time.

It was relatively busy at Hendon Central for a late Monday morning. Sashin caught the eleven-thirty tube. He managed to get a seat near the sliding doors. Within thirty minutes, he had arrived at London Bridge station. He made his way out onto the platform and navigated his way out, in and amongst fellow commuters. It was mild for September. Sashin checked his mobile phone for the temperature. The weather app showed twenty degrees Celsius. He felt warm in his light black jacket.

Soon, he arrived at the 'Ancient Egyptian Books' store. Standing outside, he saw the owner on the phone through the window. The leopard that Sashin saw outside the shop on his first visit had been replaced with a silver cat statue. The cat wore a brown, red, and blue collar, off which hung a beetle amulet. On the collar was a gold square. Sashin had to look closer to see it had the 'Eye of Horus' on it. The shop owner was having an animated conversation, gesticulating with one arm as he spoke. Sashin walked into the shop and began to scan around. The numerous piles of books that Sashin saw on his first visit were reduced to only a few. He searched around, seeing if he could spot the book 'The Secret Order of Amun'. The book was not on any of the piles. He then ran his finger across the books in one of the bookcases, but it was not there. Moving onto the next bookcase, he scanned over more book spines, searching from top to bottom. Sashin began to think that he would have to ask the shop owner to locate the book.

The owner had finished his call. He was wearing blue jeans with brown shoes and a black hoodie. His black curly hair was scruffy from running his hand through it during the phone call.

"Hello! You had a book in here the last time I came in called 'The Secret Order of Amun'. I wanted to take a look at it," said Sashin.

"That book is sold. I have it here waiting to be sent," replied the shopkeeper, leaning over the counter to pick up the book.

"Can I have a look please, before you send it out?" asked Sashin.

"You can have a quick look, but be very careful with the pages," said the shopkeeper, sternly.

He handed over the book to Sashin and stood there watching. Sashin took the book and turned so that he had his back to the owner, whose glare seemed to pierce his back. Just then, the phone rang and the shopkeeper was soon engrossed in another conversation to Sashin's relief.

Conscious of the little time that he had, he frantically flicked through the pages, skimmed over text and read a passage, 'They are there to influence the universe. Their actions influence the fabric of time and space, the universum as thought.' He then came across a drawing and immediately recognised the place. The line of sphinx statues led up to a large opening with columns on the other side, and there was a small crowd of people within the grounds by the columns. At the bottom of the drawing was the title, 'The Temple of Karnak, Luxor'. Sashin quickly fumbled in his inner jacket pocket, quickly taking a picture with his phone, turning his head slightly to watch out for the shop owner. He was still in conversation on the phone. Continuing to turn the pages now with his mobile phone in hand, he came across a page that mentioned the Theban high priests of Amun. Sashin took more pictures. Near the end of the book was another picture that showed two stone slabs, raised as if on an altar. Sashin recognised this from his past life regression as well. Beneath the picture was the title, 'Inner Chamber of the High Priests of Amun'. Sashin snapped another photograph whilst hearing the shopkeeper end his phone call. He slid his mobile phone back into his jacket pocket.

"Okay, can you hand over the book?" snapped the owner.

"Here you go," replied Sashin, feeling sweat on his forehead.

"You know a funny thing?" said the owner.

Sashin looked bemused. "What?"

"The buyer for this book was very desperate to get hold of it. He was willing to pay me extra to reserve it and post it to him. Do you believe in conspiracy theories?" asked the shopkeeper.

"I do, yes. I find them interesting," responded Sashin.

"I phoned around to get hold of other copies of the book. Here's the thing – everywhere I contacted, they had all sold out. It's like someone is buying up all copies of the book. Whoever they are, it feels like they don't want this book out in circulation," explained the shopkeeper.

"Right," replied Sashin, nodding slowly.

"Do I sound crazy?" asked the owner.

"No, not really. I mean, you've phoned around, and it's odd that the book is selling everywhere at the same time," replied Sashin.

"Sorry you didn't buy the book earlier, but maybe it's for the best," said the shopkeeper, looking concerned.

"I don't know about that," mumbled Sashin.

"What?" asked the shopkeeper, staring intently.

"Oh, nothing. Well, I'd better get going," added Sashin.

Walking out of the bookshop, he felt crushed. The book was his last hope of gaining some answers. Now all Sashin had were a few photos from which to make sense of things.

He refocused his mind on work and walked towards the Dream Ventures office with his head down in a trance. It was twenty past one when he arrived at the office. He was early and decided to take a seat near the entrance. There was now a receptionist sitting nearby, and she asked Sashin if she could help. He pointed out he had a one-thirty meeting, and the receptionist enthusiastically rushed off. She soon returned with Alexis, who ushered him into the main office. Walking through the door, he waited until it closed behind him and then gave Alexis a hug. She reciprocated the gesture, but it felt a little awkward as she hastily pulled away.

"Can I talk to you after the meeting? I have a proposition for you regarding one of your curated trips," asked Sashin.

"Yeah sure. I have about half an hour free after," replied Alexis.

A few of Alexis' staff sat at their desks working as Alexis escorted Sashin to one of the large meeting rooms. Sashin took off his laptop bag and took a seat.

"Would you like tea or coffee?"

"Tea please, white with one sugar," answered Sashin.

"Coming right up," said Alexis.

When Alexis returned, she was accompanied by Eddie Mann.

"Hi Sashin, how are you doing? Have you decided if you're in or out?"

Smiling, Sashin replied.

"Oh, I'm well and truly out. I've got enough going on at the moment, thanks."

"Oh well. Never say never, right?" replied Eddie, pointing his finger at Sashin like a gun with his forefinger and thumb raised.

"Right then, let's get started," said Alexis. She connected her laptop to the screen on the far wall and brought up Sashin's mind map of the training schedule.

"From the left, a new team member starts and goes through a fast track route to get started. I think we need to be clear on what the fast track route is. Moving along the map, there's further training to help develop team members to become proficient at growing their teams through effective recruiting and duplication. Finally, for the long term, they have the capability to become a trainer and train the trainer," explained Alexis.

"So for the fast track, I was thinking of a way to get people started fast. Eddie mentioned the idea of incentivising new team members," added Sashin.

"Yes, I talked about this in my email," responded Eddie. He got up and walked towards the television whilst talking.

"What puts people off from getting involved in a business is the cost. Now, networking is nowhere near as expensive as a traditional business. But think of this, 'get four, pay no more.' This is the fast track mechanism – a new member gets four new members and gets a free business, no subscription, and on top of that receives a fast track bonus. Just the thought really excites me. The growth from this alone will be huge."

"How much of a bonus are you talking about?" asked Sashin.

"It could be between one hundred and two hundred pounds," answered Eddie.

"We'll let our finance guys crunch the numbers on that to see what's sustainable," added Alexis.

"The main activity new members should be doing at the start is just inviting. Inviting prospects to see a presentation, this can be getting people to the weekly presentations here or to an online presentation," said Eddie.

"The online presentation is ready to go now. So people can literally be sent a link to the site," explained Alexis.

"And I think you should hold two presentations a week starting a month from now to allow some momentum to build," said Sashin.

"Good idea," replied Eddie, pointing again. He then continued.

"Now for training, once members begin building a team, they will need to understand how to deal with objections and fully understand the prospects' circumstances. Not everyone will be ready or eligible to do this. So the training needs to be geared around reading people, understanding their needs, and then overcoming objections. At the same time, always remember to invite people to view a presentation as a parallel activity. There is a great piece on the colours of personality that I can share with you and that can be incorporated into the training."

"Sounds good. We've finalised the promotion levels for rank advancement. We also have a bibliography of books that we can recommend for learning and self-development. There's four categories, one for the student, one for the salespeople, one for the business owner, and then one for the trainer or mentor," said Alexis.

"That's the key, self-development. You don't want to be like other networking companies that train their members without developing them. This should be a journey that helps you evolve and develop yourself through the process and experience, so whether you succeed or not in the business, you still have that take away," added Sashin.

"Wow! You sound like you've been in the business before," remarked Eddie.

"No, I just pay attention and occasionally get excited," replied Sashin.

"You're onto something there. I think self-development is really important, and we should encourage it as a company," responded Alexis.

"This is just the start, but longer term you could have training events around the world where members come together, travel and receive training," suggested Sashin.

"That works. I've seen it before in other companies. Now for longer term training, it's all about teaching duplication and training people to be trainers to their team and the wider network," explained Eddie animatedly, standing up from his chair.

"We'll launch the fast track in two weeks, but you can still talk about it in upcoming presentations to create excitement. The training will be finalised in about four weeks. I think we have a really good roadmap. Oh, and congratulations Eddie, on jumping two ranks already to Ambassador. We literally have the direct commissions and monthly residuals tied down. Next, we're looking at weekly team bonuses," said Alexis.

"I've got a suggestion that just came to me as you were speaking," offered Sashin. "Think about travel currency and training currency, hear me out on this. It's another form of incentive where each of these types of currency would be paid out to encourage members to travel by using the product and to go to training events. The currency would not be redeemable for cash. And longer term, think car bonus or even a home bonus," he added with wide eyes.

"Woah, woah, steady on tiger. You're talking step twenty-five, and first we have to get past step five. But I tell you what – as a parting gift, you can give a full outline of these ideas, and I'll run it past finance for analysis," replied Alexis.

"That's what I get for opening my big mouth," joked Sashin.

"Well, I'm glad you have the commissions sorted out because I ain't messing about and eager to make some money!" interjected Eddie.

Alexis smiled at him faintly and announced, "Our two hour meeting is officially wrapped!"

"Right, great meeting. I hope to see you both soon," said Eddie.

"My time is nearly up. I have a few weeks left, and then I'll be moving on to my next project," said Sashin, extending out his hand.

Eddie shook his hand tightly.

"Sashin, you have my number, so whenever you're ready to get on board, give me a call. This is going to be huge."

"I'm sure it will be," replied Sashin.

After Eddie left, Alexis offered Sashin another tea, but he declined and opted instead for water. She led him into the main office area, where they sat on the sofas in the middle.

Chapter Twenty-Five

"So you wanted to talk to me about one of the trips?" asked Alexis, sitting cross-legged on the sofa.

Sashin took a moment to take in the sight of her relaxed again.

"Yes, it's the curated trip for Egypt. I have a proposition that I think will benefit both of us," he said.

"Right, I'm listening," replied Alexis, looking intrigued.

"I want to go on the trip and test out your guides, as in really test them. I will give you feedback. I'm not asking to get paid for doing this. It gives me the opportunity to experience the trip, as I really want to visit Egypt," explained Sashin.

"We've only just finished curating the trip and confirming with our contacts and suppliers out there. I've already got some of my staff lined up to go out and test the trip, which isn't for a month or so yet," responded Alexis.

"I understand. That's why I'm suggesting this – I'm ready to go as soon as possible. Like I said, I can give you feedback as well as record some videos that you may be able to use for footage for one of your promotional videos," added Sashin.

"Yeah, I guess that's not a bad idea, but this would normally be done by our direct staff. As you will potentially be a consultant doing the work, I will arrange for your flights and accommodation and a driver whilst you're there. Maybe if I say you're a friend they might be more relaxed and you will be able to get a better idea of what they're like rather than them putting up a front just to get the business. Are you travelling alone?" asked Alexis.

"No, I will be travelling with someone," answered Sashin.

"Oh right, who with?" asked Alexis.

"My sister, Reshma," responded Sashin.

"Okay," replied Alexis, looking relieved. "I think that can be arranged."

"Can you run through the trip because, to be honest, I'm not looking to do the whole thing but a streamlined version of it with just the main parts like Luxor," said Sashin.

"That's not how it works. You can't just pick and choose parts of the trip. It's meant to be a twelve day tour that covers Cairo, the Giza Plateau, Luxor, Abydos with a Nile cruise, Aswan, and back around to Luxor and Cairo," answered Alexis.

"There you go, you've got duplication there. The back end of the tour that goes back to Luxor and Cairo – what happens there?" asked Sashin.

"Boat rides, Karnak Temple, and a drive to Sakkara. But yeah, I guess there's quite a few things that you wouldn't need to do if you didn't want to," replied Alexis.

"So let me just focus on Cairo and Luxor then, as I don't need to do Abydos, Aswan, or Sakkara. Your guys can do the whole thing when they go out there. I'm planning to be in Egypt for no more than five days. I definitely want to see the Temple of Karnak. Also, I think twelve days is maybe a bit much as most people normally go for a ten day holiday. So, we could look at a ten day alternative that cuts out some of the activities like the boat rides. Once you've done one, you've done them all," said Sashin.

"Okay, there will be an internal flight from Cairo to Luxor, just so you're aware. But that's doable. I will want full feedback from you and suggestions to improve, if any, which I doubt as we've worked really hard on the best experience and people. And your suggestion for a ten day version isn't bad. I'll think about that," responded Alexis, smirking.

"That's brilliant. I really appreciate this and it means a lot to me," said Sashin.

"You've done a great job for us launching the network and helping with the long term plan. Consider this as thanks for that. It will take up to a week to organise, so just be on standby. I'm thinking the first two days you can do Cairo and then maybe a day or two in Luxor where you can visit either Dendera or the Valley of the Kings along with Karnak," suggested Alexis.

"Hmm, I'm not sure. I don't know much about Dendera or the Valley of the Kings," replied Sashin.

"It's a good thing you're going on this trip then," chuckled Alexis. She continued.

"Have a think about it. I'll finalise the itinerary and let you know. But once I've done it, you have to do the tour I've set out."

"Okay boss," said Sashin grinning cheekily.

He got up and put his laptop bag up and over his shoulder. Alexis uncrossed her legs and also jumped up. Walking together towards the exit, Alexis began to speak, almost whispering.

"I would like to go out with you again."

"Good, let's do that when I get back," replied Sashin.

Alexis gave Sashin a hug, and the energy felt warmer this time.

"Speak soon," he said on the way out.

Alexis smiled and held up her hand.

The walk back to the station was busy as it got closer to rush hour. Borough High Street bustled as commuters ran past, rushing to get to the station to catch their train. Approaching the 'Ancient Egyptian Books' shop, Sashin stopped for a moment and stood outside, looking in through the window. The owner could not be seen. Sashin had that crushing feeling again of disappointment, like his stomach was being compressed. Yet he remembered that he had taken some photos on his mobile phone, and the thought brought him back to life. He continued walking towards the station.

The platform was very busy. Sashin battled to get on the tube and just about managed to find the only remaining seat. He thought he would put the journey back to good use and pulled out his phone to look at the pictures he had taken of the book 'The Secret Order of Amun'. Scrolling past the first picture, which was the drawing of the 'Temple of Karnak', he got to the second and realised that he had taken the picture in haste and had to zoom in in order to read the writing. After mentioning the 'universum as thought,' the text went on to say that the Order's purpose was for advancement of the human spirit and that they studied mysticism and esotericism. Amun-Ra was considered the king of gods, the creator god.

Sashin became conscious of the passenger next to him looking over, and he put his phone down for a moment. He felt a little paranoid after his chat with the bookshop owner. With the passenger now looking away, Sashin resumed looking at the photos. He swiped to the next one and zoomed in. Having taken photos of the pages in random fashion, it felt disjointed reading the extracts. However, reading through the text, the page referred to Theban High Priests as being spiritual adepts who studied practices from around the world, using various kinds of meditation, including kundalini meditation, to expand consciousness and activate the third eye. There was mention of the chamber that the priests used for meditation and projecting consciousness. 'That must be it,' Sashin thought. That was a reference to them using astral travel, but it was unclear as to why. The next photo was the last one of the chamber itself.

The train came to a standstill. Sashin jumped up, realising he had arrived at Hendon Central. He was so engrossed in analysing the photos that he lost track of where he was. When he got home, he connected his mobile phone to his desktop computer to study the photos on a bigger screen. He noticed one photo he swiped past without looking at on the tube. The page briefly mentioned Thoth as the scribe of the gods. He was said to have been born from the lips of Ra at the beginning of creation. 'But what does Thoth have to do with anything?' thought Sashin. The page went on to read that Thoth was the master of reincarnation and that he reincarnated as Hermes Trismegistus. There was further mention of emerald tablets and the 'Halls of Amenti', none of which made any sense to Sashin, as he did not know in what context this was being mentioned. He clicked back to the photograph of the 'Temple of Karnak' and took a moment to focus on the drawing.

Sashin's mind was busy working as he tried to figure out how to get to the inner chamber. He was aware that this was going to be a challenge. His concentration was broken by the ping of his phone. It was a message from Reshma.

Reshma: Did you manage to get the book?

Sashin: No, it has been sold to someone else. I had a quick look through and took some random pictures before handing it back to the owner. I'm really crushed that I couldn't buy it. I was hoping it would provide some answers.

Reshma: It's not the end of the world. You may get some answers from the trip.

Sashin: Well that temple that I saw in my regression is the Temple of Karnak in Luxor. I was able to find that out. The owner said a funny thing too. He thinks someone is trying to buy up all remaining copies of the book.

Reshma: Really? That sounds crazy. Why on Earth would someone want to buy up all the books? What's so special about it?

Sashin: I'm not sure, but maybe someone doesn't want information to get out about the 'Order of Amun'.

Reshma: Well, don't let it get you down. Let's make the most of being in Egypt and see what we can find.

Sashin: Yes, you're right.

Chapter Twenty-Six

During the week, Sashin was back in the office and ventured over to Dev, who was preparing heavily for his social media campaign for 'Star Group'. Krish worked intermittently from home as he had to ferry his parents over to Southampton, who were embarking on a Mediterranean cruise with their circle of friends, all of whom were going to meet at the port. Working away intently with a frown on his face, Sashin broke Dev's train of thought.

"Cheer up."

Dev looked up and replied.

"I'm in the zone, gearing up for this campaign. It's a big deal for me, so I want to really make it work."

"I'm sure you will," replied Sashin.

"Thanks. I've got plenty to get on with, so what's up?" asked Dev.

"Listen, I'm going to Egypt in about a week or so. It's partly..." before Sashin could finish, Dev interrupted.

"Is this to do with your past life thing with Egypt you mentioned on Friday?"

"Partly; I'm going to test out a curated trip for Alexis that her company has put together, especially for Egypt. I will be seeing just how good her guides are out there, because these trips offer a private tour. And I'll also get to experience Egypt and explore the past life connection," replied Sashin.

"Right, I see. Well that sounds like a win-win, also known as a company perk," said Dev grinning.

"I still have to do some work, but it also means something to me too. I'm hoping I'll get something out of it," responded Sashin.

"I hope so too. That way it's not just all work. Are you going alone?"

"No, I'm taking Reshma as my helper," answered Sashin, smiling.

"Cool, keep me posted," said Dev.

"I'll probably need a favour from you," Sashin said with a pleading look.

"Let me guess? Airport drop off," remarked Dev.

"Spot on buddy," replied Sashin.

"Okay, just give me advance notice," he sighed.

"Thanks," responded Sashin.

Sashin felt a buzz in his pocket and took out his phone to see that he had received a message from Alexis.

Alexis: Your trip is all organised. I've emailed you the flight tickets, details of your accommodation, and the itinerary. You fly out next Monday afternoon at two o'clock from Heathrow to Cairo with InterJet. Then, Wednesday morning you have an early flight at 9am to Luxor, a one hour flight. You can get brunch or wait for lunch when you arrive at the hotel. You've got two days in Luxor, and then you fly back on Friday on a nice afternoon flight at half past two. You have a free day when you arrive on Monday. You meet your tour guide on Tuesday morning at the hotel, who will take you to the Giza Plateau. Wednesday is a bit trickier, as you will have to meet your tour guide in Luxor. He will contact you.

Sashin: That's brilliant, thanks so much x.

Alexis: No worries, tell me all about it when you get back x.

Sashin looked up and waved his phone.

"Alexis just confirmed. The flight is next Monday at two in the afternoon, which means we have to be at Heathrow for just after eleven o'clock."

"That's not too bad. I can log on first thing in the morning at home and then come pick you up at yours for about a quarter past ten. Can Reshma get dropped off at your house? It will make life a lot easier?" asked Dev.

"That should be fine. I'll let her know," replied Sashin.

"I'll bring Krish along too," said Dev.

"For company on the way back," responded Sashin cheekily.

"So he's not missing out," replied Dev, breaking into a chuckle.

During lunch, Sashin made his way out to the line of shops that was down the road from the office to get something to eat from the mini-mart. On the way, he messaged Reshma to let her know the flight details for the following Monday. She responded while Sashin was in the shop to let him know she had booked the time off. Sashin then messaged her back.

Sashin: Can you get to my house in the morning for ten as Dev will be picking us up and dropping us at Heathrow?

Reshma: I'll check with Ketan, but it should be fine.

Sashin: Okay, let me know asap.

Reshma: Will do.

Reshma: Oh, it's hot, isn't it at the moment?

Sashin: Yes, it's in the thirties.

Reshma: I better pack light clothing.

Sashin had picked up a Ploughman's sandwich, a bag of sweet chilli crisps, and a bottle of coconut water from the mini-mart. He made his way back to the office and was met with a courier who had brought in a number of boxes.

"We've finally got our large screens and hubs!" said Dev excitedly.

"It took long enough. Let's get this setup. Krish is going to be well surprised tomorrow," replied Sashin.

They both eagerly unboxed the monitors and found that there were wireless keyboards in separate boxes as well.

"We've got wireless keyboards as well," said Sashin.

"Great! It's about time," replied Dev.

After setting up the monitors, hubs, and keyboards, Sashin and Dev stood back to admire their work, both nodding in approval.

Dev went over to make a cup of coffee. Sashin connected his laptop to a hub and saw the large monitor come to life.

"It makes a big difference working on a large screen," called out Sashin.

Dev steadily walked back with two mugs. He placed one by Sashin, and sat down, eager to connect up to the new hub.

"Thanks," said Sashin.

"No worries. These monitors came at the right time," said Dev as he successfully connected his laptop.

Sashin accessed his email and opened up the itinerary message from Alexis. On Monday, they would be met by a driver at Cairo airport who would take them to the Marriott Mena House hotel. A welcome dinner was arranged for between seven-thirty and ten in the evening at the main restaurant. Breakfast would be at half past seven on Tuesday morning, followed by a meeting with their tour guide, after which there would be a private visit to the Sphinx. There would be a stop-off at the souvenir shop afterwards. Lunch was organised for half past twelve followed by a private visit to the Giza Plateau.

As Alexis had mentioned in her message, there would be an internal flight on Wednesday morning at nine o'clock to Luxor. They would be met by a driver at the airport and taken to a Dream Ventures-owned hotel. Contact details were provided for a tour guide who was expected to contact them to arrange a private visit to the 'Temple of Karnak'.

The plan for Thursday was optional. They could choose to have a free day or visit the 'Valley of the Kings'. Sashin smiled reading this. He was impressed that Alexis had listened to him about being unsure what the 'Valley of the Kings' was.

The flight back was arranged for two-thirty on Friday afternoon from Luxor to Heathrow with InterJet.

It looked like an impressive itinerary to Sashin. He leant back in his chair with his hands behind his head, taking in the details on his new large screen. His phone pinged with a message from Reshma.

Reshma: Getting dropped off in the morning is fine. Ketan will also pick us up on Friday evening after we land.

Sashin: That's great. Tell him thanks. I'll email you the itinerary. We can go over it at the airport if you want.

Reshma: Okay.

Chapter Twenty-Seven

It had been a few days since Sashin had last astrally projected. He had successfully managed to avoid it by mentally closing the door on the very notion. However, having gone to sleep that night, he had the image of the text from the book 'The Secret Order of Amun' running through his mind. He kept thinking of Thoth and the 'Halls of Amenti'. He fell asleep with the question on his mind as to what the halls were.

It was a strange feeling, but when Sashin began to regain consciousness and lucidity, he found that he was floating through the air at great speed. He could see in the distance the pyramids as he started to approach. The Great Sphinx of Giza was on his right with the three pyramids behind it. He floated past the Sphinx and landed in front of the great pyramid. The pyramid emitted a faint yellowish glow. Sashin noticed that a similar glow was coming from the Sphinx.

He turned to look, and his vision became four-dimensional again. He saw the glow coming from beneath the Sphinx and walked towards the great pyramid. There was an entrance above. Sashin floated up towards it, gliding through the entrance. As he did, he saw the particles of the stone that made up the blocks of the pyramid. Once inside, he saw the glow emanating from below. He floated down through the ground. Below, he found himself in a hall. There were hieroglyphs on the walls on either side. The glow came from ahead. Sashin walked forward towards the light.

He came to a central area that led to various hallways. Four columns stood in the centre. On one of the columns, he saw a person lying down with what looked like their astral body leaving their physical one. Sashin walked closer to take a good look. Underneath the drawing, he saw hieroglyphs, and the word 'Ka' came to mind, as he seemed to have a memory of the word.

In the centre of the four columns was a raised stone slab, upon which were glowing objects. Taking a closer look, Sashin saw a number of tablets glowing with a greenish yellow hue. He reached out to touch one, but his hand went straight through. It seemed like residual energy from the tablets had left an imprint, like a hologram. Sashin hovered his hand over the energy and felt a vibrating resonance. Looking up, a number of sarcophagi could be seen against the wall. One of the tablets showed a similar drawing as on the column of a person, with their astral body moving to a sarcophagus.

Walking away from the stone slab, Sashin ventured further down one of the halls. There were more stone columns on either side of the hallway with hieroglyphics on them. At the end of the hall were two holes in the wall, one above the other. Inside each hole was a crystal glowing brightly. Sashin proceeded cautiously and drew nearer to the crystals. As he got closer, he felt a strong vibration. He looked at his hands, which glowed. His whole astral body began to glow as he moved closer to the crystals. He felt a wave of refreshing rejuvenation come over him and suddenly felt stronger and more alive. He took in some deep breaths as he felt energy surge through his astral body.

With a quick leap, Sashin flew up rapidly through the stone ceiling, arriving in the inner chamber of the pyramid. It was dark. Sashin flew through the entrance and appeared outside. He then flew over to the Sphinx and landed nearby. The glow continued to emanate from within the Sphinx. Sashin ascended and flew through the weather-worn head. Inside the body of the Sphinx, he was astounded to find an entrance that led to a staircase underneath. The glow was coming from below. Sashin made his way down the stairs.

At the bottom was an opening to a large hall. The square entrance glowed orange. Walking through it and into the hall, he saw many large bookcases standing in rows. It was an ancient library. Many of the books gave off a glow that was different to that of the tablets. The books were actually there. Sashin scanned the various bookshelves to see what titles they held. There seemed to be sections that covered different subjects. In one area were books about alchemy. Quickly walking over to another section of the hall, Sashin saw books about medicine and herbal treatments. In another section were books on mathematics, while at the far end of the hall were two sections for astronomy and one for magic. "Incredible," Sashin whispered.

A sound of thunder caused Sashin to look up. 'That's new,' he thought. Returning to the entrance of the hall, he walked back up the stairs and flew out of the head of the Sphinx into the open. In the distance was a large black cloud. The thunder sounded again, and there were flashes of lightning. The cloud began to move. Sashin felt a chill run through his body. The cloud began to shrink and morph into a face; it started to become distinguishable. It was Bakenkhons. This was something Sashin had not seen before. Such a feat made Sashin realise that Bakenkhons was growing in power, maybe through the assistance of the black magicians. Sashin had seen enough to have his curiosity satisfied regarding the 'Halls of Amenti' and decided it was a good time to exit. His next move would be to physically travel to Egypt to try and get more answers and be prepared to face Bakenkhons again.

Sashin focused on his house, closed his eyes, and teleported with ease into his bedroom, where he merged with his body and snapped back in.

Chapter Twenty-Eight

The days flew by and Monday came around quickly without any further astral incursions. Sashin had finished all his packing on Saturday and had his suitcase and hand luggage ready by the door. He was wearing a T-shirt, jeans and had a light bomber jacket for the flight. He saw the familiar white Audi Q5 pull up on his driveway. Opening the front door, Reshma pulled out her suitcase from the boot and had a large handbag over her shoulder for her hand luggage. Ketan waved, and Sashin reciprocated the gesture.

"Hiya! Are you all set? Have you got everything?" asked Reshma.

"Yes, all ready to go. Got my passport in my jacket pocket," replied Sashin.

Reshma stationed her suitcase by Sashin's and sat down on the sofa.

"Do you want tea or coffee?" questioned Sashin.

"No, leave it. Save it for the airport," responded Reshma.

"Saves me having to wash," said Sashin.

"What, two mugs?" replied Reshma, breaking into laughter.

Suddenly, the sound of a blaring horn came from outside. Sashin looked out of the window to see Dev had arrived, with Krish, in his new Jaguar SUV, a recent purchase from a dealership in Liverpool.

"You head out, as I've got to set the house alarm," said Sashin.

Reshma took her suitcase out and Krish helped her. Sashin left his suitcase just outside by the front door as he activated his alarm with the fob on his house keys. As he walked out and closed the door, he heard Krish shout across.

"You can sort yourself out!"

"Thanks," replied Sashin.

Krish smiled cheekily. Sashin loaded up his suitcase and hand luggage.

"Press the button at the top, and the boot will close automatically," said Dev.

"Very snazzy," responded Krish.

"Right, ready?" asked Dev.

"Ready!" responded Reshma and Sashin.

"Which terminal is it?" asked Dev.

"Terminal 2," replied Sashin.

"Oh no! I thought it was Terminal 5. I better put my foot down," said Dev with panic in his voice.

Dev updated his satnav and sped off. The journey was relatively traffic-free thanks to travelling during the quieter afternoon hours.

"The new screens are great," said Krish.

"I knew you'd like them. They make a difference, don't they?" replied Sashin.

"Oh yes, definitely. They took long enough to come," added Krish.

It had been nearly one hour since they left Hendon. From the rearview mirror, Dev saw Reshma looking at her watch.

"Don't worry Reshma. We're nearly there – look," he said.

"Ten minutes past eleven – not bad driving Dev," said Sashin.

"I'm the best!" responded Dev emphatically.

Krish turned around and smiled wide-eyed.

The car stopped outside the departures terminal. In large letters above, a sign read 'Terminal 2, The Queen's Terminal', and Sashin quickly got out of the car and began unloading the luggage from the boot. Reshma went off to find a trolley,and returned shortly with one. Krish and Dev got out of the car and stood side by the side. After loading the trolley, Sashin leant in and whispered to Reshma.

"You take the trolley in. I will be with you in a bit. I'm just going to have a quick word with the guys."

"About?" asked Reshma.

"I'm going to tell them the truth. I think they deserve to know, as they're my close friends. And I don't know what's going to happen in Egypt," replied Sashin.

"Nothing's going to happen. That's why I decided to come with you," said Reshma.

"I meant in the astral. You know it's affected me before in the physical plane," responded Sashin.

"You have to stay positive and strong, Sashin. Are you sure you want to tell them?" asked Reshma.

"Yes, it's time," replied Sashin, turning away to walk towards Krish and Dev.

"Okay Sash, have a great time, and don't work too hard," said Dev, extending out his hand.

Sashin shook his hand and began to speak.

"Listen guys, I'm going to keep this short and to the point."

Krish looked at Dev, who looked back at him.

Sashin continued.

"In my past life, I was an Egyptian adept, which is a high priest, and I was part of an order. In my group, I had a friend, and somehow something turned sour between us. We obviously both died, but he is still alive on the astral plane. I can travel to the astral planes. This person has a serious grudge and is intent on finding me and settling a score."

"Like a negative entity?" said Krish.

"Yes, like a negative entity," replied Sashin.

"A negative entity attachment?" asked Krish.

"Not exactly. I knew this person; we have history," responded Sashin.

"I knew it! I *knew* you were going out to Egypt because of this past life stuff!" yelled Dev.

"Well, as you can see It's more than just past life stuff. It's a big deal for me. Yes, I am going out there to get answers, but it's also a work trip.

Now, when I go to sleep, I travel, astral travel and this is where this person can find me," explained Sashin.

"What? Like a Nightmare on Elm Street?" asked Krish.

"No!" cried Sashin.

"This sounds mind blowing Sash, and I'm sure this all seems real to you, but it sounds out of this world," said Dev.

"I know you might think I'm crazy – I can tell by the way you're looking at me. But this is real, and it is happening, which is why I'm telling you. Something could happen to me while I'm out in Egypt, and if it does, then I want you to explain what I told you to Alexis," said Sashin.

"You haven't told her?" asked Dev.

"Nope, it would be too much, too soon. I wouldn't want to jeopardise our working relationship. It would make things awkward. It will be different once I've finished the project," replied Sashin.

"Well, stay safe and come back in one piece whether it's here or out there, wherever out there is," responded Dev.

"The astral plane," replied Sashin.

"Right," said Krish, looking dumbfounded. Thinking for a minute, he looked at Sashin and spoke.

"Well, whoever this guy is, make sure you take him down."

Krish slapped him on his shoulder. Sashin nodded and walked away to join Reshma in the terminal, who waited near the entrance.

"Let's get our suitcases checked in," he said.

"Bag drop is over there," said Reshma pointing at the Interjet sign.

After dropping off their suitcases and clearing security, they both made their way airside. Whilst weaving in and out of passengers in the duty-free section, Reshma grabbed hold of Sashin's arm and pulled him over so he could see a café ahead.

"Let's get a cup of tea and a snack," said Reshma.

In the café, they sat down with their mugs of tea. Reshma had ordered a Danish pastry, and Sashin had a granola slice.

"Here's the itinerary," said Sashin, pulling out the printed email from Alexis out of his hand luggage. He straightened out the pages and set them out on the table. Reshma read over the first page.

"Right. So once we get to Cairo airport, the driver will meet us when we arrive – he should be holding a sign with your name," she said.

"I missed the bit about the sign," replied Sashin.

"You need to be paying attention to this!" scolded Reshma.

"Relax, you're coming along as the tourist," said Sashin.

Reshma rolled her eyes.

"The itinerary looks good. Three days, but full-on days with the option to do something on the last or have it as a free day. Without a tour like this, you would be a bit lost as to what to do, right?" she said.

"Yeah, exactly. That's the good thing about a curated trip like this," responded Sashin.

"Giza Plateau – I've always wanted to visit there!" shared Reshma excitedly.

"We've got an hour. What do you fancy doing, have a look around or sit?" asked Sashin.

"Let's have a mooch around the shops," replied Reshma.

The hour went by quickly, and after buying a bottle of water each, the pair made their way over to the gate for boarding. Once on the flight, they found that there was an older gentleman on their row who was sitting by the window. Sashin sat in the middle of the row of three, and Reshma had the aisle seat. There was in-flight entertainment much to Sashin's excitement.

"There normally isn't in-flight entertainment for short haul flights. I'm impressed," he said.

"Is this airline owned by the company you're working with?" questioned Reshma.

"I think it might be, you know," answered Sashin.

The captain had announced mid-flight that the journey was ahead of schedule and that the flying time would be reduced to four hours and twenty minutes. With one hour left to go, the flight attendants were doing the rounds with a food trolley. A petite flight attendant leant over and spoke.

"Vegetarian or non-vegetarian?"

"Vegetarian," answered both Sashin and Reshma. This was followed immediately by the passenger in the window seat shouting out.

"Non-vegetarian for me!"

The attendant thanked them and handed out boxes to each of them, before moving on quickly to the next row.

Reshma observed the box, which had 'snack box' written on the top. She opened it up to find a wrapped chunky sandwich, a bag of crisps, a mini packet of biscuits, and a small bottle of water inside.

"Complimentary snack box; this is great," said Reshma beaming.

"What sandwich did you get?" asked Sashin.

"Cheddar and caramelised onion chutney. You?" questioned Reshma.

"Cheddar and cucumber. Do you want to swap?" proposed Sashin holding up his sandwich.

"No chance," replied Reshma snappily.

Deflated, Sashin unwrapped his sandwich and continued to watch the movie on the in-flight screen. An hour later, the seatbelt sign blinked on as the flight attendants collected any remaining rubbish and did their last-minute checks. The captain made an announcement to prepare for landing. The window passenger slid up the window blind, allowing the sunlight to flood in. Sashin saw the plane tilting to one side as it began to descend. The thud of the wheels could be felt in Sashin's stomach as the plane hit the runway. They soon exited the aircraft with their hand luggage, behind a line of passengers eager to get off.

Once in the airport, they both cleared security and headed over to the baggage belts. The baggage collection area was stuffy and it seemed like the air conditioning had stopped working. A group of distressed travelling students approached a female staff member standing near the belt with a walkie-talkie, complaining that it was too hot. The lady with a stern look on her face pressed the button on her walkie-talkie and spoke into it. She then ordered the group back by holding out her hand with her palm facing forward.

"Let's get our suitcases quickly – it's chaos here," said Reshma.

Sashin made his way over to the conveyor belts stealthily and waited as suitcases started to appear on the moving silver belt. Within a few minutes, the motion stopped, and luggage was littered along the belt. Several passengers approached the female staff member, who was becoming visibly more and more agitated. Finally, she snapped at the irate passengers, telling them to be patient, and then began screaming into the walkie-talkie. The belt started moving again shortly afterwards. Reshma joined Sashin.

"Sash, it's a quarter to seven already. I just want to get to the hotel and get something to eat."

"I don't want to get to the hotel too late. I'm keeping an eye out for the luggage," replied Sashin.

They spotted the first suitcase, a black case with a red border. Sashin asked the family in the front to make way for him, but they ignored his first request, so he spoke louder.

"Excuse me!" he yelled, after which two people turned and made some room.

He grabbed and pulled the suitcase off the belt, rapidly wheeling it over to Reshma.

"Here's yours," he said.

Keeping his eyes focused on the belt, Sashin visualised his dark silver case, which had a gold ribbon tied to the handle, a trick his mum, Ushma, had taught him. He grew weary as he watched suitcase after suitcase being pulled off the belt. Finally, his case appeared without obstruction as the crowd around the belts had dwindled. With his suitcase in hand, he rushed over to Reshma and ushered her to follow.

"There's arrivals," he said, pointing up at the overhead sign.

The arrivals hall was a small area next to the exit. There were many people holding up signs, and some had their mobile phones held up with a name on the screen.

"Keep a lookout for my name," said Sashin.

"What do you think I'm doing?" replied Reshma, sounding irked.

Manoeuvring closer to the exit, Sashin spotted his name on a white piece of A4 paper written in black felt tip. A stocky man, slightly shorter than Sashin, stood waiting. He was wearing a short-sleeved white shirt and had short black curly hair and a moustache.. Reshma waved, which was met with a jolly smile back.

"Sashin Nayi," said the driver.

"Yes, that's me."

"My name is Tarek. Come, come," he said, taking the suitcases from them both.

They followed Tarek outside and were immediately hit by the evening mugginess. A line of yellow and white taxis stood outside, which they passed, and then continued past the next two lanes. Reshma turned towards Sashin and whispered.

"Where is he parked?"

"Can't be too far now," replied Sashin.

They eventually came to a car park further back, where Tarek led them to a black Hyundai saloon car. He loaded up the suitcases and offered to take the hand luggage which both Reshma and Sashin declined.

"I'll jump in the front," said Sashin.

A few minutes into the drive, Sashin wiped his forehead with his hand. The driver immediately pressed a button on the dashboard.

"AC," he said.

"Yes, good," replied Sashin, giving a thumbs up.

The journey took just under an hour, much to Reshma's chagrin. Pulling up outside the Marriott Mena House, Reshma breathed a sigh of relief.

"Finally," she said.

With the suitcases waiting by the car, a porter appeared with a trolley and took the cases, giving a ticket to Reshma. Sashin gave his thanks to the driver and turned to Reshma.

"Let's get checked in. We can drop our things off in the room, and then head straight down for dinner," he said.

"Sounds like a plan. I'm starving!" replied Reshma.

It was dark outside as they both walked into the illuminated reception area, with the light glistening off the white marble floor. The reception desk was to their right. A young woman with shoulder-length hair and wearing a light blue shirt greeted them.

"Welcome to the Marriott Mena House. Could I see your passports please?"

Sashin took out his passport from his jacket, which was in his hand luggage. Reshma handed hers over from her handbag. After scanning the passports, the woman, whose name badge read 'Nour Ahmad', handed them back.

"You have booked two adjoining guest rooms with garden views. Welcome dinner is at the Pavilion. There is also an Indian restaurant and an Italian restaurant. The pool bar is closed. Breakfast is served from six in the morning at the Pavilion also. You have half board, which covers breakfast and dinner with your booking. Here are your key cards. Please enjoy your stay."

"Thank you very much," responded Sashin.

Reshma grabbed Sashin by the arm and pulled him away.

"Let's get moving and drop off your hand luggage and then we'll head straight down to the main restaurant, Pavilion," she said.

In the room, Sashin put his hand luggage on top of the stand by the wardrobe. Reshma rushed through the adjoining door and started speaking fast.

"Before you go to sleep, I have to cleanse the rooms."

"What, how?" responded Sashin.

"I will meditate in both rooms with this," she said, holding up her mala.

There was a knock on the door. Sashin responded to find the porter had arrived with their suitcases.

"Do you have the ticket?" asked Sashin.

Reshma handed it over. After wheeling in both suitcases, they headed downstairs to the main restaurant, Pavilion. The Pavilion was a buffet restaurant. There was a small table that had been set up near the entrance with Dream Ventures leaflets and a welcome pack. The pack contained a fan, a pair of slippers, a bottle of wine, and a personal note to each of them welcoming them on a Dream Ventures trip.

"This is nice," said Reshma.

"It is, isn't it? It gives a personal touch," replied Sashin.

There were many tables available as it was past eight-thirty, and most guests had eaten and left. After their meal, Reshma and Sashin went for a walk around the hotel to explore, ending up in the lobby bar.

"Do you want an after dinner drink?" asked Sashin.

"Just a green tea for me," replied Reshma.

"Okay, suit yourself," responded Sashin.

Reshma took a seat and put the welcome packs on the table. Sashin ordered a double shot of Johnnie Walker Black Label from the limited selection of whiskies on the drinks menu along with a green tea. Sashin brought the drinks over and joined Reshma. The sound of a piano could be heard. Sashin turned to see a lady sitting at the piano playing a haunting piece. He was moved by the music and sat in silence for a moment.

"Is this the evening entertainment?" said Reshma.

"I think it might be the only entertainment. Nice though," replied Sashin.

After finishing their drinks, they returned to their rooms. Reshma came through into Sashin's room and sat on his bed cross-legged.

"Right, come and join me. We're going to meditate. I'm going to play some cleansing frequencies on my phone. We'll do your room and then mine," she said.

"Do I have to?" responded Sashin.

"Yes! It's for your own benefit," replied Reshma.

The music began, which sounded like Tibetan singing bowl harmonics. Sashin sat on the other side of the bed with his feet on the floor and closed his eyes. Reshma chanted faintly. For a few minutes, Sashin took deep breaths in and out. From total black, an image started to form. It was the pyramids. The image became vividly clear, and he meditated on it, but was soon awakened by Reshma, who tapped him on the shoulder.

"Onto my room now," she said.

In Reshma's room, the same thing occurred during the meditation. The image of the great pyramid appeared, and it was very clear. Sashin pondered why the pyramid kept appearing in his mind. Was it because he astral travelled to the very place he was in now? It was unclear. After the music stopped, he opened his eyes from the meditation. He got up and stretched out his hands, while also leaning back.

"Right, I'm going to go to bed. We've got an early start tomorrow," he said.

"I'm tired too. Okay, good night. Get me up in case I don't get up," replied Reshma.

"You will get up, and you can wake me up," joked Sashin as he walked through the adjoining door to his room.

Chapter Twenty-Nine

Reshma barged in at six in the morning and ordered Sashin to get up. He rubbed his eyes and groaned back to acknowledge her. He got up feeling a little groggy from the after effects of a day of travelling. After showering, he felt a lot better and alive. He shouted at her through the adjoining door.

"What are you wearing today?"

"Shorts, trainers, and a hoodie, which I'll keep in my handbag. It's hot today, so keep it light!" yelled Reshma back through the door.

Sashin opted for denim shorts with a T-shirt and trainers. He put a sweatshirt in his rucksack just in case. At seven-thirty, they both headed downstairs to the Pavilion restaurant. Upon arrival, a woman checked their guest details on a laptop. Reshma gave the room numbers, and the lady asked them if they preferred breakfast in the restaurant or outside. Sashin immediately opted for outside. Walking through the main restaurant and out, they were greeted with a clear blue sky and pleasant sunshine. There were tables and chairs arranged on a stone patio. Further back was a pool, and beyond that, the pyramids could be seen.

"Would you like to sit here with a direct view?" asked the waiter who had come over.

"Yes please," replied Sashin.

They were seated by the pool. The pyramids looked majestic and seemed very near.

"This is beautiful! We're so close to the pyramids," mused Reshma.

"I didn't realise we were this close. I'm sure you're pleased about that – not far to travel," replied Sashin, smirking.

"It's perfect," responded Reshma.

During breakfast, Sashin received a WhatsApp message from an unknown number. He opened and saw that it was from Rami Hamdy. Rami was the tour guide who worked with Alexis.

Rami: Hello sir, I am Rami. I will meet you in the reception area at nine o'clock and take you through the details of the tour for the day.

Sashin: Hi Rami. I look forward to meeting you. See you at nine o'clock.

Sashin looked up at Reshma.

"The tour guide is meeting us at nine o'clock in reception," he said.

"Okay. I'm going to go for a full English breakfast. Do you want anything?" asked Reshma.

"I'll join you," responded Sashin.

After breakfast, they headed back to the room with twenty minutes to spare before meeting Rami. Sashin took two water bottles from the fridge and put them in his rucksack.

"Don't forget to take water – you'll need it," he said to Reshma.

"I'll take one bottle in my handbag, and you take another in your rucksack. Otherwise, my bag will be too heavy," replied Reshma.

"So I have to carry a heavy rucksack?" said Sashin, rolling his eyes.

"You'll survive. Have you got hand sanitiser?" asked Reshma.

"I forgot to put that in my rucksack. Good shout," replied Sashin.

At ten minutes to nine, Sashin ushered Reshma out of her room.

"But we're early," she said.

"It's better to be," he replied.

They initially waited by the reception area but then took refuge around the corner in the lobby, where there were cushioned seats by low tables. A man walked towards reception wearing a pink polo shirt, sunglasses and blue jeans. He exchanged words with Nour at the front desk. Sashin had the inkling to get up and walk over. As he did, the man turned, eagerly smiling before he spoke.

"Sir, nice to meet you."

"Rami, hi! Nice to meet you too," said Sashin, shaking his hand. We're just sitting over there. That's my sister," said Sashin, pointing to Reshma.

"Okay great. Let's sit, and I will tell you about the trip," replied Rami.

"Reshma, meet Rami, our tour guide."

"Hello Madame, nice to meet you," said Rami.

"No need to say Madame. You can call me Reshma," she replied.

"And you can call me Sashin."

Rami sat next to Reshma and opened up a map.

"The Giza Plateau is close. We will get there quickly," said Rami.

"We can see the pyramids from out back," replied Sashin.

"Yes, yes, they are very near. It's a good hotel, " said Rami, nodding his head. He continued.

"You will spend two hours at the Sphinx, and you'll also have some time in the souvenir shop. When you are ready, we can have lunch for around forty-five minutes. Then I will take you to the Great Pyramid, where I'll take you on your private tour which will be two hours," explained Rami.

"Okay great, all set?" Sashin asked whilst looking at Reshma.

"All set," she replied.

Following Rami outside from the air-conditioned reception, they felt the heat, which was in the mid-twenties Celsius. A white Hyundai was parked outside.

"This must be a popular car for drivers," said Sashin.

They got into the car and, as Sashin sat down, Reshma passed him hand sanitiser.

"I saw you shaking hands. I don't want you to get Tutankhamun's curse," she whispered.

"What's that?" asked Sashin, looking bemused.

"The Egyptian version of Delhi belly," replied Reshma, quietly. She was paranoid about getting ill whilst abroad.

Within ten minutes, they arrived at the Great Sphinx of Giza. A tour bus was already parked, and a group of people were walking up to the statue. After getting out of the car, Rami took them over to an area in front of the Sphinx. The area looked like a square of new decking. The group they had seen earlier had already started to walk around the Sphinx and take pictures. Admiring the decked area, Sashin noticed that it was stone decking. He looked up at the Sphinx and was immediately surprised to see just how big it was.

"It's absolutely huge! Look how big the paw is," he said.

Reshma stood looking, stunned.

"I was not aware how massive it is. You just can't tell from the pictures," she replied.

Sashin began to take pictures on his mobile phone of the front. He handed his phone to Reshma and asked him to take some pictures of him standing in between the paws. He then took a selfie with Reshma.

"Let's walk around it. I'm going to take a video," said Sashin.

Rami stood by the decking, inhaling a vape. Sashin gestured to him that they were going to walk around. Exhaling smoke, he waved back, gesturing to go ahead. They proceeded to walk around. Sashin began recording on his phone, looking in awe at the paw.

"That must be around twenty feet tall."

When they were at the side of the statue, Sashin raised his phone to capture the top of the Sphinx. There was scaffolding against the side.

"Looks like they're doing some kind of restoration work," Reshma commented.

"It looks different on the physical plane," said Sashin.

"What do you mean?" asked Reshma.

Sashin paused the video.

"I'll tell you in a bit," he replied.

"I was not prepared for what I'm feeling energetically. There is high energy here," said Reshma, looking slightly fazed.

"Are you okay?" asked Sashin.

"Just feeling a little woozy," responded Reshma.

"Well, it *is* hot. Drink some water," said Sashin.

As they neared the back of the Sphinx, Sashin resumed the recording. Some of the brick work looked new on the side of the statue, and Sashin commented on this to add some narrative to the video. However, when they got to the back, he noticed something at the bottom that immediately caught his eye. There was a white wooden frame around a metal mesh grille. The frame was filthy with dirt and stood upright to cover something. Sashin knelt down and became very animated.

"Wow, oh wow," he muttered quietly.

"What is it?" asked Reshma.

Sashin pulled the grille away to reveal an opening. They both looked down to see a metal ladder against a metal frame. Another metal post was positioned in front of the ladder and up against the stone to offer support. Sashin paused the recording and then held his hand out below and started recording again. The light from the phone was activated by the darkness below, giving illumination and a clear view of a tunnel.

"That tunnel leads down to a library," answered Sashin.

"How do you know?" asked Reshma.

Having stopped the recording, Sashin replied.

"I travelled here in the astral last week. The Sphinx looked different, and I was drawn to it. I flew into it and went underneath it. There is a large library there. I would say bigger than the reputed library of Alexandria, with a vaster range of books. There are books on topics such as astrology, magic, mathematics, and herbology. The whole statue was giving off energy. I could see it glowing and it was coming from underneath. You can sense that energy on the physical plane."

Sashin felt a rush of adrenaline and excitement, debating whether to go down or not. He felt a pull inside to do it.

"Right, I'm going down to take a look," he said.

"Are you out of your mind?" commented Reshma.

"I'm interested to see if I'm proven right or wrong," replied Sashin.

"I don't think you're supposed to go down there," said Reshma.

"You can keep a look out or come down with me," added Sashin.

"You already saw what's down there astrally! Leave it at that," responded Reshma.

Just as Sashin was about to grab the top of the ladder he heard a voice coming from behind him.

"That leads straight down to prison if you ask me," said a man with an American accent who was wearing a white T-shirt with khaki shorts and light-brown boots. He had black-grey hair with a goatee and an African American complexion.

'Crap!' thought Sashin. His urge to see if he was right about what was under the Sphinx was quashed.

Rami had come round the back and saw Sashin by the opening.

"No, no! It is forbidden!" he yelled as he waved his hand frantically.

He returned the frame with the grille over the opening and slowly got up.

"It's fascinating," said Sashin.

"It sure is. I think it might be tunnels created by the Romans," replied the American.

Sashin started to walk away with Reshma around the other side of the Sphinx, accompanied by Rami. Reshma whispered.

"I don't think they want anyone to know about that opening or what's down there. I just get the feeling."

They walked back around to the front where the decking area was.

Rami stood in front of them and asked them to look up at the statue's head.

"The whole Sphinx was buried under sand, with only the head visible. They had to dig away the sand to reveal the whole thing," he said.

"When was that?" asked Reshma.

"In 1817. The excavation was led by Giovanni Battista Caviglia. The team of archaeologists uncovered the Sphinx's chest completely," replied Rami. He continued.

"There between the paws is the Dream Stele erected by Pharaoh Thutmose the Fourth as a small shrine. Here, let me take some photos of you."

Sashin and Reshma stood between the paws by the Dream Stele as Rami took pictures on Sashin's mobile phone. A lady with long, curly, dark brown hair, was seen nearby. She wore a white short-sleeved shirt, khaki chinos, and brown walking trainers. She called over a group who began congregating around her. "Gather round seekers!" she said, ushering more people towards her.

As they walked back towards Rami, the lady began addressing the group. Sashin took his phone back from Rami and gestured to Reshma to get close to the group. They stood on the edge of the congregation as the lady asked a question.

"Does anyone know what is under the Sphinx?"

Sashin looked at Reshma with wide eyes, pleasantly surprised.

Various answers were yelled out.

"There's nothing under it!"

"A tomb!"

"A UFO!"

"Tunnels!"

"A secret chamber!"

A couple stood near Sashin on his left. He turned to them and introduced Reshma and himself. They reciprocated the gesture.

"Hi, this is Ian and I'm Yasmin. We're from Manchester," said Yasmin with a thick Mancunian accent.

"Who is that lady?" asked Sashin.

“You’re telling me you don’t know? You must be dead new to the group. That’s Lisa Perez, the host of the ‘Seekers of Truth’ podcast. She’s famous in the world of paranormal and conspiracy theories. You know, not mainstream. We love a bit of fringe radio, podcasts, or TV, don’t we Ian?” replied Yasmin.

“Oh yes! We live for this stuff,” said Ian enthusiastically.

“The podcast listeners are referred to as ‘Seekers’. Look at my T-shirt,” said Yasmin, pointing to hers that had the word ‘Seekers’ across it with an alien face below the writing.

“Welcome to the group,” she added.

“Oh no, we’re not part of the group. We just happened to catch her talking about the Sphinx. I found it interesting,” responded Sashin.

“Okay, well listen carefully to what she says,” said Yasmin.

Both Reshma and Sashin drew their attention to Lisa as she continued on from the variety of answers yelled across to her about what lay under the Sphinx. Lisa began to explain.

“There has been a lot of speculation about what is under the Sphinx, considering it has been found using lidar that there are tunnels and a chamber underneath. Look down and see what you’re standing on. Why would this stone decking be put down here in front of the Sphinx? You don’t see this kind of decking anywhere else. What if this was put here to conceal an opening of some kind? The clairvoyant Edward Cayce claimed that there is a ‘Hall of Records’, an ancient library under the Sphinx.”

“See, I told you,” said Sashin.

“Looks like you’re not the only one who has paid a visit down there with their powers,” whispered Reshma.

They turned their attention back to Lisa.

"The 'Hall of Records' is said to have been built by refugees from Atlantis to preserve their knowledge, but there is definitely something under there. We know that they have found tunnels already. This is a cover-up."

Sashin felt a touch on his shoulder. He moved his head to see Rami's hand.

"We should go to the souvenir shop now," he said.

Before he began to walk away, Sashin lifted his arm up, which got Lisa's attention.

"There's an opening around the back, at the tail of the Sphinx. Evidence of a tunnel!" shouted Sashin.

Lisa's eyes widened, and she whispered the word, "What?"

"Follow me!" she cried. In a frenzy, the group marched behind her.

Ian and Yasmin were the last behind the group. They uttered some words in excitement before they joined the others.

"You should've started with that. That's mint!" With that, they were off to join the rest.

Reshma tugged at Sashin's arm.

"We better get out of here quickly," she said.

They caught up with Rami who walked ahead. Making it back to the SUV, Rami took them to a strip of souvenir shops that were a ten-minute drive from the Giza Plateau. There were two bazaars within walking distance of each other, a papyrus shop and a perfumery a bit further away. Rami gave them instructions.

"You can spend up to an hour here. Have a walk around. If you see anything you like, then let me know and I will help you get a good deal, okay?"

"Okay," replied Sashin, nodding his head.

Rami walked off with his vape in hand. He headed towards a small kiosk where a man was making Egyptian tea.

Reshma leant over and whispered into Sashin's ear.

"I bet he's earning commission from here, like in India."

"Really, actually, yeah, now I think about it. Still, better to have someone who knows their way around," replied Sashin.

After discussing a strategy for looking around the shops, they decided to try the ones further away first and make their way back to the bazaars last. The first stop was the papyrus shop. There was not much to pique either of their interests, so they moved onto the perfumery. It was like a living room in the perfumery. There were sofas arranged in the centre of the shop with glass cabinets behind them housing various oils and fragrance bottles of different colours and ornate designs. The shopkeeper introduced himself as Abdullah the chemist and started to bring out bottles for smelling. Sashin found some of the fragrances to be overpowering, and combined with just having come out of the heat, he felt a bit queasy. The air conditioning in the shop helped, and he stood up to walk around the shop to get away from smelling more of the oils. Reshma seemed okay and was enjoying the experience. Abdullah had now introduced her to flower extracts, which she found pleasant. It was the lotus extract that she was particularly fond of.

"I like this one," she said, turning to Sashin.

Abdullah became animated at hearing this and attempted to negotiate a deal by offering three other scents at a discounted price if Reshma took all four. Sashin ushered Reshma over, pretending to be interested in a bottle in a cabinet. She came over, and he lowered his voice and spoke discreetly.

"Only get what you're interested in. Don't be pushed into buying more. Also, Rami said he could haggle a good deal. We should go and get him."

"You like this bottle? I can get it out of the cabinet," said Abdullah.

"No no, it's fine, just looking," replied Sashin.

"We will come back in a bit," said Reshma.

"No, no, you must stay and try more scents! I have many!" responded Abdullah with panic in his voice.

"We will come back," said Sashin.

They hurried out of the shop and passed the crystal shop, heading over to the bazaar. There, Rami sat and drank tea with his aviator sunglasses on. Sashin walked over and explained that Reshma wanted to buy a bottle from the perfumery. Rami shot up and briskly made his way over, ordering them to follow him. In the perfumery, he spoke to Abdullah and managed to get the price reduced much to Abdullah's annoyance. Happy with her purchase, Reshma suggested that Sashin should buy something so as not to be left out. They all made their way back over to the bazaar, where Rami resumed his seat and asked for a top-up of tea.

There were two bazaars very close to each other. One was called the 'Golden Beetle Bazaar,' which is the one Sashin gravitated towards. He walked in and started to look around. There were brown units in two lines full of ornaments and souvenirs. Various statues adorned the units. Along the walls were shelves that contained plates, mugs, and other paraphernalia. Reshma had wandered off and was hovering near the counter. She started to wave and Sashin looked over. He read her lips as she uttered, "Come here". He walked over.

"Look at these," she said, drawing Sashin's attention to a silver necklace. There was Egyptian writing on the silver oblong that was attached to the necklace. Reshma asked the shopkeeper to take it out of the cabinet so that they could take a closer look. Once it was taken out, they were able to inspect it better. The shopkeeper spoke as they turned the oblong pendant over.

"This is a cartouche. The name of the wearer is written in Egyptian. It is double-sided and custom made. Look, see the hieroglyphics."

"You should get it made up with your name. I think it's lovely," said Reshma.

"It is nice. And I guess a decent piece of memorabilia," replied Sashin.

"I've just had a thought. What was your Egyptian name? It began with an A," asked Reshma.

"Ahmenemat," responded Sashin.

"That's it. You should get one side with Sashin and the other with Ahmenemat," said Reshma.

"How much is this cartouche?" asked Sashin.

"In Egyptian pounds or British pounds?" questioned the shopkeeper.

"British pounds," replied Sashin.

"One hundred and fifty pounds," replied the shopkeeper.

"One hundred and fifty?!" cried Sashin, looking at Reshma incredulously.

"I cannot take off much as this is a custom-made piece of real silver," remarked the shopkeeper.

"Wait here. I'll get Rami," said Reshma.

She rushed out of the shop and stood near the entrance waving and yelling over at Rami who nearly choked on his tea at hearing Reshma shout. She returned with Rami who took one look at the cartouche and gave a stern look.

"This is a custom-made piece," he said.

"We know," replied both Reshma and Sashin.

Rami spoke to the shopkeeper in Arabic. The shopkeeper then looked at Sashin.

"The best I can do is one hundred and twenty British pounds," he said.

Sashin gave an unresponsive look.

"You should get it, Sash. It's a really nice piece. Don't be tight," said Reshma.

Sashin reluctantly produced his wallet and handed over his credit card.

"Write the names down here that you want translated. Give me half an hour to have your cartouche ready," said the shopkeeper.

"Let's get lunch, and then you can collect it before we go to the pyramids," added Rami.

Rami took Sashin and Reshma to a restaurant that was a few minutes' drive away. There were vegetarian options, much to Sashin's relief. After lunch, which took around forty minutes, they returned back to the 'Golden Beetle Bazaar,' where Sashin picked up his freshly emblazoned cartouche.

"Okay, make sure you have water and have used the toilet. I have water bottles in the car. I will now take you on a private tour of the pyramids," said Rami, smiling.

In the SUV, as they were approaching the pyramids, Rami began to give a commentary as he pointed.

"There are three main pyramids for three different rulers. The Pyramid of Khufu, also known as the 'Great Pyramid of Giza', the Pyramid of Khafre, and the Pyramid of Menkaure. We will start at Menkaure and end at the Great Pyramid."

Rami parked in front of a tourist coach in the visitor car park.

“Get your things ready and put your sunglasses on. It's very hot. Let’s go,” he said.

“Put your cartouche on,” said Reshma.

Sashin took it out of his rucksack and put it on.

“How does it look?” he asked.

“Great,” replied Reshma.

On the walk towards the Pyramid of Menkaure, Rami explained that they had two hours, so this would mean they would have to go in and out of each pyramid quickly, allowing for more time at the Great Pyramid. Arriving at Menkaure, they saw a large stone pathway that led up to the pyramid.

“This is not open that often to the public, but Dream Ventures clients get full access to this tour,” said Rami.

Sashin looked at Reshma and smiled smugly. Rami spoke to the guard at the entrance and led them down some wooden stairs, which led to a long, descending wooden path with slats. Everyone had to crouch to get through the low hallway. The humidity immediately hit Sashin as he walked down. Once at the bottom they were in a chamber and could see a stone lintel ahead that required them to crouch again to navigate. This led to a corridor that they were able to stand up in. At the end of the corridor was another chamber.

“This is the largest chamber in the pyramid, the upper chamber,” explained Rami.

Sashin began recording on his phone as soon as they started to descend from the entrance, as he knew he had to show some footage to Alexis of the tour when he got back. Taking a few minutes to look around, Reshma commented.

“Wow, this is amazing!”

“Wait until you see the lower chamber. Follow me,” said Rami.

They descended again down a wooden path to the lower chamber. Sashin found the chamber to be quite small.

"It's a good thing I'm not feeling claustrophobic," he said.

On the way out, Sashin felt the granite walls.

"Amazing craftsmanship," he commented.

Once outside, Rami pointed out that they were to make their way on to the main causeway, and it would be a straight walk down. The causeway was a long wooden path that made it easy for tourists to navigate from one pyramid to another.

"All together, it is three kilometres to walk from one end to the other," said Rami.

They soon arrived at the Pyramid of Khafre.

Sweat marks appeared on Sashin's T-shirt as he struggled with the heat. He took out his water bottle and took a few sips. They followed Rami through an entrance that led to a descending corridor.

"All the pyramids have these kinds of entrances with inner chambers. This will go down and then up," said Rami, turning around.

At the bottom, they straightened up after crouching.

"This is the King's Chamber. Now, we go up," instructed Rami.

Ascending up a wooden platform, they once again had to crouch. At the top was a corridor that they were able to walk through relatively comfortably, which led to an inner chamber. Once in, Rami held his arm out with his palm facing towards them, a signal to stop.

"There is another private group here, so we will have to wait to see Khafre's sarcophagus," whispered Rami.

Sashin observed the group ahead and noticed that Lisa Perez stood in front.

"Look! It's Lisa and that group from earlier," said Sashin to Reshma.

After ten minutes of waiting, Sashin grew restless, and Reshma also grew weary. The group finally began to walk towards them and exited. Yasmin and Ian walked past them.

"Ooh, hello again seekers. Fancy meeting you two! You must try meditating in the sarcophagus; it's something else, I tell ya," said Yasmin.

"I think I'll try that," replied Reshma.

Ian nodded excitedly and then waved.

"See you guys, and enjoy the rest of your trip," he said.

At the sarcophagus, Reshma stood looking.

"Which way should I enter?" she asked.

"That part looks like where the head would lie," said Sashin, pointing at a small stone step that resembled a pillow.

"We don't have much time here because of waiting for the other group. Only one of you can go in the sarcophagus. Then, we must move on!" Rami animatedly said.

Reshma got in and laid down. It was dark and there was a dull silence as she closed her eyes and heard the faint echoes of Sashin's and Rami's voices. She soon felt calm and drowsy. Colours appeared before her eyes, bright colours that appeared in rainbow waves. This was followed by a brief feeling of levity in which Reshma's body began to feel very light, as if she were floating almost on water. Rami's voice interrupted the serenity.

"Time to go," he said.

Reshma got up feeling very light and flimsy.

Rami helped her out.

"You will have more time to do this at the Great Pyramid," he said.

They left the chamber and made their way out. More people came in, and they had to intermittently stop in the low corridors to let others pass. Once outside, Rami led them back onto the causeway. The wooden path ended to give way to the desert and the Great Pyramid could be seen ahead. They made their way across the sandy, rocky ground to a road, which they crossed.

Rami shared, “The timeline of ancient Egypt runs across different dynasties with a number of rulers belonging to the same family. The Great Pyramid is also dedicated to Khufu, the second king of the fourth dynasty. The son of Khufu is Khafre.”

A wooden path led up to the pyramid that they joined. The sheer size of the structure made Sashin stop in his tracks and take in the view. He pulled out his mobile phone and took some pictures before he recorded some video.

“I can’t believe this was made by man all those years ago,” said Sashin.

“About four thousand, six hundred and twenty-four years ago,” replied Rami.

At the foot of the pyramid, narrow stone steps led up and Rami took the lead, followed by Reshma. There were several sets of narrow stairs to climb. A few tourists stood ahead and some sat on large stones taking pictures. They manoeuvred around the bystanders, eventually arriving at the entrance. Rami walked up to a moustached man, sitting on a brown cushioned chair. He wore dark blue jeans with a blue cardigan and a light blue shirt. After an exchange of words, they were let through. A narrow, cavernous corridor awaited them, high enough for them to walk through without stooping. This led them to a set of stone steps, at the top of which was a narrow corridor leading up to a wooden path. They each had to crouch to get through. Once at the top, Rami stood in between two paths that continued to ascend. He stopped them and brought their attention to where they were.

"This is the grand gallery. As you walk up, take a look at the whole thing," he offered.

Walking up one side on the long wooden plank, Sashin observed the area; it had a high ceiling, and he began to experience a strange feeling, like a tingling sensation in his fingers that seemed to travel down his arms. His throat began to feel dry. He pushed on in awe as he filmed the gallery on his phone.

Ahead, there was only one wooden path on which to further ascend. Swiftly making their way up this singular path, they reached the top, where there was a low corridor. It reminded Sashin of the temple from his earlier astral experience that he thought was a dream. It was where he had seen Jyoti trapped inside the temple and had to crouch low to enter.

Once they all passed under the low corridor, they were inside an inner chamber.

"This is the King's Chamber. There is a sarcophagus," remarked Rami, pointing to the back of the rather small chamber.

"I'm feeling a bit strange," whispered Sashin to Reshma.

"Maybe you're just hot and a bit tired," replied Reshma.

"No, it's something else," replied Sashin.

"Come and sit here on the floor. Let's meditate for a while. It might help," suggested Reshma.

Reshma sat down on the floor with her back to the chamber wall and ushered Sashin to come and sit next to her. Sashin joined her by taking off his rucksack and placing it in between his crossed legs. He began to take deep breaths and saw that Reshma had closed her eyes and placed her hands on her legs with her palms facing up. Sashin did the same.

At first, he felt a sensation of fatigue, which soon gave way to drowsiness. Colours appeared out of the blackness, which faded into a vague image. The image became clearer; it was the pyramids he'd seen outside and in his vision when he had meditated in the hotel room. Only this time he could see all three pyramids as if standing from a short distance away. His attention moved to the sky as the image seemed to shrink to reveal the night sky. Above the pyramids were several stars. Sashin pondered what the image was trying to show him, and presumed that there was a relationship between the pyramids and the stars.

The image then shifted rapidly, and Sashin saw the seven chakras on the human body. It was an image that Sashin had seen several times on the physical plane and astral plane. It was the poster that Reshma had in her study room and the statue of the meditating monk in the 'Lane Side' pub at the astral intersection. The image of the chakras seemed to overlap the pyramid. Whispering voices could be heard nearby. Sashin could sense that a group of people had entered the King's Chamber. He slowly opened his eyes to see Rami standing nearby.

"It's okay, you carry on," he said.

"That's alright. I'm going to get up now," replied Sashin.

Reshma too had opened her eyes and stretched out her arms above her head.

"Take a picture of me before we go. I'll stand by the wall there," said Sashin, pointing to the opposite end of the chamber.

He handed his mobile phone to Reshma, then crossed to the other side and stood by the wall. Reshma took a picture.

"Put your hand on the wall, I'll take another photo," she said.

Sashin reached out to lean on the wall. As soon as he touched the stone, he felt a tingling sensation in his feet like a wave of electricity that worked its way up his legs and then to the base of his spine. He let the sensation continue without resisting as the wave continued up his back to his neck and then up to his forehead. Sashin felt a vibration in his forehead, and suddenly images flooded his mind. He recognised the 'Halls of Amenti' and the sarcophagi from his astral travel there. His attention was drawn to the emerald tablets and the one in particular that showed the projection of the astral body.

He then saw a man with the head of a bird and a protruding beak. Swirling images of papyrus pages then appeared with a page showing spells and a drawing of some sort of pentagram. The chakra system then flashed before his eyes with a recollection of him meditating with the 'Order of Amun'. Sashin's forehead felt warm, and a tingling sensation grew stronger to the point where it felt like his head was being electrocuted. His ears started ringing, first as a dull sound and then louder and more resonant. Everything went black.

"Sashin? Sashin, get up. Get up!" said Reshma, frantically shaking him.

Sashin opened his eyes and found himself looking up at the chamber ceiling. He lifted his head to see that he was on the floor on his back.

"You passed out," said Reshma.

"Yeah, I had a strange experience touching the wall," he replied.

"You may be dehydrated. You need to drink water. Let's go outside to get fresh air," said Rami.

"I'm not dehydrated," whispered Sashin.

"What happened?" asked Reshma.

He promised to explain once they were outside, as he found it difficult to talk while navigating the low corridor. They made their way back down the grand gallery area, which was now becoming more crowded with an influx of new groups. Back at the cavernous corridor near the entrance, Sashin discreetly talked to Reshma.

"I touched the wall and all these images flashed into my head. Energy rose up through my body. I saw these emerald tablets and halls under the pyramid known as the 'Halls of Amenti'. Then, I saw the chakras and pages of papyrus that contained magic spells."

Now emerging outside, they all congregated onto the wooden path causeway.

"Are you okay?" asked Rami.

"I'm fine. I guess I just feel a bit tired and dizzy," replied Sashin.

"We'll walk back to the car," instructed Rami.

"It sounds like you had a download," said Reshma.

"A what?" remarked Sashin.

"A download. I've read about this. It's where you can be in a certain place and touch something and get fast access to higher information. It's very high frequency communication that has a message for you connected to your past. That message might be different for me if I had a download. But the vision was trying to show you something," explained Reshma.

"In that papyrus of spells I saw, there was an image of a pentagram. I know this sounds a bit out there, but what if that spell you cast in your house came from that page? What if there is a connection?" pondered Sashin.

"That spell was from the 'Order of the Golden Dawn'," replied Reshma.

"I saw a man with the head of a bird, I don't know who that is," said Sashin. He caught up with Rami and asked him the question.

"Rami, do you know who the man is with the head of a bird, from ancient Egypt?"

"That is not a man that is a god. I think it is Thoth that you mention. Did the head have a long beak?" asked Rami.

"Yes he did," replied Sashin.

"That is Thoth. He has the head of an ibis. He was an advisor to the gods," responded Rami.

"Did he practise magic?" asked Sashin.

"Yes, he practised many things. He wrote about these in the emerald tablets. As for magic, there have been people who have tried to interpret his writings from ancient papyrus. I think there are four different books about the book of Thoth. Personally, I don't think there was a book, I think the knowledge was in his papyrus, and we may never know the real truth," answered Rami.

Sashin slowed down his pace to join Reshma.

"That spell worked against Bakenkhons because it came from Thoth. It was Egyptian magic," said Sashin.

"Woah, well, it would make sense, wouldn't it?" replied Reshma.

They returned to the car. Rami took them back to the Marriott Mena House. Once there, Rami escorted them out and walked them to the entrance of the hotel.

"I hope you enjoyed your tour," he said.

"Yes, I did very much. You are an excellent tour guide," responded Sashin.

"Thank you so much for a great experience," added Reshma.

"I'm glad you enjoyed it. Be sure to let Alexis know of my service," said Rami.

"Will do," replied Sashin.

Chapter Thirty

The following morning, Tarek had arrived just after six o'clock in the morning to take Sashin and Reshma to the airport. After clearing security, they spent a short time airside before boarding their flight. The flight was short and only took one hour. At Luxor airport, baggage collection was stress-free. It did not seem that busy, as there were only two other groups of people waiting for their luggage. The exit could be seen near the baggage collection belts.

As they neared the exit with suitcases in hand, they saw a lady standing with a white piece of paper. She wore a red cap from which draped her long black hair. She wore a light pink shirt with blue jeans and trainers. Sashin's name was on the piece of paper. He approached her, acknowledging the paper.

"Hello. Welcome! My name is Yara. I will be taking you to the hotel."

During the drive, Yara began to talk about the town.

"A lot of the hotels are along the Nile here. This attracts a lot of tourism. Your hotel is one of them."

"Wow, lovely view," replied Reshma as they approached a strip of hotels overlooking the river Nile.

They shortly arrived at the hotel. Yara had pulled the suitcases out of the boot and said she would be taking them back to the airport on Friday. She handed over her business card to Reshma. Both Sashin and Reshma stood by the entrance and looked up to read the sign, "Dream Luxor Resort & Spa'.

"Looks like a nice hotel. Is this owned by Dream Ventures?" asked Reshma.

"Yes, that's what it says on the itinerary," replied Sashin.

"Very nice," responded Reshma with an approving smile.

The reception was a large opulent area with a white marble floor featuring a patterned circle at its centre. At the front desk, they were greeted by two members of staff. They were informed that check-in was at two o'clock and that they were welcome to leave their luggage in the storeroom which they accepted.

"Lunch is being prepared in the main restaurant 'Rosetta'," said the receptionist.

"Let's get lunch and contact the tour guide," suggested Sashin.

"Yes, I'm hungry now," responded Reshma.

In the main restaurant they were seated.

"You go up first, I will keep an eye on the hand luggage," said Sashin.

Reshma made her way over to the buffet and came back a few minutes later.

"Right, you go up now. There's quite a large selection," she remarked.

After Sashin had returned with his plate of food, he pulled out the itinerary from his rucksack and laid it out on the table while he began to eat.

"The company is called 'Travel in Luxor' and the contact is a guy called Saeed," said Sashin.

"Find out where we meet him and what time the trip is," commented Reshma.

Sashin finished his lunch and pulled out his mobile phone.

"Do you want anything else?" asked Reshma.

"A cup of tea," responded Sashin.

"Any desserts?" said Reshma.

"I'll have a look myself after I've messaged this guy," replied Sashin.

Sashin: Hi Saeed, this is Sashin. We are supposed to meet for the trip to the Temple of Karnak. Where shall we meet you, and at what time?

Saeed: Hello Sashin. I am currently out doing a job, and I will meet you. Where are you staying?

Sashin: We are staying at the Dream Luxor Hotel & Spa.

Saeed: I will meet you at the Al Amir Perfumery Luxor. This place is not very far from your hotel. Ask reception to show you the way.

Sashin: What time?

Saeed: It will be an evening tour of Karnak, so meet for six o'clock.

Sashin: We will need access to an inner chamber on the right hand side of the temple. It was used in the past by the Order of Amun.

Saeed: How do you know about this?

Sashin: From my research.

Saeed: I need to talk to someone. I will come back to you.

There was a pause. Ten minutes had passed when Sashin's phone pinged. Sashin was eating the last bit of pastry on his plate and had to find a napkin to wipe his hands, which were sticky from the dessert.

Saeed: I can't promise you that we can get to the chamber, but you will need cash to pay the guard in Egyptian pounds just in case. You will also need a torch, as it can get dark in the evening.

Sashin: Okay, we will see you at six by the Al Amir perfumery.

Saeed: Okay.

On their way past the front desk, the receptionist advised them that their rooms were ready earlier than thought and that they could check in.

"Your rooms are on the third floor and are opposite each other. Do you need your bags taken upstairs?"

"It's fine. We can manage," replied Sashin.

"Lifts are just over there on the right," said the receptionist pointing.

After dropping off the suitcases and securing their passports in the safe, Sashin said he would meet Reshma in reception after she freshened up.

Once downstairs, Sashin walked over to the front desk.

"Hi, I need some help. Where can I get a torch?" he said.

"There is a hardware store about ten minutes from here. I will give you a map and mark where it is," replied the receptionist.

"Could you also mark on the map the Al Amir Perfumery Luxor?" asked Sashin.

"No problem. That is also about a ten minute walk from here," said the receptionist.

Reshma appeared from the lift and had changed into a sleeveless T-shirt.

"Just be careful walking around as there is a protest taking place near the town centre," warned the receptionist.

Sashin gave Reshma a wide-eyed look. Once outside, Sashin opened the map and attempted to get his bearings.

"We follow this road down and then turn right," he said.

"Try not to look like a tourist," said Reshma sternly.

After turning right, they proceeded further along. Sashin had folded the map and was discreetly looking at it to ensure they were on the right path. A line of shops could be seen on either side in the distance.

"I think the hardware shop is down there somewhere," said Sashin.

Just then a group of people walked past them with Egyptian flags. As they both neared the line of shops, more and more people were now appearing, some with rucksacks, some were shouting and chanting in Arabic. They were now in a sea of people. The shouting was getting louder.

"I think they're protesters. We need to get into the shop quickly," said Sashin.

They were surrounded by protesters, and the entrance to the shops was blocked by a train of people. Just then, a man grabbed Reshma by the arm, she flinched and turned around. The man grabbed her breasts. Reshma immediately pushed him away and shouted.

"Get off me!"

Sashin put the map into his back pocket and lunged forward. He grabbed the man around his neck and pulled him back. The man struggled to get free as Sashin grabbed on tight. Suddenly, out of the corner of his eye, Sashin saw something coming towards him. He felt a sharp pain on his cheek and the side of his nose. Someone had punched him in the face. He let go of the man and dropped to his knees, quickly looking up to see both men had fled. His face throbbed with pain, and Sashin felt blood start to drip from his nose onto the pavement.

"Sashin! Are you okay?" said Reshma in a panic, helping him up.

"Have you got a tissue?" asked Sashin.

Reshma quickly fumbled in her bag and pulled out a packet of tissues, handing one to Sashin. Covering his nose and tilting back his head, Sashin said something to Reshma that sounded muffled.

"Are *you* alright?" he asked.

"Yes, just a couple of arseholes. Should we go to the police?"

"No point – that could take us out for the whole day," replied Sashin.

Pinching his nose to stop the bleeding, Sashin felt pain as he pressed and a slight crunching sound.

"It feels like that idiot broke my nose," said Sashin.

The crowd of protesters began to subside, and there was an opening to a café.

"Go in that café there," said Reshma, taking Sashin by the arm.

Once inside, Reshma inspected Sashin's face.

"Let me take a look. The bit under your eye has come up, and your nose looks a bit out of line. I don't think it's broken," she said.

"Are you sure you're okay?" asked Sashin.

"Yes, I'm okay," replied Reshma.

Sashin noticed toilets at the far end of the café.

"I'm going to the toilet to have a look, I'll be back in a bit," he said.

Inside the toilet, Sashin was met with a grubby, humid, and smelly space. There was a cubicle with a hole in the floor and one with a western toilet. He walked over the sink that looked like it had seen better days with scuff marks and cracks in the basin. In the mirror, Sashin saw that his nose looked slightly wonky. He grabbed the main body of his nose, which caused immediate pain that he fought by clenching his teeth. He then sharply jerked his nose straight, which resulted in a clicking and crunching sound. The pain was excruciating. Sashin slammed his hands on the sink.

"Ah crap!" he yelled as blood began to drip from his nose again into the sink.

He took a tissue from the dispenser on the wall to his left and curbed the bleeding. Waiting a few minutes for the dripping to stop, he pinched his nose and held on through the biting pain. There was a knock at the door.

"Sashin, are you okay?" said Reshma.

Sashin walked out. Reshma took a look at his face and commented.

"Your nose looks better. What did you do?"

"Something stupid," replied Sashin.

"Your eye is coming up though," added Reshma.

"Well, we're not at home, and it's the last thing we need, so I tried to straighten it," said Sashin.

"Yeah, that's not a good thing to do," replied Reshma.

"Let's get these torches and head straight back to the hotel," said Sashin.

"You need to get some ice on your face to stop the swelling," suggested Reshma.

"I feel really bad about what happened. I should've defended you better," said Sashin, deflated.

"You didn't know! That guy came at you from behind. We were just in the wrong place at the wrong time. Those guys were out for trouble, to provoke," replied Reshma.

The hardware store was a bit further up. There was a comprehensive range of torches that Sashin was able to choose from. After purchasing two, they made for the exit, diligently looking around once outside. No protesters could be seen, and only distant yelling could be heard.

Back at the hotel, Sashin approached the front desk. The receptionist looked up from her touch screen computer.

"Hello again," she said.

"Can I get an ice pack?" asked Sashin.

The receptionist looked bemused.

"An ice pack?" she asked.

"Yes, we were attacked outside by some protesters, and I got hit in the face," replied Sashin.

"Oh, I'm so sorry to hear this. I did say to be careful. Protesters can get very violent here," remarked the receptionist.

"Yes, we know," responded Reshma.

"I can get an ice bucket sent up to your room with a tea towel. You can put the ice in the towel," said the receptionist.

"That will be fine," replied Reshma.

"One other thing. Is there a cash machine near here?" asked Sashin.

"We can offer this in the hotel. You can withdraw money or convert currency," responded the receptionist. She lowered her voice and continued.

"I shouldn't be telling you this, but there is an ATM that is just a few minutes away. You walk out and turn right and walk down, there are two machines there. You will get a better rate. Don't say I told you, please."

"Of course, thanks," replied Sashin.

Back in his room, Sashin prepared a change of clothes for the evening tour. There was a knock at the door. A man with a cream shirt and black trousers stood at the door with a silver bucket full of ice and two hand towels.

"Here you go sir," said the man.

Upon hearing the knock, Reshma immediately came through to Sashin's room.

"Give me a towel," she demanded.

Reshma added ice cubes to the towel and wrapped it up into a ball.

"Grab the top and apply it to your face, and keep it there for a few minutes. It will help with the swelling and pain," she added.

Sashin applied the bulging towel to his face and immediately felt it cool and quickly turn to a chill.

"It feels really cold," he said.

"It's supposed to," replied Reshma.

I'm going to get ready. Knock for me in half an hour," instructed Reshma.

"I'm going to have a quick shower," said Sashin.

"Make sure you apply the ice to your face again afterwards," responded Reshma.

After showering, Sashin applied the towel filled with ice to his face and soon began to lose patience as his cheek and the side of his nose began to feel numb. He had put on a freshly ironed T-shirt and packed a thin hoodie in his rucksack along with a bottle of water. When he knocked on Reshma's door, she had on a fresh shirt and she handed him a light jacket.

"Can you fit that in your rucksack?" she asked.

"Just about," replied Sashin.

At the cash machine, Sashin stood for a moment contemplating how much to take out.

"How much should I take out? A hundred pounds, which is about five thousand, nine hundred and ninety Egyptian pounds?"

"Yes, that's fine. Any cash left over you can use to buy things in the shops or at the airport," replied Reshma.

Making their way to the Al Amir perfumery in the balmy heat, the numbness in Sashin's face was wearing off and the murmurings of pain began to return. He still felt on edge as a plethora of emotions crossed over him. He felt down about the attack, but he did not want this to overwhelm him or detract him from getting to the Temple of Karnak in his search to find some semblance of what happened in his past. Touching his eye, he felt it was swollen. He took off his rucksack and rummaged inside to find and put on his aviator sunglasses.

"Stay vigilant," he said.

"Hey, it's okay. There's hardly anyone about," replied Reshma consolingly.

Upon reaching the Al Amir perfumery, they were met with a large arched shop front painted in gold. The name shone brightly in blue neon above them. A shopkeeper looked through the window to see them and came over with his hands out, smiling.

"Come in, come in," he said.

"No thanks. We're waiting for someone," replied Sashin.

The shopkeeper continued to welcome them into the shop.

"No, it's okay," said Reshma.

The shopkeeper touched Sashin's shoulder, continuing the haranguing.

"I said we're not interested. Leave us alone," snapped Sashin as he turned to break contact with the man's arm.

The shopkeeper raised his arms in despair, giving him a look of disdain as he walked back into the shop.

Sashin's phone pinged. It was a message from Saeed to say he was nearly there. Shortly afterwards, a black Hyundai saloon parked beside them. The window slid down.

"Sashin?"

"Yes," replied Sashin.

"I'm Saeed."

The air conditioning was on in the car to both Reshma's and Sashin's relief.

"We are very near the Karnak Temple. It won't take long," said Saeed.

They soon approached a car park. There were three coaches parked and several cars. Getting out of the car, a number of small shops could be seen near the entrance of the temple grounds. There was a bookshop that seemed to sell souvenirs, T-shirts and sunglasses as well. This was next to a minimarket which was next to a shop selling all things electrical. At the end hung a selection of clothes with a sign above that read 'Book Shop Clothes Glasses'. On the other side were a number of chairs and tables with parasols next to a café and a shop selling soft drinks.

It was now dusk, and Sashin removed his sunglasses and put them in his rucksack. As soon as they walked past the shops and through the entrance, Saeed spoke to two people sitting at a desk. Sashin and Reshma were both asked to put their bags in to be scanned. Once through, they were in a large open area in the middle of which sat a model of the whole temple under glass. Sashin stopped for a moment and looked at the model.

Saeed pulled out what looked like a small torch from his jeans, which turned out to be a laser pointer that he used to show the entrance to the temple.

"We will start here by the Sphinx. These have the head of a ram. Where did you want to go?" asked Saeed.

"Here," replied Sashin, walking around the model and pointing. Saeed shone his pointer to where Sashin had indicated.

"We go past the courtyard into the main temple grounds and then turn right here. Down this corridor and turn left, and the chamber is just there on the right," added Sashin.

"This corridor is guarded by security. Like I said, we can try and gain access. Do you have money?" asked Saeed.

"Yes. How much is it to get access?" asked Sashin.

"To pay the guard, if he is the right person to accept, is one hundred British pounds," answered Saeed.

"One hundred pounds? You must be joking!" yelled Sashin.

"Fifty pounds is what we will pay," said Reshma nonchalantly.

"I know this is not ideal, but we can try. Do you have the money in Egyptian pounds?" replied Saeed.

"Yes," responded Sashin.

Saeed then led them out onto stone paving and to a modern entrance that looked like it had been built especially as a prelude to the main temple entrance. A brown sign read 'Karnak Temple' above which led them through to the main site. Walking ahead, they turned right to approach a wooden bridge with the juxtaposition of modern railings on either side. Sashin stopped, recalling his past life regression. The entrance to the temple was just as he had seen. As they drew near, he saw the two rows of sphinxes on either side.

"I saw this in my past life regression," whispered Sashin to Reshma.

"Yes! This is the place that you're most connected to," replied Reshma.

The sphinxes were illuminated with floor lights. Lights could be seen in the main temple as well, effects for the night tour.

"The reason for the ram's head is because this animal can smell water from a distance. The ram showed the ancient Egyptians a way to survive, so they worshipped this animal. It was the sacred animal of Amun-Ra," explained Saeed.

Walking through the opening to the temple, Sashin was in awe at how huge the walls were. The temple courtyard was lit up. The image of Amun-Ra was projected on a stone column and was quite the spectacle. They followed Saeed into the centre.

"This is the open court that has different shrines and temples for different gods and pharaohs. The temple on the right over there is dedicated to Ramses the Third. You can see the statue on the left lit up with one leg forward, which shows that he was the living king of Egypt at the time. Do you want to go in?" asked Saeed.

"No, let's move on to the main part of the temple and the chamber," replied Sashin.

"Fine, follow me," responded Saeed.

A few people stirred around the courtyard. They were led to a statue, where they stopped.

"There are two statues here facing each other of Ramses the Second. By his legs is a small statue of his wife, Nefertari. Past this point we enter a great sight, 'The Great Hypostyle Hall'," said Saeed.

Rows of columns could be seen lit up. Sashin immediately recognised this part.

"These columns were once bright and colourful. I saw them in my regression," said Sashin.

Using his laser pointer, Saeed brought their attention to the tops of two columns and began to speak.

"These columns were once painted and were very beautiful and colourful."

Sashin looked at Reshma and gave a nod of approval.

"Over time the paint has worn away, but here you can see where the colour has stayed for three and a half thousand years," added Saeed.

"That's amazing. Can you imagine walking through here in ancient times?" remarked Reshma.

"I did!" replied Sashin.

Saeed continued.

"The columns have pictures and hieroglyphics on them and imitate papyrus."

Saeed pointed to an opening on the right.

"This is the third pylon, known as the great gate, which leads to the back of the temple and the corridor. How do you know of this corridor? It is not common knowledge. And how do you know of the chamber and the 'Order of Amun'?" asked Saeed inquisitively.

"I have done a lot of research," answered Sashin.

"Or you must know people who know this knowledge," added Saeed.

"Maybe a bit of both," said Reshma.

"Have your torches ready, as it is dark in the tunnel. Get your money ready too," instructed Saeed.

Sashin produced the torches from his rucksack and handed one to Reshma.

"Where is the statue of Amun that used to be by the entrance to the pylon?" asked Sashin.

"The statue is moved during the festival to the Temple of Luxor," replied Saeed.

"Is that where it is now?" said Sashin.

"I don't know," answered Saeed.

Two monuments stood before them as they drew close to the back of the temple.

"These are two obelisks. The first one is dedicated to Thutmose the First and the second to queen Hatshepsut," explained Saeed.

They had arrived at the entrance to the corridor. A security guard stood watching as they approached.

"Okay, get your money ready. You will need around three thousand Egyptian pounds," said Saeed.

Saeed spoke to the guard in Arabic, and the conversation soon erupted with the guard looking angry and holding up his hands. Saeed attempted to placate him by calling over Sashin.

"Hand him the money," instructed Saeed.

Sashin handed over the money confused, unsure if the guard had agreed to allow them in. He spoke as he started to extend his arm.

"Are we allowed through?"

"Yes, yes, he's just nervous. We won't have much time inside," explained Saeed.

The guard eagerly counted each note and then looked up annoyed. He shouted at Saeed and then immediately looked around and lowered his voice. Saeed spoke back in Arabic and held his hands up as if giving an ultimatum. The guard reluctantly relented and gave way.

He opened the door, giving them access. The corridor was dark and there were no lights anywhere. Sashin shone his torch, followed by Reshma. Saeed led the way and it felt like minutes had passed by the time they reached the end of the corridor. It veered off to the left, and there on the right was an entrance.

It was just as Sashin had seen in his past life regression. The torchlight revealed two stone altars. He walked over to the altar on the right while Reshma shone her torch on him to allow him to see. She stood in the corner with Saeed.

"Give me a minute," said Sashin.

He placed his hands on the cold stone. A strong feeling of melancholy came over him, a sense of being alone and lost.

"Could I have died here, all alone?" said Sashin as a tear rolled down his cheek.

"Is he okay?" whispered Saeed.

"It's been a long day. He has an emotional blockage connected to this place," replied Reshma.

Saeed looked bemused. He pulled out his mobile from his pocket and signalled to Reshma that he was going to make a call while walking towards the chamber entrance, where he stood outside in the dark hallway. Reshma could hear his voice faintly but was unable to make out what he was saying.

Suddenly, shouting could be heard in Arabic coming from outside. The security guard came running down and ordered them out. His supervisor was spotted, and the guard started to panic.

Saeed rushed through the entrance.

"We have to go. His supervisor is on his way over," said Saeed.

They quickly made their way back through the dark corridor. The guard was hysterical and told them to switch off their torches, which meant they had to walk back in complete darkness. When they reached the entrance, a man could be seen walking towards them. Seeing them come out from the corridor, he started to shout.

"What are you doing?!" he yelled.

The security guard panicked and pointed at Sashin, Reshma, and Saeed, shouting as he did.

"He's calling us intruders. Run!" said Saeed.

"The rat!" yelled Sashin.

They ran straight ahead. The supervisor gave pursuit. Saeed ran off, leaving Sashin and Reshma.

"Where's he going?" said Reshma.

"This way behind the columns," replied Sashin as they headed into the Hypostyle Hall. The supervisor could be heard running.

"They're over here!" shouted a voice. Sashin peered from behind a column to see a man wearing blue jeans and a white T-shirt waving his arms. The supervisor approached him, and the man pointed in a direction away from where Sashin and Reshma were standing. The supervisor ran off.

"Who is that guy and what is he doing?" whispered Sashin.

"He's with me," came a voice from behind them.

Sashin turned around to see a woman with long dark brown hair wearing a dark green top with a gold pattern. She had gold hoop earrings and gold bangles on.

"Come with me if you don't want to go to prison. The Chamber you went to is not open to the public," she said.

"Who are you?" asked Reshma.

"My name is Dina. Your guide Saeed phoned me to tell me that you wanted to see the chamber used by the Order of Amun, that you went inside," answered Dina.

"Why would he phone you to tell you?" asked Sashin.

"Because I have knowledge of the Order," replied Dina.

She continued.

"Come with me, I will explain."

Dina led them out of the Hypostyle Hall and quickly through the courtyard. They then exited through the entrance and were back near the front entrance and the model of the temple. Once in the car park, she shared more.

"Saeed has left you. I will take you back to your hotel."

The lights on a white car flashed as Dina pressed the button on her key.

"Get in the back. My friend will join us soon," she said.

Once in the car, Dina turned and began to speak.

"So why are you interested in that chamber?"

"You go first. Tell us what you know about the Order," asked Sashin.

The man in the white T-shirt opened the passenger side door and got in.

"This is Darius. What are your names?" asked Dina.

"I am Sashin, and this is Reshma."

"Hello. We need to go now, as they have called the police," said Darius.

Dina started the car and drove out of the car park.

"We are descendants of the Order of Amun," said Dina.

"Of Ahmenemat or Bakenkhons?" asked Sashin.

"Neither; we are descendants of two other members of the Order, but we are familiar with those names. Both of them died around the same time. I don't know how or what happened but we know this affected the Order," replied Dina.

"Now, can you tell us what your interest is with the Order and why you wanted to go to the chamber?" questioned Darius.

Sashin looked at Reshma and tentatively responded.

"I think I am the reincarnation of Ahmenemat," replied Sashin.

"Is that so?" said Dina as she looked in the rear view mirror, clearly interested.

"I've discovered that I have the ability to astral travel. Now this is going to sound far out, but I have met Bakenkhons on the astral plane. He calls me by the name Ahmenemat. Something happened between us during the time of the Order. When I am on the astral plane he hunts me down. He is working with these black magicians from the lower planes," explained Sashin.

Dina looked over at Darius. Silence.

"The Order was using that chamber for astral travel. Their aim was to push the boundaries of human consciousness for progression and knowledge," said Dina.

"Yes, I know they were using that chamber for astral travel. I found a book called 'The Secret Order of Amun' that mentioned this," replied Sashin.

Dina briefly looked over at Darius again. Reshma noticed it this time and felt uncomfortable. She discreetly tapped Sashin on the leg and gave him a wide-eyed look and directed her gaze over to the front. He knew she was trying to bring his attention to something.

"Do you have the abilities of Ahmenemat to astral travel? Do you remember?" asked Dina.

"No, not exactly. I have had to learn as I go," answered Sashin.

"Which hotel are you staying at?" asked Dina.

"The Dream Luxor," replied Sashin.

"Okay, that's not very far," said Dina.

"You need to understand what happened," said Darius.

"What do you mean?" asked Reshma.

"Between Sashin and Bakenkhons, you came here to find out the truth, right? I don't think you will find it here," said Darius.

"Where will I find it?" asked Sashin.

"On the astral plane," replied Darius.

"If you are the reincarnation of Ahmenemat, then you may very well have the ability to find the truth," added Dina.

The car pulled into the Dream Luxor car park.

Dina turned around and spoke.

"We can pick you up tomorrow afternoon and bring you to my house."

"To do what exactly?" asked Reshma.

"To try and recreate what the Order was doing in the chamber. With our guidance, you could access the one place where you can find the truth, a record of all that took place," replied Dina.

"The Akashic records," said Sashin.

"Yes, you know of it?" asked Darius.

"I've heard of it. I also know it's very hard to get to," responded Sashin.

"For most, yes. For you? Maybe not," said Dina.

"We can pick you up at three o'clock tomorrow. That will give you the morning to relax," she added.

"We'll think about it," responded Reshma.

"Here – take my number and let me know," said Dina, handing over her mobile phone. Sashin added her number.

Back in the hotel, Sashin heard a knock on his door. It was Reshma. She walked in with the bottle of red wine from the Marriott Mena House.

"I could do with a drink after today. Do you want a glass?" she asked.

"Yeah, I could do with one," replied Sashin.

"Your eye is really swelling up," said Reshma.

"Yes, I know. The ice is melting. I'll have to fish out the remaining solid pieces and use them before I go to bed," responded Sashin.

Reshma poured out the wine into two glasses, which were situated by a kettle on the worktop.

Sashin noticed that he had received a message from Alexis earlier but had not heard it during the commotion at the Temple of Karnak. The message read:

Alexis: Hi Sashin, I hope all is going well x

Have you decided what you want to do tomorrow? Do you want to go to the Valley of the Kings?

Sashin: Hey Alexis, had a long day today. We have met some locals and are thinking of meeting up with them tomorrow instead x

"I don't fully trust Dina and Darius. She kept looking over at him when you were talking. I just get a feeling that they're not telling us everything," said Reshma after she took a sip of wine.

"Yes, I know you were trying to tell me in the car. They did help us get away and are willing to help me get to the

Akasha. If I can get to the records, then at least I finally have the chance to find out the truth. It's the only chance I have left," replied Sashin.

"Okay, I suggest you sleep on it. If we do decide to do this, then we have to proceed with caution. There's one day left, so let's get through it without any issues," said Reshma.

After two more glasses of wine, they retired for the night.

Chapter Thirty-One

Sashin was woken up by a knock at the door. He got up and walked towards the door, yawning. It was nine o'clock. He opened the door to Reshma, who was dressed in a sports vest and jogging bottoms and sweating.

"I've just been to the gym. It's nice," she said.

"Oh, I knew I forgot something! I didn't bring any gym wear," replied Sashin.

"Don't worry," but before Reshma finished her sentence, there was a look of shock on her face as she pointed wide-mouthed.

"Oh no! Look at your eye," she remarked.

Sashin rushed over to the long mirror that was by the door and stared at his face.

"Great, I've got a black eye. I've never had a black eye in my life," he said despondently.

"I've got concealer. That will cover it up if that makes you feel better," suggested Reshma.

"Yeah, go on then," replied Sashin.

Be ready in half an hour, and I'll bring it over. We'll just make breakfast," said Reshma.

Sashin got ready. His nose was still sore, and rubbing it while washing his face caused a pang of pain. He heard this phone ping and saw that Alexis had replied.

Alexis: No problem. There will be a Dream Ventures rep in the hotel between ten and twelve. In case you change your mind, you can speak to Armani Khalaf, who will be set up near reception. Normally the rep does a welcome session first thing in the morning, but as it's just the two of you, she will come in a bit later.

Sashin: Great, thanks for letting me know.

He made his way over to Reshma's room. She was drying her hair and pointed out where the concealer was in her makeup bag. She spoke through the roar of the hairdryer.

"Put a little bit on your finger and rub it slowly under your eye until it blends in."

Sashin followed Reshma's instructions using the long mirror by the door.

"How does it look?" he asked.

"Put a bit more on," replied Reshma.

"How about now?" said Sashin.

"It will have to do. We'd better get going," urged Reshma.

It was busy during breakfast. It seemed as if many guests had the same idea of going for a late breakfast. After having navigated the moving crowds of people around the buffet, Sashin and Reshma sat down to eat. A tall and slender waiter approached them with a mug of tea.

"Tea?" he asked.

"Yes, thanks," replied Sashin.

"So, have you decided what you want to do today?" asked Reshma.

"Yes, I think we should meet Dina and Darius and give what she suggested a go," replied Sashin.

"Right, but like I said last night, just be careful. I know they helped us, but I don't know," said Reshma.

"Yes, I know. I get the feeling that they are keeping their cards close, but I do think they want to help. They also want to know the truth about what happened. I got that impression," added Sashin.

"What are you going to do after breakfast? Do you want to venture out for a bit? I know you might not want to, considering what happened yesterday," asked Reshma.

"I'm happy to just stay in the resort and walk around for a bit. I have some things to send to Alexis, some photos and videos. There should be a Dream Ventures rep near reception now until twelve, so I will drop by and see her," responded Sashin.

"That's fine, I don't mind. I might take a peek in the spa. We can get a snack before we go at lunchtime," said Reshma.

"That sounds like a plan. I will message Dina to confirm that she meets us in reception for three," replied Sashin.

After breakfast, Reshma went off to have a look at the spa. Sashin had a look in reception. He walked around but did not see anyone there. It was when he turned the corner from the reception area that he saw that there was a sign pointing to the lobby bar area. There he saw Armani, who was wearing a grey sweatshirt with 'Dream Ventures' written on the front. She offered Sashin some leaflets of things to do in Luxor, one of which had her mobile number and email address.

"Alexis had mentioned that you might want to do the Valley of the Kings excursion. The information is there in the leaflets. I know you're going back tomorrow, so if you don't do it today, maybe next time," said Armani, smiling.

Sashin thanked Armani for her help and then embarked on a walk around the hotel. He found a small library area where a few guests were reading. For the next two hours, he carefully curated an album of a few photos and videos that he sent to Alexis. He then added a message.

Sashin: Here are some photos and videos of the last two days to give you an idea of the tours. I will fill you in properly when I get back.

Reshma wandered past, and Sashin called her over.

"I got a massage done in the spa; it was good. I feel very relaxed now. Maybe you should get one done," suggested Reshma.

"No, I'm good. Let's get that snack and then get ready to go," replied Sashin.

There was a café situated outside, near the main restaurant. They had a light snack there and then made their way back to the rooms. Sashin checked his eye to see that the concealer was beginning to wear off and the black hue was re-emerging. He felt despondent at the thought of having to cover it up again and decided to leave it. After a brief conversation about what they would need to take, they decided to travel light.

"You don't need to take much, maybe just a bottle of water for the ride. And keep your wits about you," said Reshma.

At just past three o'clock, Dina and Darius walked into the large reception area. Sashin spotted them clearly from where he was sitting, while Reshma attempted to go incognito, reading a magazine held firmly in front of her face. Dina wore a casual black jumpsuit with white trainers, which caused Sashin to stare momentarily. He found her somewhat attractive, but dismissed the notion immediately. He did not want his judgement to be clouded. Darius wore a white T-shirt again with a black biker jacket, blue jeans, and black trainers.

"Where do they think they're going, clubbing?" joked Reshma as she peered around the side of the page.

Sashin smirked as Reshma lowered the magazine. Dina waved. They both got up and greeted Dina and Darius.

"I'm glad you want to do this. Let's get going," said Dina.

Her white Kia saloon sat in the car park at the front of the hotel. It was hot outside, and once he got inside the car, it felt like a sauna.

"Have you got air conditioning?" he asked.

"Sorry, it's not working properly. You'll have to do with the windows down," responded Dina.

As the car drove off and was on the main road, the air blew in through the window, which slightly alleviated the discomfort of the heat. Ten minutes into the journey, the car slowed down due to a traffic jam ahead. A horse and carriage rode past the window using the only available part of the road to navigate past the traffic. A sprawl of buildings could be seen in the near distance. Electric wires were strewn across the top of the buildings. The traffic finally began to move, and they neared a light brown building that looked like a block of apartments. Dina parked in a bay at the front.

"Here we are," she said.

"I thought you said a house?" remarked Reshma.

"It's a two-bedroom apartment that Darius and I share. We're like roommates," replied Dina.

"Oh, so you are not together?" asked Reshma.

"No. We're just friends brought together by our connection with the Order. Sharing helps with the bills," responded Dina.

"It's funny because we were studying at the same college and we got talking about our ancestors, and that is where we found out that we were both descendants," added Darius.

Sashin and Reshma were led inside and taken up a flight of stairs.

"We're on the second floor," said Dina.

Entering the apartment, Sashin and Reshma took off their shoes.

"Thanks," said Darius in gratitude as he and Dina removed their trainers.

The apartment had a small hallway that led into an open plan living room with a kitchen area at the back and a small breakfast bar, under which were several stools.

"Help me with this," said Dina, addressing Darius, who helped her move the dining table at the far end of the long room to the centre.

They both removed the items from the table, including a scented candle and placemats. The table was moved around. Dina turned to look towards Sashin.

"You will lie on this table, which will be like the altar in the chamber, but don't worry. I will get you a pillow for your head," she said.

Darius disappeared and returned shortly, handing over to Dina what Sashin thought was an odd looking pillow. It was white and quilted with edges that were slightly curved in. On each edge was a speaker within the pillow.

"This is a speaker pillow. Darius will play a 528 Hz solfeggio frequency. Just relax and listen to the frequency, which will bring your brain waves down to theta, this will help you astral travel faster and deeper. It is said that the records are stored behind your neck. Records of your body are directly connected to your chakras, which is why this pillow will help. If the frequency is distracting, then just say by raising your hand," explained Dina.

"You seem to know a lot about this stuff," Reshma noted.

"It's what we have heard from stories passed down to us," replied Dina.

"Once you have projected, then press this switch here so we know," said Darius, holding a box with a red button on it. He pressed it to demonstrate, which resulted in a "yes" coming from the box.

"We used to use this to train dogs," mentioned Dina.

Reshma looked bewildered.

Sashin got up on the table and laid his head on the pillow. Looking up, he could see the ceiling fan.

"It's important that you remember who you are and what you were once capable of. The Akashic records are on the causal plane, which is a higher plane," added Dina.

'Yes, I remember Rajarshi mentioning the causal plane,' thought Sashin.

"I saw flashes of the Akasha above the astral intersection," replied Sashin.

"What is that?" asked Darius.

"It's the place between the different planes that you go past when you travel to a higher plane," answered Sashin.

"Oh, you mean the astral highways," responded Darius.

Sashin turned his head and spoke.

"Does kind of sound better," he said.

"Are you ready? Darius will start the frequency," said Dina.

"Okay," said Sashin as he closed his eyes.

Darius pressed the screen on his phone, and the solfeggio frequency began to play through the speakers in the pillow.

At first the sound was distracting, and Sashin found it difficult to relax with the noise. He then began to let go and immerse himself in the sound. His brain waves began to slow down. Entering a meditative state, he felt the onset of a trance. A wave of energy moved up from his feet to his forehead, where he felt it pulsating. Sashin's body became one with the resonance of the frequency. His attention was now on his astral body, and as the pulsating feeling enveloped his entire body, he floated straight out without much thought.

'Dina was right,' he thought.

The frequency made separation ten times easier. Sashin floated to the ground and walked over to the box. He held out his hand and could feel the energy of the box clearly. With his astral body resonating, he merged the energy of his hand with the button and pressed it down, triggering the "yes" response. Dina stood up from the sofa and looked over at Darius.

"Cool, right?" said Reshma.

Darius nodded his head in awe.

Sashin floated up and hovered above his physical body, where he adopted the lotus cross legged position. He visualised the images of the Akasha from the astral highway and focused on the higher causal plane. He remembered when he achieved rapid speed, turning his attention inwards, and asked his higher self for guidance. There was sudden propulsion as Sashin flew straight out of the house over the apartments and, like a rocket, shot up higher and higher.

A tunnel of white appeared before him that he flew into at great speed. Colours of light swirled around inside like a kaleidoscope. The coloured lights then became a rainbow of lines as Sashin flew on at great velocity. Outside the lines was a great expanse of space; it was like Sashin was travelling through a tunnel in outer space. Something caught his eye as he looked out past the lines of colour. It was a train that was riding through space.

Through a window, he saw passengers on the train dressed in white. Some looked like they were walking down the aisle, passing the window. By the window sat a group. One of them was dressed in a white suit and looked out of the window, staring directly in Sashin's direction. The man drew his head closer to the window and looked intently, trying to focus his gaze. Sashin recognised the face. It looked very similar to his own, except older.

'How peculiar,' he thought.

Turning his head forward, Sashin sped on. Ahead, he could see the tunnel beginning to veer downwards. Now shooting down, he saw an opening draw near. As he flew out of the tunnel, he began to slow down. Below he could see a liquid ocean of a substance like water, effervescent and ethereal. A large structure stood before him in the near distance. It was a long building of white stone with a large golden dome on top with glass windows. A huge gold balcony extended from the rear of the building, with ornate railings running along its sides.

Sashin hovered towards the balcony. On the floor was a symbol, a large lotus flower with a circle inside it, and within the circle an inverted triangle. Inside the triangle was another symbol, which looked familiar. He had seen such a symbol in a book at his parents' house. It was a Sanskrit symbol, but he was unaware of what it meant.

Lowering himself towards the balcony, Sashin uncrossed his legs and landed straight in the middle of the large symbol. There was an arched doorway ahead that was closed. Sashin proceeded slowly, looking around, and as he approached the doorway, it began to open. He stopped still and waited in anticipation. The doors appeared to glide open by themselves;

there was no one there. Sashin walked forward, and as he was about to walk through the entrance, he heard a low humming sound. He walked down a hallway that led to the inner circular building.

Once inside, he was dumbstruck by the sheer size of the inside of the building. There were many levels, around which stood bookcases in the walls. But instead of books, the cases contained glowing blocks, iridescent in nature. This reminded Sashin of the holographic emerald tablets he'd seen under the Great Pyramid. He felt like he was in a massive library. In the centre were black platforms, squashed shiny oblongs that levitated. There were many that went all the way up to the top. As Sashin stared up, he saw the glass dome through which the sky was a hue of orange, blue, purple, and yellow.

He walked around looking at the various blocks in the bookcases. Curious, he went over and touched one. Immediately, the block expanded, causing Sashin to move back quickly in panic. From the block, a wide rectangular frame was formed, and within the frame was a viscous substance that formed a film over it that looked like that of a mirror. Sashin put his hand through the substance. It went right through, and he could feel a dull pull on his arm. He cautiously put his head through to take a peek on the other side of the substance. There was a sudden rush as he felt his sinuses expand as if he had inhaled a decongestant. He breathed in deeply, feeling disorientated. The feeling began to settle, and Sashin could see the life of a woman called Amira Lakhi.

Amira had experienced domestic abuse shortly after she got married. Her husband would beat her and subject her to humiliating demonstrations of power, sometimes in front of her children, which made her very depressed. The abuse went on for several years until it had become too much for her to bear.

'I can't take it anymore. I've had enough. My life is hell,' were common thoughts that ran through her mind.

On one particular occasion, she waited for her husband and when he came home and started to show aggression, she dowsed him in white spirit and set him alight. Amira was later convicted of manslaughter and sent to prison. She eventually made it out after a long and gruelling legal battle.

Sashin pulled out his head and gasped. The thoughts he experienced were somewhat overwhelming. He walked over to another block and touched it, quickly moving out of the way. A frame appeared again, and he put his head through. This time he saw a young boy, aged ten, his name was Adam, who was being bullied at school on a regular basis. The boy suffered from deep depression and became withdrawn.

'I'm worthless. I'm nobody. I want to die. I want to kill myself,' were the thoughts of the boy.

Sashin pulled himself out again, feeling sadness. He went over to another block. He witnessed a middle-aged man who had grown despondent at work, unappreciated, unable to progress.

'I'm just not appreciated. I hate this place. I deserve more,' were his thoughts.

Sashin pulled out.

"Why are all these thoughts so negative?" he said out loud.

"Because this is the nature of humankind," came a reply.

The humming sound was now behind him. Sashin turned around quickly. A gold hovering seat moved towards him. In it sat a young woman. She wore a gold helmet with a headpiece that formed a symbol similar to the one on the balcony. She had a shimmery white outfit on with shoulder pads and a breastplate that gave way to a dress. White boots could be seen with golden heels where the dress ended. Sashin nearly mistook her for an android, but her face was clearly human, which made him think twice.

"I am the custodian of the Akashic records, the records of all that was, is, and shall be. This is not an easy place to find. How did you get here?" asked the custodian in a monotone voice.

"With some help. I wasn't sure I would make it here," replied Sashin.

"What is it you seek?" asked the custodian.

"My records from a past life," answered Sashin.

"I must scan your *mayavirupa*," said the custodian.

'My what?' thought Sashin.

Closing her eyes, she momentarily sat silently. Her eyeballs moved under the eyelids. In an instant, her eyelids flicked open, and she pointed up two levels where a white light had appeared on a bookcase.

"You must take the platforms to reach the higher records," added the custodian.

"Oh no need – I can fly up there," responded Sashin.

Sashin attempted to ascend and nearly fell off the platform. He swiftly prevented himself from falling forward by grabbing onto the rail next to him.

"Here in the Akasha, space operates differently. You will be unable to perform certain abilities that you can on the astral plane. You must respect the ways of the Akasha," explained the custodian.

Just then, a crackling sound could be heard. Energy began to shoot off some of the bookcases from all sides, merging in the centre to form a long and tall twister of energy.

The dome opened, and the energy escaped through into the sky.

"Occasionally the energy from the records will build up and must be dissipated," explained the custodian.

"What happens if it isn't?" questioned Sashin.

"Too much energy building up could be problematic," replied the custodian.

A levitating platform glided towards them, on which Sashin embarked. The custodian followed, hovering over. The platform rose and moved towards a higher floating one. This platform then began to ascend until it reached the next level up. Sashin stepped off and walked over to the bookcase where the white light was shining on an iridescent block. Sashin touched the block. The custodian immediately spoke.

"Now, stand back," she said.

"Yes, I know," replied Sashin.

Sashin leaned forward and placed his head through the viscous surface once again, now beginning to get the feel of it.

He was immediately transported to Egypt, to his life as Ahmenemat. He was one of a group of four that were part of the 'Order of Amun'. The Order held high prestige and wielded great power. Their ethos was to be visionaries and free thinkers, learning esoteric practices for spiritual development. Ahmenemat was the most accomplished of the group. He meditated daily and practised chakra meditation, working with priests from the temple for spiritual guidance. Ahmenemat was happily married to a woman named Sitamun. He felt good about what he was doing with the Order; he felt he had a higher purpose and was keen to learn and be an attentive student. Bakenkhons was also an accomplished member of the group. He and Ahmenemat were good friends and would sometimes meditate together, sometimes apart. The Order was using astral travel to navigate the astral realms in order to communicate with beings from the higher planes. Ahmenemat had successfully reached these higher planes. The higher dimensional beings were providing knowledge and wisdom to the Order. It was this knowledge that helped to build the pyramids.

"They used astral travel to learn how to build the pyramids," said Sashin out loud.

Bakenkhons grew increasingly frustrated with being unable to reach the higher planes. Ahmenemat had observed a noticeable change in him – he became withdrawn and more defensive. Ahmenemat reached out to see if he could help. Bakenkhons expressed his frustration at not being able to ascend to the higher astral planes, to which Ahmenemat responded by consoling him and telling him to keep trying and to continue with the daily meditation exercises. But Ahmenemat had a lingering notion that something was not quite right. One day, Bakenkhons decided to astral travel alone. Ahmenemat, lying beside him on the stone altar, also went astral and followed him. To his surprise, he found that Bakenkhons had travelled to the lower astral planes. There Ahmenemat confronted Bakenkhons, who lost his temper, accusing Ahmenemat of spying on him.

"No good can come from travelling to these lower planes. Please stop," pleaded Ahmenemat.

Bakenkhons seemed furious after this incident.

Ahmenemat was a keen student of the teachings of Thoth. He had read the emerald tablets and was working his way through his writings on papyrus. He was particularly fascinated by the process of soul projection.

Sashin then realised that the record came to an end. What he was able to see from the remaining insight was that after doing his daily meditation, Ahmenemat had astral travelled to contact the higher level beings, but something had gone wrong. His astral cord had become detached, and he began to panic. His astral body was in free fall, and he felt completely lost.

Using the knowledge he had learnt from the teachings of Thoth, Ahmenemat propelled his soul through time and space. He reached the 1990s at the time Ushma was giving birth in the hospital with Satish by her side. The baby was stillborn and had already passed before Ushma had given birth. Ahmenemat transferred himself into the stillborn baby and was reborn.

Sashin withdrew from the frame and took a moment to take a number of shallow breaths.

'What happened to me? I don't remember anything. Being reborn must have wiped my memories,' he thought.

"I have to find out what happened. How can I access the records of Bakenkhons?" asked Sashin.

"Do you have any more information, like a full name?" asked the custodian.

"Just the name Bakenkhons," replied Sashin.

"That is insufficient information. I will not be able to access his records. If he was present, then I could scan," responded the custodian.

They were interrupted by a large thud that came from above. Sashin looked up to see someone had landed on the dome.

"That's Bakenkhons! That's the person," said Sashin.

"How did he get here? Did you bring him with you?" asked the custodian.

"No. He must've followed me here, just like Rajarshi said he would. I'm afraid my coming here has led him right to the Akasha. Are you able to scan his *mayavirupa*?" replied Sashin.

"Yes, I can," said the custodian.

She closed her eyes momentarily.

"There," she said, pointing opposite at two levels up to where a beam of light had appeared on a bookcase.

"Right, I must be quick," said Sashin.

He leapt onto the black platform as it began to move towards him.

"Can these things move any faster?!" yelled Sashin.

"The platforms are not designed to move fast," replied the custodian.

Sashin ran and jumped for the platform that was descending from above. He pulled himself up and then ran forward again to reach the next platform. Jumping up, he grabbed at the platform, but his hand slipped, and he fell back onto the platform below. Getting himself up, he saw below that Bakenkhons had entered the library. In a panic, Sashin jumped again and managed to pull himself up successfully.

"Can you stop him from getting up here?" asked Sashin.

"The Akashic records are open to all that make it here. I cannot stop him from accessing any part of the records, but I can try to keep you apart. I will reconfigure the library, but first you must make it off the platform," replied the custodian.

Sashin took a running leap onto the deck of the higher level. As soon as he landed, he ran to the bookcase and heard a loud rumbling sound as each of the levels of the library began to move and turn. Sashin touched the illuminated block and stood back for the frame to appear. He looked out over the railings to see Bakenkhons trying to get onto a platform but, with the level turning, he was taken away from the platform, much to his annoyance. Sashin quickly put his head through the frame and accessed the record.

He experienced Bakenkhons' thoughts and feelings. Bakenkhons grew increasingly frustrated with not being able to access the higher astral realms. He began to develop feelings of jealousy towards Ahmenemat. He thought the priests were treating him more favourably. Bakenkhons then had the idea of travelling to the lower realms, which he was able to do with ease. There, he encountered the black magicians, the Nyingma Pa, who offered him power and help through the use of dark magic. He found their offer attractive and allied himself with the black magicians. He showed his desire to become a more powerful astral traveller than Ahmenemat.

After being found on the lower astral plane by Ahmenemat, Bakenkhons had great resentment for him. He was concerned that Ahmenemat would tell the other members of the Order. In fact, Bakenkhons was convinced that Ahmenemat would tell the Order leading to his expulsion from the group. An idea had formed in his mind. While Ahmenemat was astral, he made his way to the chamber with a rope basket, passing two guards on the way in. He told the guards they were wanted in the main temple.

Opening the lid to the basket, Bakenkhons carefully used a stick to pick up a cobra, which he quickly grabbed by the head. Placing the snake's head on Ahmenemat's neck, the snake produced its fangs and bit in. With the snake still in his hand, Bakenkhons waited a few moments for the venom to take effect. Ahmenemat's face began to change colour to a blue-greyish hue. Just then Sitamun opened the door to the chamber and stood gasping. Startled, Bakenkhons threw the snake towards her. Instinctively, Sitamun swiftly flicked the cobra away with her arm. Bakenkhons had picked up a small stone statue and hit Sitamun over her head. She fell to the ground. Touching her head, she looked at her hand to see it was covered in blood. She began to crawl out of the chamber, screaming for help as she did. Bakenkhons followed her with the statue in his hand. The guards had returned and ran down the corridor towards Sitamun. One guard called for more help while the other kneeled down to check on Sitamun.

"He murdered Ahmenemat, and he tried to kill me!" she screamed as her head fell to the ground and lay motionless.

"What did you do?" asked Sashin, immersed.

In a panic, Bakenkhons returned to the chamber. More guards arrived and stormed through. One spotted the cobra in the corner and lanced it with a spear. Checking on Ahmenemat, they saw that he was dead and, on closer inspection, noticed the fang bites on his neck. Turning to Bakenkhons, they raised their spears, and one guard lanced him in the chest. Bakenkhons fell to the ground, landing on his back. Knowing that he was about to die, he closed his eyes and astral projected. Immediately travelling to the lower astral plane, he found the Nyingma Pa and asked them for their help. They used dark magic to retain his astral body on the lower plane, but as a result, his etheric body had undergone deterioration. His astral body was stuck on the astral plane for centuries, until Sashin began to travel, when Bakenkhons sensed the presence of Ahmenemat and was drawn to him. He vowed to make him suffer for what had happened to him.

Bakenkhons had started to make his way up the platforms and was now one level down.

"Unfortunately, the one you call Bakenkhons has made his way up the library. You must withdraw from the record," said the custodian.

Bakenkhons made a leap off the platform, and a 'bang' could be heard as he landed on the floor. He ran towards Sashin, who had pulled out of the record and saw Bakenkhons charging towards him with clenched fists. The prospect of being punched in the face again, even if it was his astral face, was not one that Sashin wanted to entertain. He held up his arms together with his shoulders extended out to guard his face. Bakenkhons took a swing and hit Sashin's arms, causing him to slide back.

"I know what you did. You're a murderer!" yelled Sashin.

"You made me do it. And because of you, I have been stuck here for centuries," replied Bakenkhons.

"You're delusional!" yelled Sashin.

"Enough! You cannot bring this chaos to the Akashic records," said the custodian.

Bakenkhons took another strike, which Sashin averted.

"I'm going to take everything from you," snarled Bakenkhons.

"Leave now!" shouted the custodian. Her voice reverberated throughout the library. This made both Sashin and Bakenkhons turn to look at her.

"Leave immediately!" she yelled.

Sashin turned to run around the level to get to the platform on the other side, and Bakenkhons took pursuit. The whole level started to spin in the opposite direction, and Sashin felt like he was running on a treadmill. The whole level started to tilt, causing Bakenkhons to slip and slide down the floor. Now feeling like he was running on a treadmill with a gradient, Sashin started to feel the strain, but he pushed on and ran harder. A crackling sound could be heard as sparks of energy began to shoot off the blocks in various bookcases across the library.

"Reconfiguring the library has caused a surge of energy," said the custodian, her voice sounding panicked.

Sashin jumped for the railings. Climbing on top, he leapt for the black platform in front. Just about catching it with both arms, he pulled himself up. Bakenhons also made the leap for the platform and struggled to hang on, eventually climbing on top. The surging energy created a vortex again in the centre of the library. The custodian hovered over to the platform.

"Let's see what happens when I push you off this," said Bakenkhons.

Sashin ran towards Bakenkhons and leapt forward, pushing him off the platform and flying off himself. Bakenkhons flew into the energy vortex while Sashin grabbed onto the custodian's chair, causing it to flip to one side.

"What are you doing?" shouted the custodian startled.

She began to hover down to ground level as Sashin tried to hang on with fatigue setting into his arms. Nearing the ground, he let go and landed in a squat position. Standing up, he turned to see Bakenkhons caught in the energy vortex. The dome opened, releasing the energy out into the sky, taking him with it.

"Time to go," said Sashin.

"I hope to never see you again," snapped the custodian.

Sashin made his way over to the outer balcony where he assumed the lotus position. Levitating above the ground, he shot off into the sky and saw Bakenkhons in the distance hovering above the dome. The tunnel of white appeared ahead, and Sashin flew straight in. Travelling through the kaleidoscope of colours once again, he neared the end of the tunnel and rocketed out into a blanket of white light.

Chapter Thirty-Two

Sashin opened his eyes to see the ceiling fan spinning around. The frequency sound had stopped. He turned his head to see Reshma on her mobile phone. Seeing that Sashin was awake, Dina jumped off the sofa. There was an aroma of garlic and herbs. Sashin lifted his upper body and leant on his arms, looking over to see Darius in the kitchen area.

"So, how did it go? What did you find out?" asked Dina.

"I accessed the records and found out the truth. Bakenkhons and Ahmenemat were good friends, accomplished members of the Order. They would astral travel together. But the problem was that Bakenkhons grew frustrated because he couldn't progress. He grew jealous and resentful. So he turned to the lower astral plane, where he allied himself with the black magicians. Ahmenemat caught him on the lower plane, and this led to Bakenkhons seeing me, I mean Ahmenemat, as a threat. So he decided to kill me using cobra venom as well as kill my wife in the process," replied Sashin.

"Oh my God!" gasped Reshma.

Darius came into the living room. Dina looked over at him, and they made eye contact. Reshma noticed this body language from the car journey home the night before.

"He was there in the Akasha. Going there was like putting a pin on a map, and I led him right to the Akashic records. I also saw from accessing his past that Sitamun, my wife who eventually died, had alerted the guards. They raided the chamber and saw Ahmenemat. They speared Bakenkhons, who, in his dying breath, travelled to the lower plane, where the black magicians using dark magic kept his astral body stuck in the astral plane. But this corrupted his body and mind. He blames me now for what happened to him. When I started to astral travel as me in my current incarnation, he sensed it and found me," explained Sashin.

"He is a crazy man who is surrounded by dark magic. You have to understand, and this is very important, that he will *not* stop. Every time you astral travel, he will be there waiting for you," said Dina.

"Yes, I know. I confronted him once, but he had the help of the black magicians. I'm tired of running," replied Sashin.

"Then don't," responded Darius.

"You must make a stand – it's the only way," added Dina.

"Woah, woah, woah. Steady on people. This guy is a cold-blooded killer. I'm not going to have my little brother just take him on!" yelled Reshma.

"Well, then you underestimate him and what he is capable of," replied Dina.

"I'm only looking out for my brother. If he is going to do this, he needs to be fully prepared," added Reshma.

"He is prepared. He made it to the Akasha, with a little help maybe, but he still did it on his own. There is no real way to prepare apart from having the will," responded Dina.

"She's right Reshma; it's okay," said Sashin.

Reshma gave a reluctant nod.

"Now you know what happened to Ahmenemat and Bakenkhons and the impact it must have had on the Order. I didn't get a chance to see enough to know whether the Order continued," added Sashin.

Dina gave Darius another fleeting look. This time, Sashin noticed and it gave him mixed feelings of curiosity and uncertainty.

"I think we should head back to the hotel," he said.

"When you do decide to face Bakenkhons, which for your sake I hope is soon, you will need to do the same like we did here. If you don't have a table, then lie on the floor," said Dina.

She turned to look at Reshma and continued.

"You must be there too to watch over him. And call me. Give me a video call so that we can help you as much as we can, like today, even if we won't be there with you."

"Okay. Thanks for helping me today," replied Sashin.

"You're a connection to our forefathers, to the Order. For us, this is important," replied Darius.

"Okay, we'd best go," said Reshma.

"Are you sure you don't want to stay for dinner? Darius is making koshari and fattah," suggested Dina.

"No, that's okay. We'll get something at the hotel," responded Reshma matter-of-factly.

On the car journey back to the hotel, Sashin thought about the day. Making it to the Akasha filled him with amazement as well as a growing belief in himself at what he was able to accomplish, even if it was with a little push. Bakenkhons now knew that Sashin had seen the truth.

'The next time we meet will be different. It's time to face this head on,' he thought.

Back at the hotel car park, before Reshma and Sashin exited, Dina turned around.

"Let me know when you are ready – we will be ready to help," she said.

"Well, nice to meet you both," replied Sashin, opening the car door.

"Bye," said Reshma.

In reception, Reshma expressed her thoughts.

"It's great what they did to help you get to the Akasha, but I still feel like they're hiding something. It seems like, yes, they share a connection with you through the Order, but they are very interested in what happened to you, too eager to help," she said.

"I got a funny vibe in the house after I woke up. Maybe they genuinely want to help with some agenda of their own, which is a little unclear. But still, apart from you, they're the only ones that understand what's going on," replied Sashin.

"Yeah, I guess so," responded Reshma.

"Anyway, let's get ready for dinner. Be ready for six o'clock," suggested Sashin.

"Definitely, I'm starving," replied Reshma.

There was a small queue for the main restaurant at just past six. They managed to get a table straight away, as the restaurant was just beginning to fill up. After dinner, Reshma's phone pinged, she looked and saw that it was Ketan.

"It's Ketan," she said, waving her phone.

"Have you called him today?" asked Sashin.

"No, I haven't yet," replied Reshma.

"You should call him."

"Okay," responded Reshma, walking towards reception.

Sashin still had a glass of red wine left and a plate of baklava pieces. As he sipped his wine, his phone pinged. It was Alexis.

Alexis: Hi, just seeing how today went with the locals. All okay, or do you regret not doing the Valley of the Kings tour?

Sashin: It was fine. We had a more relaxing day today. I guess Valley of the Kings will have to be next time. Maybe we can do it together.

Alexis: I've already been, lol, but happy to go again with you. See you next week for the debrief x

Sashin: See you next week. I'll fill you in on the whole trip then x

Reshma had returned to the table.

"Everything okay?" asked Sashin.

"Yeah, he's fine. I think he's beginning to miss me now. So it's confirmed for tomorrow. Ketan will be picking us up from Heathrow. We should land at around eight-fifteen," replied Reshma.

"Great. Yes, it's about five hours and forty-five minutes' flight time," said Sashin.

"So tell me, what was it like in the Akashic records? Did you find out anything about me?" asked Reshma.

"I didn't have time to search. It's like a huge library. As soon as Bakenkhons turned up, I was just trying to get out of there. I managed to throw him into this energy vortex, which kept him away long enough for me to get away," replied Sashin.

"Energy vortex, what and how?" asked Reshma.

"The records give off this energy, which builds up and creates this spiral of energy. The custodian of the records, who hovers around in a golden chair, has to discharge the energy through the dome in the ceiling to prevent the build-up," answered Sashin.

Reshma looked bemused.

"Wow, that sounds incredible and scary at the same time," said Reshma.

Sashin looked sullen all of a sudden, with an introspective look on his face.

"Everything okay?" asked Reshma.

"I'll tell you more tomorrow. I'm tired; I'm gonna get an early night," answered Sashin.

In the morning after breakfast, Reshma produced the business card she was handed when they were dropped off at the hotel.

"I'm going to send Yara a message just to remind her that we need a transfer back to the airport," she said.

"I'm sure she remembers. That's her job," responded Sashin, smiling.

Reshma shortly received a message back from Yara confirming pickup at eleven o'clock, which gave them just over half an hour to finish packing. Yara walked into reception a few minutes early. Sashin and Reshma exited the lift to see Yara at reception. She turned to spot them and began waving enthusiastically. Sashin handed in the room key cards while Yara took the luggage.

"We hope you enjoyed your stay. And I hope the eye gets better," said the receptionist.

Sashin was lost for a response and instead gave her a nervous smile. Once at the airport, they made their way to the bag drop area for InterJet and then through security. The airside area was relatively limited and Reshma and Sashin were able to traverse it in less than twenty minutes. They took refuge in an Irish-themed pub for some lunch and drinks, whilst keeping a keen eye on the electronic board, waiting for their boarding time to appear. Once it popped up, they readied themselves and made their way to the gate. Reshma suddenly stopped and had a panicked look on her face.

"I haven't bought any souvenirs, a fridge magnet, or sweets," she said.

"Really, you've had all this time, and you realise now?" replied Sashin unamused.

"Come on, quickly," said Reshma, scurrying back to the shops.

Sashin followed with less enthusiasm. At the duty free shop, Reshma took her basket containing a Sphinx statue, an Egypt fridge magnet of the pyramids, and a box of baklava over to the checkout.

"Are you getting anything?" asked Reshma.

"No, I'm good," replied Sashin.

"Here, I'll get you a fridge magnet," responded Reshma.

"How kind," said Sashin sarcastically.

They then rushed over to the gate as Sashin partly pulled his hand luggage and carried it up the escalator. A queue had formed at the gate, but people were already boarding, and they were both soon on the plane. This time the only seats that were taken were their own in the row of three, with the left one unoccupied. Reshma took the aisle seat while Sashin sat in the middle. Reshma turned her head to Sashin and began to talk, almost at a whisper.

"When you were astral at the house, I connected to the wi-fi and did some research on Thoth, the emerald tablets, and his book of magic. It turns out Thoth reincarnated as Hermes Trismegistus, who wrote the 'Hermetica' which is the basis of the teachings of the 'Order of the Golden Dawn'. Well, to be exact, the basis of the Second Order, which is called the 'Rosae Rubeae et Aureae Crucis', taught magic and astral travel. I learnt about the 'lesser banishing ritual of the pentagram' that I used on my house from reading about the 'Order of the Golden Dawn'. How interesting is that? You see? This is all connected," explained Reshma wide-eyed.

"That's the reason why Bakenkhons couldn't get into your house. That ritual came from Thoth's magic," replied Sashin.

"I think we should do the ritual at your house. I mean you've raised the stakes now by going to the 'Akashic records' and finding out the truth. And you threw him into that energy vortex, he's going to be even more pissed off so he may come to find you at your house," said Reshma.

"I told the black magicians when they decided to pay a visit, by no means ever come back again," responded Sashin.

"Do you think that will stop Bakenkhons? You don't want him to come to you in your home; you want to be the one to find him on your terms," replied Reshma.

"I'm willing to take that chance. If he comes, then I will face him," answered Sashin.

"Okay, but think about it, but not for too long," added Reshma.

"There's something I have to tell you that's been playing on my mind," said Sashin.

"What is it?" replied Reshma.

"I didn't really want to say anything at Dina's house because we were both unsure as to whether we could completely trust them. But here goes. I was a student of Thoth's teachings. I was learning about soul transmutation. This is something Ahmenemat was doing outside of the Order. When I died on the astral plane, I panicked. I was lost, my chord had been cut, and I was free falling. I propelled my astral body into the future, where I found Mum and Dad. Your brother died in childbirth and I inhabited the body of the baby and was reborn. I'm so sorry to tell you this, but I'm not your real brother," said Sashin glumly.

Reshma grabbed hold of Sashin's arm and gave a consoling squeeze.

"Look. That was the soul contract of the baby, to pass during childbirth as part of his or her soul journey. You're still my brother," she said reassuringly.

Sashin nodded silently.

It was eight forty-five UK time when the landing announcement was made. By eight fifty-five, the plane had landed. Shortly after, Sashin and Reshma made their way through passport control, and it was relatively quiet in the baggage collection area. With suitcases in tow, they made their way to arrivals. Once they were outside, Ketan stood by the white A5 as Reshma rushed forward with her suitcase.

"Hey honey!" she said, giving Ketan a hug.

"Hey Sash. Oh, what happened to you?" asked Ketan, looking shocked.

"We got caught up in a protest," replied Sashin.

"What the, how did that happen? Aren't you supposed to be the protector?" asked Ketan.

"What? Like you were?" responded Sashin, squinting his eyes. Ketan's comment had touched a nerve.

"It was just a couple of idiots causing trouble. Don't worry about it," reassured Reshma, glancing over at Sashin.

During the car ride home, Ketan asked about the trip. Sashin remained quiet, still seething from Ketan's jibe. Reshma expressed her enjoyment.

"It was an amazing experience, and we got to see and learn so much. Didn't we, Sash?"

Sashin nodded in agreement, catching Ketan glancing in the rear view mirror. Back at home, Sashin unloaded his suitcase from the car, turning down help from Ketan, who stood by the boot. The passenger side window slid down.

"Have you thought about what I said about on the plane, about doing the lesser banishing ritual? Since I'm here, we might as well do it," suggested Reshma.

"You're persistent about this. It's late and I just want to relax," replied Sashin.

"Now is the best time to do it," said Reshma.

"It's up to you, as long as it doesn't take too long,"

"It won't. So I take it that's a yes?"

"Okay," responded Sashin.

Reshma quickly got out of the car and shouted over to Ketan.

"We just have to do this ritual!" she said.

"What now?" replied Ketan, rolling his eyes.

Once inside the house, Reshma asked for white candles. Sashin only had a pack of tea candles that he found in the back of a cupboard in the kitchen.

"Those will do. I will need four. You can wait in the kitchen," said Reshma looking at Ketan.

"Do you want a beer?" asked Sashin.

"Oh yes, I'll have one," replied Ketan.

"Er, you're not drinking until you've done the ritual with me," ordered Reshma.

"Great," mumbled Sashin.

"Can I watch TV?" asked Ketan.

"Okay," replied Sashin, putting on the television on the wall in the kitchen.

"Keep the volume down," yelled Reshma.

Reshma lit the tea candles and placed them in each corner of the living room.

"I will stand in the centre of the room and start by making the Qabalistic cross. I'll then face each direction and draw pentagrams in the air that I will then join, and then I will invoke the archangels. I will finish off with the Qabalistic cross," explained Reshma.

"Right," replied Sashin, intrigued.

"First, I'll face east. Just stay quiet," said Reshma.

Facing east towards the lit tea candle, Reshma imagined herself growing large and tall to the extent that she was a towering figure above the earth. She saw herself as the centre of the universe, with an intense white light touching the crown of her head. With her right hand, she touched her forehead, imagining the white light pulling down to her head, and at the same time, she uttered the word *'ahtah'*. She then moved her hand down to her chest, stomach, hips, and then stopped near her groin and said, *'malkuth'*.

She brought the light down from her crown to the ground beneath her feet. Touching her left shoulder, she spoke *'ve-geburah'*, then touching her right shoulder, said *'ve-gedulah'* all the time seeing the light move from shoulder to shoulder. She then outstretched her hands and brought them together at her chest, saying *'le-olahm, amen'*.

Reshma then proceeded to draw a pentagram in the air, starting from the east, from bottom left, tracing the shape up and then down, then left, right, and then back to the start. She visualised it glowing in blue flames. As she pointed to the middle of the pentagram with two fingers she said, *'yod heh wav heh'*. She then did the same in the southern direction and said *'adonai'*; then to the west she said, *'eheieh'* and to the north uttered *'agla'*. Whilst drawing the pentagrams, Reshma moved methodically in a circular motion. She then pointed east and imagined the pentagrams connecting in a sphere of blue flaming light. Now, with her arms outstretched, she spoke.

"Before me, Raphael. Behind me, Gabriel. To my right, Michael, and to my left, Uriel. For around me shines the pentagram and within shines the six-ray star."

Reshma then performed the first part of the ritual again, touching her forehead, moving her arm down her body to her groin, touching each shoulder, and then outstretching her hands to bring them together to end the ritual. Sashin stood transfixed, as it was not like any type of ritual he had seen before. Reshma opened her eyes.

"There is one thing I have added; come and stand here in the middle," she said.

Sashin walked over and joined Reshma in the middle of the living room.

"The four flaming pentagrams are all around us, and I want you to imagine them burning with blue flames. Now, push them out towards the end of the house," instructed Reshma.

Sashin closed his eyes and visualised the flaming pentagrams shining blue and pushed them out towards the walls of the house.

"Right, it's all done! See, not so bad," said Reshma.

"Pretty impressive," replied Sashin.

"Ketan, we're going!" shouted Reshma.

Ketan appeared out of the kitchen.

"Thanks for the beer," he said.

Reshma slapped Sashin on the shoulder.

"You made the right decision to do the ritual. Thanks for an amazing trip. Speak soon," she said.

"Hope the eye heals before you get back to work," added Ketan.

Sashin's expression was blank. He was pleased to see him leave.

Winding down with a beer, Sashin sat relaxed on his sofa and watched television. The day of travel weighed down on him as his eyes became heavy and slowly started to close. He jolted himself awake, cognisant that he was falling asleep. Again, his eyelids began to slide down, and there was momentary blackness. Sashin forced himself awake again to find that he was standing in the centre of the living room in front of the television.

'That's odd. I was literally just on the sofa,' he thought.

He turned around, shocked to find himself sitting down asleep.

'But how? I didn't even try,' he wondered.

It was apparent to Sashin that becoming astral now required less effort. He had slid out of his physical body through the mere act of falling asleep whilst watching television. 'Had the experience of travelling to the Akasha with the help of Dina and Darius somehow accelerated his ability to astral project?' The thought had crossed his mind. Realising that his physical body was exhausted, he brought himself back so he could head up to bed.

However, there was a sudden eruption of sound as if fireworks were going off outside. Waves of crackling could be heard. Sashin walked over to the kitchen and through the window, he saw sparks of blue flying in all directions.

'Well, I'll be damned. She was right,' he thought.

Sashin heard a familiar voice. It was Bakenkhons.

"What is this magic that I face again?" he said.

"It would be futile to try to break through," uttered another voice that Sashin recognised. It was the black magician who had entered his bedroom previously.

Sashin ran upstairs and looked through the spare bedroom window to get a view from above, but he was unable to see Bakenkhons. He only caught a glimpse of shadow entities flying around the house and heard voices below. He ran back downstairs, and there were now multiple explosions taking place around at all sides. Sashin spotted blue sparks illuminating the darkness outside. He edged closer to the window again to hear the voices.

"We nearly broke through last time," said Bakenkhons.

"You will not break through; this is very powerful magic!" responded the black magician.

"Yes, we can. We just need more shadow wraiths, a lot more. Let us return to the lower plane and bring back a small army," snapped Bakenkhons.

"That is if you can find enough willing to sacrifice themselves. This could take a long time, and for just one man," replied the black magician.

Sashin felt a wave of anger come over him, like heat building up to a crescendo in his head. He took a minute to process what was happening and began to calm down. He nodded his head from side to side in stark disagreement with what he had just heard. The voices subsided. He made his way back to the living room and returned to his body by sitting back down into it. He awoke knowing that it was time to act quickly.

Chapter Thirty-Three

On Sunday afternoon, Sashin received a message from Alexis.

Alexis: Hi Sashin, let's meet in the office on Tuesday for your debrief of the trip. After that, you have your wrap-up meeting with Suzanne. So I suggest you get in an hour before, say nine o'clock?

Sashin: That's fine and works for me. I'll see you at nine on Tuesday.

As he sat in his kitchen, he had an uneasy feeling of being an astral prisoner, confined to his house. The events of two nights ago still played on his mind. He needed a distraction, and this came in the form of a lunch invitation from his mum, Ushma. She had phoned during breakfast and informed Sashin that they had been shopping in Wembley the day before and that she had bought lots of goodies. They'd gotten so many in fact that they needed his help to finish them off. Sashin happily accepted and reminded his mum that he did not eat as much as he used to. Ushma dismissed this and told him to treat it as a cheat day.

He turned up at his parents' house later than Ushma had suggested, which was half past twelve due to having had a slightly late breakfast. As soon as the door opened, Ushma stood there with her mouth agape, staring at Sashin's face.

"Oh *beta*, what happened to you? Did this happen in Egypt?"

"I don't remember telling you about Egypt," said Sashin.

"Reshma told me," replied Ushma.

Once inside, Ushma started to call out to Satish.

"Come look at your son's face, look."

Satish jumped off his recliner to see what the commotion was. Seeing Sashin's eye, he held up his arms.

"What is this? I've never seen you with a black eye!" exclaimed Satish.

"Just a run-in we had in Egypt with some protesters," replied Sashin.

"You can tell us all about it," said Ushma, ushering them both to the dining table.

"This is Indian tapas. There's kachori, Gujarati samosas, Punjabi samosas, batata vada, chilli paneer, fafda, dhokra, and gulab jamun for dessert," announced Satish.

Sashin's eyes lit up, and he felt his mouth water at the delectable selection.

"Lovely. But the only thing with Punjabi samosas is that it depends on how they're made. If the outside is too thick, then it gets, what's the word I'm looking for? Stodgy. That's it, it gets stodgy," commented Sashin.

"Cut it in half then. If you don't like it then at least you haven't wasted a whole samosa," replied Ushma, rolling her eyes.

Sashin sat down at the table as Ushma brought over plates and cutlery. Satish also joined him and began to speak.

"So what happened to your face, son?" asked Satish.

"We got caught up in a group of protesters. Just bad timing I guess. Two guys were causing trouble, one of them groped Reshma. I went to restrain him, and I got punched in the face for it," replied Sashin.

"Bloody bastards!" yelled Satish.

"But we got away, which is the main thing," said Sashin.

"When we first came to this country in the fifties, there was a lot of racism. It was a tough time for your mum and me. We got lots of abuse. Things started to get serious when this group of yobs started to vandalise the houses of Asians. Then they started to attack people. They started on me a few times, the bastards. There was a guy in the community who got beaten up; he was hit over the head with a wooden bat and suffered bad head injuries. So we all started to panic. What we did is, we all got together with friends and neighbours who, like us, were immigrants and formed like a society group," explained Satish.

"Oh right. I don't think you've ever told me this story," responded Sashin.

Satish continued.

"We learnt how to defend ourselves, anything from boxing to karate, meeting up and just exchanging ideas. There was no real organisation to what we were doing, just doing what we could. Then one time, when I was walking home, I was surrounded by a group of yobs. One of them went to hit me from behind, and I hit him back. They were trying to get me on the floor so that they could kick me, but I just started to punch back, I even got two of them down. But there were too many of them. Some of the guys from our group saw this, and they came running over. There was a big fight, and we managed to scare them off. After that, we didn't get hassled again. We were forced to fight. Indians are seen as very weak people who don't fight, but we had to fight back. Kirit, the guy who got hit over the head, was in a coma, and when he woke up, he didn't really have any quality of life, you know. That was taken away from him."

"That's very sad. I appreciate what you guys did. It must've been hard for you, but you came here for a better life. Your decision has affected future generations, giving Reshma and me a better life," said Sashin, pausing for a moment as he became introspective.

"What is it, *beta*?" asked Ushma.

"For the future generations," mumbled Sashin as he ate a Punjabi samosa.

After taking his last bite, Sashin continued.

"You made a decision to come here. And then to fight back, which impacted yours and the lives of your group and your fellow Indians."

"I told you this story because your black eye reminded me of that time. We got bullied, got hit, but we got back up. We continued on and kept going," replied Satish.

"We didn't give up hope," added Ushma.

After lunch, Sashin pondered over what his dad had said. In a funny way, it was just what he needed to hear. He thought about what he had seen in his Akashic record regarding his rebirth.

"I have to ask you, when I was born were there any complications?" asked Sashin.

"Why do you ask?" enquired Ushma.

"I just wondered, that's all," responded Sashin.

"You were a miracle child. The doctor said that you weren't moving, that you might be a stillbirth, and both mine and your dad's hearts sank. But then you started to move and cry. It was such a relief," replied Ushma.

Sashin then thought about how he had been brought up in an Indian household. He saw himself having the best of both worlds, a past rich in Egyptian culture and one now in Indian culture.

Chapter Thirty-Four

Monday morning came around quickly, and Sashin was back in the office. Both Dev and Krish arrived shortly afterwards.

"How was your trip, Sash? Did you sort out your issue with that astral entity person?" asked Dev.

"Ooooh! Look at the shiner. I never would've thought you would get into trouble. Passive Sashin, drives at fifty five to stay alive, and all of that. It reminds me of my younger days," chuckled Krish.

"What happened to you then?" asked Dev.

"At this rate, I'll have to have a script ready for every time someone asks. We went out in Luxor to get some torches and got caught up in a protest on the streets. This guy groped Reshma, so I grabbed him, and his friend punched me from the side. It all happened so fast," explained Sashin.

"What a couple of arseholes!" yelled Krish.

"That's what Reshma said," replied Sashin.

"Then what happened?" quizzed Dev.

"We managed to get out of the crowd. Those guys ran off. I didn't go to the police," responded Sashin.

"Yeah, they wouldn't have done anything, and you probably would've wasted your time. Glad you're both okay apart from the shiner," said Krish.

"In Luxor, we met a lady called Dina and her friend Darius. They're both descendants of the 'Order of Amun', the same Order that I was a part of in my past life. They helped me to reach this place on the astral plane. Now, you're going to have to keep an open mind. This place is known as the 'Akashic records' where all memories and thoughts are stored, like in a gigantic library. It was here that I was able to see my past and that of Bakenkhons, the person who has it in for me. The thing is, we used to be friends in the Order, but he grew jealous of my ability to astral travel to areas he was unable to reach, and he became resentful. Out of frustration, he turned to these black magicians that are on the lower astral plane, very negative beings who offered him power and help. I followed him to this lower plane, and as a result, he thought I would tell the rest of the Order, which would lead to him being kicked out. After this, he murdered me whilst I was astral travelling and then he killed my wife, who walked in on him in the act. Before she died, she alerted the temple guards who came and saw what had happened and killed him. However, whilst he was dying, he kept his astral body on the lower plane with the help of the black magicians. Fast forwarding to now, he's been stuck on the astral plane for centuries. When I started to astral travel in my current incarnation, he was able to sense me and find me. He blames me for what happened to him," explained Sashin.

"Wow! This sounds even more wild than what you explained at the airport. It appears you had a traumatic past life death," said Dev.

"Yes, it was a traumatic death and reincarnation," replied Sashin.

"So what's your next move?" asked Dev.

"Bakenkhons is quite the name, isn't it? He sounds crazy," commented Krish.

"I have to face him, have it out, and confront him with what I now know. Maybe try to appeal to his better nature," answered Sashin.

"But do you really think this guy is willing to negotiate? Think about it; he's now got these black magicians helping him, and he's killed you before. So what's to say he won't do it again?" asked Krish.

"Exactly, I'm with Krish on this one. You confront this guy and his legion of doom, and he's hellbent on destroying you, but then what? How are you going to talk your way out of that?" added Dev.

"Then, I stand my ground and face him and the black magicians head on. I'm tired of running," replied Sashin.

"If this Bakenkhons has the help of these black magicians, then why can't you get help out there in the astral place?" enquired Krish.

"I already used that lifeline and got the help of a spirit guide, but I don't think he's going to help again. He said I have to remember who I was," responded Sashin.

"Well, I hope you sort this all out Sash. It's a lot to take in. I'm finding it hard to process," added Dev.

"I understand. It is a lot to take in, but I told you both for a reason. Being able to talk about it with you guys is really helping me cope in some ways rather than having to keep it all in," said Sashin.

"That's what we're here for. I for one consider myself open minded, and I find it fascinating," said Krish, looking over at Dev with a judgemental look.

The following morning, Sashin waited for the seven-thirty tube to London Bridge. Hendon Central was filled with commuters for the morning rush into central London. He had prepared notes for his debrief with Alexis and had held back a few pictures and videos, which he intended to share with her at the meeting as an added bonus. On the tube, Sashin scrolled through his album to ensure he had curated the right photos and videos as a final check. As the train pulled into London Bridge, the familiar mass exodus of passengers occurred.

However, he felt a strange sensation as he caught a young man staring over in his direction. He saw it just out of the corner of his eye, and when he turned to look, the man turned away. Sashin shrugged it off as an overly inquisitive, bored passenger. Exiting the train whilst descending down the escalator, he had the urge to turn and look behind. And lo and behold, the man was there on the other side, also making his way down on the adjacent escalator. He looked like he was in his early thirties with a Mediterranean complexion and curly black hair wearing a denim jacket. Paranoia did not tend to be one of Sashin's usual traits, and he continued on without much more thought about it.

Sashin noticed a buzz about the Dream Ventures office as soon as he had walked into the reception area. He saw through the glass in the double doors that there was more staff around than normal. People walked around, while some were engaged in conversation whilst standing.

"Hello, Sashin," said the receptionist.

Sashin turned around in surprise. The receptionist had never addressed him by his name, let alone remembered it.

"You remembered my name," he replied.

"Yes, Alexis is expecting you," responded the receptionist, beaming.

"I'll go right through," said Sashin.

Walking through the double doors, he saw Alexis in the middle seating area, where he had sat with her before. Alexis was talking to two other people who he had not seen around the office. 'They must be new,' he thought. Alexis turned to see Sashin, and he immediately noticed her eyes light up as she gave an emphatic smile that very quickly turned into a look of shock. Her mouth opened as she held out her arm to touch his eye, barely making contact with his face.

"What happened to you? Tell me this didn't happen in Egypt," she said, altering the volume of her voice mid-sentence to a lower decibel.

"If I had known I would get this much attention for having a black eye, maybe I would've gotten one earlier," replied Sashin, breaking into a chuckle.

"Well, tell me?" insisted Alexis.

"Okay, yes, it did happen in Egypt," responded Sashin.

"I knew this was a bad idea sending you out there," Alexis began, but before she could finish, Sashin interjected.

"It was a great idea – me going out there. I just got caught in a protest with Reshma in Luxor. We had a run in with a couple of idiots, one of which touched Reshma inappropriately, so I went to restrain him, and the other guy he was with hit me," explained Sashin.

"Come with me to one of the side meeting rooms," said Alexis, looking around cautiously.

They entered one of the smaller meeting rooms that resided at the back of the office, away from the larger rooms.

"I'm so sorry to hear this, Sashin. I feel so bad," said Alexis.

"Hey listen, it's not your fault. We ventured out, and it was just bad timing," replied Sashin.

"Do me a favour and don't tell Suzanne that it happened in Egypt if she asks, which she's more than likely to do," said Alexis.

"What, are you asking me to lie? Well, I would never have thought," responded Sashin, grinning.

"Not a lie exactly, just a slight fabrication of events? I just don't want to bring attention to the trip that I sent you on and have her start asking questions," she added.

"It's okay; I'll say it happened over the weekend," suggested Sashin.

"So, tell me all about the trip then?" asked Alexis.

Sashin bent down and opened his rucksack, pulling out his laptop and a collection of notes that he had made on pages torn from a notepad. He flicked through the pages, ensuring each was in the right order. Looking at this laptop, he realised he had taken it out due to habit and did not need to use it.

"In Cairo, what was the name of the driver at the airport?"

"Tarek," replied Alexis.

"Yes, that's him. He was a nice enough chap. He was a friendly and jovial guy who got us to the hotel in an hour. The journey was long, and the car was a bit stuffy, but he did put the aircon on. The Marriott Mena House was a nice hotel with a spectacular view. I think that's what makes it. Thanks for the welcome pack and for the half board basis. That was a nice touch. Which reminds me, you should have a torch in your welcome pack because the inside parts of the pyramids can be dark. You don't want members venturing out looking for a torch," he added.

"That's okay. I wanted you and Reshma to experience what our members would receive when they go on the same trip or type of trip," responded Alexis.

"The tour to Giza was amazing, and the guide, Rami, was excellent. An all rounder, very knowledgeable; he's a keeper that one. Here, look at these photos. These are ones I didn't send you," offered Sashin as he swiped to his pre-prepared album.

Alexis, with a look of curiosity, eyed up the photos as Sashin swiped across.

"Here is a close up of the Pyramid of Giza. Now, watch this video of the inside of the pyramid. This is a first person view of walking through to the inner chambers."

As Alexis watched the video, her face lit up.

"Wow, that is amazing. I've been to the pyramids, but I must confess I never went inside. This is great. In fact, can you send me this video? I can use this for promotional material. We could use it for a virtual tour piece for those that don't want to go inside the pyramid for various reasons, such as claustrophobia or disability. I've got some ideas bouncing around my head," she suggested.

"Now this is Luxor, at the Temple of Karnak. And this is a chamber in the temple grounds that is not open to the public that I wanted to see," said Sashin.

"That isn't even part of our itinerary," added Alexis, looking puzzled.

"Yes I know. So with the guide in Luxor, Saeed, we had a very different experience. For one, we had to leave the hotel to meet him at a perfumery. He did have some knowledge, but at the chamber there was some bother with us visiting there, and he panicked and abandoned us," explained Sashin.

"What exactly did you get up to at Karnak? You were supposed to stick to the itinerary," said Alexis.

"I will explain. It was linked to my past life experience," replied Sashin.

"Oh yes, the past life situation you mentioned the other night. I did say if it's something you want to find out about, then pursue it," responded Alexis.

"That's exactly what I did. I know visiting that chamber was a bit risky and it was during your trip, but it was the only way."

In order to deflect attention away from the sensitive subject of the chamber, Sashin resorted to diversion as he continued on.

"So, this brings me to my last picture and video. Back to the Giza Plateau, the Sphinx in all its glory. Now, get ready for this. Around the back of the statue is an entrance, look here," pointed out Sashin as he zoomed in on the picture.

Alexis looked intently with a cheeky smile appearing on her face.

"There's something I've got to show you," she said.

Opening up her laptop, she made a few clicks on the on finger pad and then swivelled the machine round so Sashin could see the screen. She then pressed on the pad button, which brought a YouTube video to life. Sashin was intrigued and focused his attention to concentrate. He then smiled after seeing familiar faces.

"That's Yasmin and Ian," said Sashin, pointing at the screen.

"This is the Seekers of the Truth page. The group of conspiracy theorists in the video found an entrance at the back of the Sphinx. They're calling it a cover up. Wait a few seconds. There, look in the background," said Alexis rapidly.

Sashin spotted Reshma, Rami, and himself. 'That was after we had spoken to Yasmin and Ian,' he thought.

"I was the one who told the group about the entrance," remarked Sashin.

"Really? This video has gone viral; it's had over one million views!" replied Alexis, looking bemused.

"Whoa! There really is an appetite for this stuff," responded Sashin.

Alexis turned her laptop back around.

"Thanks for sharing these photos and videos. Your information has been useful. I'll look into this issue you had with the guide, Saeed. To be honest, I wasn't too sure about him. You didn't happen to meet anyone out there who you think could be a good replacement?" asked Alexis, breaking into a laugh.

"I did meet a couple of locals shortly after we were left alone at the Temple of Karnak. Actually, come to think of it, it was perfect timing," replied Sashin, suddenly going quiet as he pondered for a moment.

"You know it's funny, but I've been having some weird dreams recently. Seeing the Sphinx reminded me of one I had recently. I was in the desert, still in my pyjamas, standing barefoot in the sand. In the distance, I could see the Sphinx. I heard thunder, and there was this large black cloud coming overhead. I started to feel scared. In the cloud was a huge face, and then the cloud became a person. I saw this hooded guy come down, wearing an old fashioned robe. He flew down towards me. I saw his face, and it looked horrific. He looked directly into my eyes. As he landed on the sand and walked towards me, I felt terrified. I started to run towards the Sphinx, but I couldn't move, it's like I was stuck running on the spot. I panicked and woke up after that," said Alexis.

Sashin was jolted out of his trance by what Alexis had said, like he had been grabbed by the shoulders and shaken.

"What did you say?" he asked.

"I just said I had a nightmare in which this robed man..." before Alexis could finish, Sashin interrupted.

"Yes, this robed man. I have seen him too in my dreams," he replied.

"No way, that is really weird. Maybe it's like the nightmare man, where loads of people were seeing the same man in their dreams because of a suggestion. Maybe we've seen this man somewhere before in a picture, a movie, or in some form of media," remarked Alexis.

Sashin had a sinking feeling in his stomach. He could feel his body becoming paralysed with the thought of Bakenkhons invading Alexis' astral space.

"I have something to tell you," he said.

"Don't tell me this is going to be a complicated relationship," joked Alexis, grinning.

"Not quite, but I just need you to keep an open mind," replied Sashin.

"Oh, time's up. I don't want you to be late for your wrap-up with Suzanne," said Alexis, looking at the time on her laptop.

"It's the end of an era, even if it was a short one at that. I'm gonna miss seeing you in the office," she added.

"Well, we can see each other out of the office," replied Sashin.

"Yes, let's organise a second date," said Alexis, smiling.

Sashin packed his rucksack and made his way out of the room accompanied by Alexis.

"This way to the main meeting room where we met Eddie last time," she said.

As he approached the glass door, he saw Suzanne walking round to a chair. She was dressed less formally this time, wearing a white shirt with navy trousers and black high heels.

"Sashin, so nice to see you again," said Suzanne standing up to shake his hand.

"Time has gone quickly since I last saw you at my office," replied Sashin.

"What happened to your eye?" asked Suzanne.

Sashin looked over at Alexis.

"It happened over the weekend, I was..." he said.

"In the garden," interjected Alexis.

"Yes, I was cutting bamboo, and it hit me in the eye, bit clumsy," responded Sashin.

Alexis laughed nervously.

"Got to be careful cutting bamboo," she said.

Suzanne looked at each of them.

"You two have really hit it off. I'm pleased to say that you've done a great job. I'm going to keep this meeting very brief and informal. Glad we brought you on, Sashin. Your expertise and knowledge in network marketing really paid off. Your contract has now come to an end. Here's a little something to say thank you for your efforts," she said, handing over a bag containing a small case that was covered in a purple velvet material.

"Oh thanks," replied Sashin.

"I'm sure you two will keep in touch. We may need your services in the near future, so don't go too far. In the meantime, I wish you all the best with your next project. Is there anything you wanted to say about your time with us, good or bad?" enquired Suzanne.

"Nothing in particular. I would like to thank you for using our consultancy. Working with Alexis on the Dream Ventures launch has been really interesting and fun actually," responded Sashin.

"Well, great. Right, I have another meeting; we have members of the management team in to look at our roster of trips with a view to introducing new ones, so no rest," added Suzanne.

Alexis got up and held open the door whilst looking at Sashin, his cue to leave. As he got up and walked past Alexis, the sinking feeling returned in his stomach. There was no time to delay. He had to face Bakenkhons sooner rather than later for the sake of the people he cared about.

Walking through the buzz of people on the office floor, Alexis escorted Sashin all the way to and into the reception area, something she did not usually do, normally saying her goodbyes at the double doors.

"Let's organise our night out soon," said Alexis.

"Definitely, I'll let you know," replied Sashin.

"You can tell me what you wanted to say," she said, giving Sashin a hug and discreetly kissing him on the cheek.

The sensation was soothing, and for a moment he felt lost in her embrace. This quickly subsided to a feeling of dread, which triggered a determination in him.

'I must do whatever I can to protect her,' he thought.

Back at home, Sashin opened the bag from Suzanne and pulled out the small purple velvet case. He clicked a small latch on the side to open the case. Inside was a bottle of Bollinger champagne, with two smaller bottles at either side. Around the neck of each smaller bottle was a piece of string with a small folded card attached. He opened one card which read 'Blackcurrant Cassis', and the other said 'Strawberry Cassis'.

"Lovely," he said to himself.

Chapter Thirty-Five

Sashin pulled out his mobile phone and messaged Reshma.

Sashin: It's time.

Reshma: For?

Sashin: For me to go back in and face Bakenkhons.

Reshma: Are you sure you're ready?

Sashin: As ready as I'll ever be.

Reshma: I'm not free until Friday, early evening. I can come over and stay the night if I have to.

Sashin: Thanks, but I'm hoping you won't have to. It should be in and then back out, like at Dina's house. Which reminds me, I need to message her to join us on video.

Reshma: Okay, but you know my thoughts on those two. They did help, but just be wary.

Sashin: Yes, I know.

In the days leading up to Friday, Sashin thought hard about what his strategy was going to be. He went over all the different places in his mind that he had visited so far on the astral planes, the abilities he had developed, and the things he had experienced.

In the office, his mood fluctuated between moments of open conversation and bouts of being withdrawn and visibly introspective. Sashin deliberately avoided talking about his astral dilemma with Dev and Krish even when they brought it up. His gut feeling told him to deal with it, run towards the fear and face it. If all worked out, then he could tell them later; if not, then they would find out from Reshma.

Sashin messaged Dina on Wednesday. There had been no response all day, and Sashin grew apprehensive. On Thursday afternoon, his phone pinged.

Dina: Sorry for the delay. The network has been out here, so I could not message back. Friday evening is fine for the video call. Remember we are two hours ahead, so the earlier the better. Aim for six o'clock at the latest UK time. And prepare yourself for astral travel. If you don't have a table, then lie on the floor, make sure you're comfortable, and have your sister Reshma there for support. Above all else, just believe in yourself.

Sashin: Okay, speak to you at six tomorrow.

On Friday, Sashin left the office early, at four o'clock. He had informed Reshma that she had to be at his house for just before six. She was not entirely pleased with the time as she would have to drive over during rush hour on a Friday, but she did say she would try to finish work a little early by starting earlier in the morning.

Krish looked over at Dev.

"He seemed quiet today. Do you think everything is okay with all that astral stuff?" he said.

"I'm not quite sure, but you're right, he was quieter than normal. Maybe he's just trying to make sense of everything. I mean, if something was bothering him, he would've said something to us, right?" replied Dev.

"I just hope he's okay," responded Krish.

Sashin arrived home at twenty minutes past five. He prepared the centre of his living room by placing a blanket on the floor and a pillow at the top. The doorbell rang at quarter to six, and it was Reshma. She walked in with a bag and pulled out a round purple candle.

"This is a scented candle that will help to charge the energy in the room," she said.

Reshma lit the candle and placed it on a side table, which she positioned near the blanket on the floor. Sashin picked up his mobile phone and made a video call. The phone continued to ring without any response.

"Did you agree on a time to call?" asked Reshma.

"Of course," replied Sashin dryly.

Sashin cut the call and stood looking puzzled at this phone. The phone immediately sprang to life. Accepting the incoming video call, Dina appeared on the screen with Darius next to her.

"I was waiting for Darius. We're ready. Are you?" she asked.

"Yes, Reshma is here, and I'm about to go astral."

"Great, we're here and watching. Just remember when you were here at our house and do the same thing. Allow yourself to relax and guide yourself to where you need to go," added Dina.

"Finding Bakenkhons won't be a problem; it's when I find him that it will be," responded Sashin.

He lay down on the blanket. Reshma sat on the sofa cross-legged.

"If things don't work out, just get out of there. Okay Sash, you got this," she said.

Sashin closed his eyes. The aroma of the candle diffused throughout the living room. There was a hint of lemon amongst lavender that was somewhat soothing. As he focused his mind on his whole body, he felt tingling and the high-pitched frequency started shortly after. Sashin rose up out of his body as he somersaulted slowly up and over to be in an upright position, floating in the air. He then descended rapidly through the floor. Shooting down, he saw the concrete and then the dirt in the ground as the particles of his astral body moved through them.

Further and further down, he went at great speed until he appeared amongst dark grey clouds that he rapidly dropped through, slowing down before he reached the ground. Sashin stood in the familiar dark and barren wasteland of the lower astral plane. All around were decrepit trees. Sashin walked on cautiously. It was quiet, and the eeriness that he could sense seemed to be endemic to this astral wasteland. As he moved on ahead, he saw movement out of the corner of his eye. Looking to his side, he observed wisps of black flying along. It was the shadow wraiths. Sashin produced his light sword, which illuminated the area around him. He looked to his left and saw the wraiths moving at pace on that side too.

'That's odd. Why aren't they coming for me?' he thought.

The shadow wraiths seemed to be keeping their distance. On the horizon, Sashin saw a line of figures. As he drew closer, he noticed that the wraiths were beginning to edge closer on either side. He turned around to see them behind him.

'It's an ambush. I knew they were up to something," he thought.

There ahead of him was Bakenkhons, who sat on a throne made out of stone with a black magician on either side of him. Closing in all around were the shadow wraiths. Sashin withdrew his light sword, which dissipated away.

"It's about time, Ahmenemat. You saved me the trouble of coming to get you out of your magical box. I thought you were going to hide yourself away like a coward," said Bakenkhons scornfully.

"I'm here, aren't I? And I know the truth. I know we were once friends and that you grew frustrated and turned to the black magicians because they offered you power. But did you know that they came to me and offered me an alliance with them and that very same power?" replied Sashin.

Bakenkhons looked clearly agitated as he turned to look over at each of the black magicians by his side. He then dropped his head and pondered for a moment.

"I know there was once good in you, Bakenkhons. You need to look within yourself and remember that," said Sashin.

Bakenkhons raised his head, and the familiar look of disdain appeared in his expression.

"As you can see, I have put together a small army," he said.

Sashin witnessed hordes of shadow wraiths closing in, forming a circle all around.

'Oh my...' he thought.

"We were planning to attack your magical box and break through, forcing you out. But now that you are here, it would be a shame to put them to waste. Take him!" ordered Bakenkhons, raising his arm and pointing towards Sashin as a command.

A streak of disappointment came over Sashin, as well as rising anger. He immediately materialised his light sword. Shadow wraiths flew towards him from all directions. Sashin took swipes as they neared, causing them to disintegrate. He then produced his light shield and lunged at the shadow entities whilst stabbing them.

Sashin had never seen such a concentration of wraiths before.

'I'm going to lose energy at this rate,' he thought.

As he continued to stab and strike shadow wraiths with his shield, the onslaught began to dissipate, giving Sashin a very short moment to think. An idea quickly emerged in his mind. He teleported away from his position to within the droves of wraiths, there he continued to swipe and stab as the wisps dissipated away. Swapping his sword and shield for a light bow, he began to fire light arrows into the air. Momentarily focusing on the arrows caused three light arrows to emerge when Sashin pulled back on the bow, which he fired into the air.

'That's new,' he thought.

He fired another three arrows, followed by another three and then another, causing explosions of wraiths all around the wasteland. Moving his bow down directly in front of him, Sashin began to shoot light arrows all around him, causing further eruptions of energy sparks as wraiths faded into the dark.

Bakenkhons had a look of disgust on his face.

"Are you going to intervene?" asked one of the black magicians.

"My astral form is weakened from my visit to the Akashic records after being thrown into an energy vortex by Ahmenemat. He continues to infuriate me!" replied Bakenkhons.

"We shall stop him," said the black magician, ushering the other one to join him.

They both hovered over towards Sashin. As another group of wraiths vanished into thin air from oncoming light arrows, Sashin held still, unable to move.

'What is happening?' he thought.

It was the astral wind. Sashin tried frantically to shoot a light arrow at the black magician in front but his efforts were futile. Two wraiths attached themselves onto him, causing a sharp sting as they disrupted his auric field. The black magicians, with hands raised, began to float over to Sashin. As a reflex action, he teleported instantly with the wraiths and the black magicians who were in close proximity to him.

They all reappeared. Sashin quickly looked around to see that he was in a side alley on the astral highway. With a light sword now in hand, he swiftly stabbed the wraiths on either side. The black magicians released their grip on Sashin in order to gauge where they were. Once they recognised their surroundings, they lunged forward and grabbed onto Sashin. He struggled to get free. When he attempted to use his light sword, it disappeared from the shock of the black magicians grabbing him, which had a negative effect on his astral body.

"Leave him alone!" yelled a voice.

Sashin turned to see that it was Britt.

"Let go of him!" she shouted.

The black magician in front of Sashin turned to look towards Britt. He raised his arm, which caused a strong gale to force her to fly back and hit the wall where she stood paralysed. Sashin grabbed the black magician by the wrist and forced his arm up, breaking Britt's hold. But no sooner had he taken action, the black magician behind him resumed the astral gale, and Sashin felt its sheer force.

Knowing that he had put Britt and others in jeopardy by coming to the astral highway, he realised he had no choice. With his eyes closed, he focused and teleported the black magicians along with himself to the astral wasteland, where a group of waiting shadow wraiths sprung into action. They flew towards him, and two grabbed hold of Sashin on either side. He felt his aura drain, as if the wraiths were syphoning off energy from his body, and this caused him to drop to one knee. The black magicians looked towards Bakenkhons with satisfied looks on their faces.

"You see Ahmenemat, I wish to be free of this prison and be reborn through you. By taking your body, I can live again in the material world in the incarnation you have taken. I can walk amongst people once again. Who knows what I could achieve in your modern world?" exclaimed Bakenkhons with a look of wide-eyed excitement on his face.

"This is not the way of the Order of Amun – you know it isn't. Look back to what the Order was trying to achieve. It wasn't this," said Sashin looking up directly at Bakenkhons.

"Prepare him! Hold him tight this time," instructed Bakenkhons as two more wraiths flew over and grabbed onto Sashin.

"The dagger!" ordered Bakenkhons.

The black magician produced the dagger from beneath his shawl and performed the same ritual that Sashin had witnessed on the astral highway – chanting as he rubbed a mala over the blade. The dagger turned charcoal black, and Sashin lowered his head in despair.

'Is this the end?' he thought.

Negative thoughts began to flood his mind, but he quickly halted them. He was reminded of what he had seen in the Akashic records, all the negativity people created in times of struggle. This reminder derailed his dark thoughts, and Sashin felt a sense of relief.

"Remember," spoke a voice in the back of his mind that sounded like Dina's.

Sashin looked up towards the sky.

"Remember who you are," said a voice that sounded like Rajarshi's.

'Where did that come from? 'he thought.

"Remember, go back to go forward," said a voice. "Know yourself," it whispered.

Sashin closed his eyes. He remembered the vision he had from when he was doing the chakra meditation. Focusing on the memory, he travelled back in time and shot forward at such an immense speed that his astral body seemed to stay where it was. This left an astral hue that gave the shadow wraiths the illusion that he was still there.

Emerging in the chamber used by the Order, he sat cross-legged before the high priest. He felt like he was actually there. The priest chanted, "uh, ew, oh, ah, eye, aa" and "ee" and Sashin almost involuntarily repeated his words. As he continued to chant, the priest gave an instruction.

"Focus on the kundalini from the base of your spine and work up through the chakras to your crown, just like we did before. But do not stop. Keep going and when you feel your crown activate and your third eye open, do not be afraid. Listen to my voice – I will guide you."

Sashin felt a warm sensation in the lower part of his back and saw a red light. Now starting to grow hotter, the feeling moved up his spine to his abdomen, and the red light changed to orange. The heat now moved to his stomach, accompanied by a yellow light. He began to feel a sense of confidence and grounding. Moving to the centre of his chest, the heat continued to rise to his throat and then his forehead. The colours changed to green, light blue, and then to purple. With a pulsing at his forehead, Sashin began to see a tunnel of light similar to when he travelled to the Akasha. Once the heat had hit the top of his head, there was an intense white light.

"My crown chakra is open," he said.

"Do not be afraid. Be one with the light," replied the priest.

Sashin could see the universe once he had emerged from the tunnel of light. He saw the stars, the planets, and the galaxies. He felt at one with the universe. He remembered what activating all his chakras felt like and his astral body became supercharged with energy as all his chakras began to spin.

He snapped back to the future in the astral wasteland, returning to his position on one knee as if he had never left. As he opened his eyes, they began to glow with a sizzling white light. He emitted a wave of energy that disintegrated all the shadow wraiths around him in a brilliant explosion of light. He stood up and looked directly ahead. The black magicians exchanged a glance and fled. Bakenkhons stood up from his throne with a look of terror on his face. Sashin advanced towards him.

"What has happened to you?" asked Bakenkhons.

Now standing directly in front of Bakenkhons, Sashin smiled.

"High energy," he said as he put his arms around Bakenkhons.

"What are you doing? What are you doing? Let me go!" cried Bakenkhons.

Sashin shot up into the sky and flew through the dark clouds appearing on the next astral plane – the material plane. As he rose alongside Bakenkhons, they became visible from the astral highway. People stopped to stare at the spectacle, looking up in awe, some pointing with eyes wide open and mouths agape. Britt stood amongst the crowd and also looked up in wonder.

"Well, what d'ya know? That's not something you see every day," she said.

Sashin reached the next level up and then rocketed up to the higher astral realm. Bakenkhons began to vibrate and convulse uncontrollably.

"Let me go!" he yelled.

Entering the higher astral plane, Sashin let go of Bakenkhons and jumped back to land on a platform next to a golden gate, the one he had seen in an earlier dream. Bakenkhons, suspended in mid-air, vibrated violently until he exploded, as particles of his astral matter shot out in all directions and then fizzled away. A clanking noise could be heard behind him. Sashin turned to see one side of the gate open. A tall being emerged with long golden hair, wearing a long white robe with a purple chest plate. The aura of the being was crystalline in appearance. Sashin used his fourth dimensional sight to see that the being vibrated extremely fast.

"His low density astral body was unable to endure the high frequency of this realm. By bringing him here, you set into motion his return to the *devachan*," explained the being.

"What will happen to him?" asked Sashin.

"He will pay his karmic debt," replied the being.

Sashin nodded and the being continued to speak.

"It is good to see you again in your current incarnation. However, you have not followed the natural astral order either and will have to return to the *devachan* when you reach the end of your current incarnation's life."

"I understand," responded Sashin.

"You made your way back to the devachanic plane. Should you wish to return again, I will be here to help you in your pursuit of knowledge and spiritual wisdom," the being added.

"Thank you," replied Sashin.

Sashin looked around to see a set of stairs with two large columns on either side. On top of each column sat the statue of a lion, and everything was in gold. He had seen this place before in a much earlier dream. Levitating into the air, he turned towards the being and held up his hand to wave. The being waved back. Sashin descended over the staircase and shot down, teleporting away.

Opening his eyes, Sashin sat up and turned his head to see Reshma looking at her phone. She stopped for a moment and looked over. Seeing Sashin awake, she leapt off the sofa.

"How did it go? Are you okay?" she asked.

"Yes, I'm fine," replied Sashin.

Just as he was about to explain what happened when he travelled back in time, he paused and remembered that Dina and Darius were still on the video call. He continued.

"I took Bakenkhons to the higher astral plane by literally grabbing him. He wasn't able to take the energy there. His astral body was forced apart, and he was returned to the *devachanic* plane, to face his karmic debt."

"That's excellent news! Well done. Speak later," replied Dina, cutting the call.

"Well, they didn't stick around, did they?" remarked Reshma.

"Something tells me they got the outcome they wanted," said Sashin.

"I'm really proud of you, Sash. It's all over," added Reshma, helping Sashin up off the floor.

"I went back and saw myself in the chamber with the high priest. I learned how to activate all my chakras; I experienced it and actually opened my third eye. I remembered who I was and what I was capable of. Because of this, I was able to travel to the higher astral realm with Bakenkhons," responded Sashin.

"Woah, you finally did it! You connected with your past self," said Reshma, looking amazed.

Three thousand miles away in the heart of the Zamalek district of Cairo, a white Kia pulled up and parked. Dina got out of the car and walked over to a large building on the corner of a busy road. The building could have been mistaken for a small hotel, with a dome on the roof and an open balcony area behind it. Between two sets of columns was an entrance with a large spiral staircase above it. Several other balconies were on either side of the building. Dina made her way up the dark staircase to the middle floor. She approached a large, dark brown door with a gold lion head door knocker. After knocking twice, the door opened, and she was ushered inside by a thin man wearing a burgundy waistcoat and tarboosh. His waistcoat was worn over a half-sleeved khaki shirt, which contrasted his black trousers. Dina approached oak double doors, which she opened and then closed behind her.

The room was dimly lit. A man sat at a desk in a black dashiki with gold embroidery. He had a goatee beard and thick black hair.

"What is the status, Dina?" he asked.

"It is done, Grand Master. Bakenkhons was taken to the higher astral plane, where he was unable to survive and is no more," replied Dina.

"Good. His actions put the Order in jeopardy once before. How did Sashin do this?" asked the Grand Master.

"I'm not sure," responded Dina.

"Impressive. He really must be the reincarnation of Ahmenemat," said the Grand Master.

An open file lay on the desk with loose papers and photographs of Sashin.

"I've read the file. These pictures?" enquired the Grand Master, holding up one particular photo.

"We have our man over in London, Karim. He has been watching, reporting back to us, and taking pictures," answered Dina.

"This woman, Alexis Zenonos, seems to be an item with Sashin. That's good," remarked the Grand Master, sitting back in his seat, pondering whilst looking at the picture of Alexis and Sashin from their night out in London Bridge.

"How so?" asked Dina.

"He works with her. I want you to befriend Alexis and offer your services for her travel company. Tell her you can be a reliable guide for her tours. Let her entertain the idea," suggested the Grand Master.

"What if she doesn't want my services?" queried Dina.

"We can be persuasive," replied the Grand Master.

Dina nodded.

The Grand Master continued.

"That way you have another connection to Sashin, to solidify the trust."

"Right," responded Dina.

"The 'Order of Amun' lives on through us, Dina. Keep an eye on Sashin, as we might need his help in the near future," said the Grand Master.

"What are you going to do about those?" asked Dina, looking over at piles of books in the corner of the room. All of them had the title 'The Secret Order of Amun'.

"They'll all be burned," replied the Grand Master nonchalantly.

Chapter Thirty-Six

A few days later, a young woman ventured down a busy city road. She looked around at the shops, restaurants, and bars on either side and wondered exactly where she was. Over in the distance, she saw the road leading up as if it rose towards the sky. Flashing lights appeared in the sky that looked like vague images.

'How weird. What is this place?' she thought.

The woman had ginger hair that came down to her chest. There were light freckles on her forehead and cheeks. She wore a light pink crop top with blue jeans and white trainers. Her necklace had a small white crystal on it. She approached a side alley and stopped as she looked down to see a man standing with one foot against the wall. He turned his head to make eye contact with her. She walked down the alley towards the man.

"I'm lost and don't know where I am. Do you know what this place is? I'm a bit confused and a bit scared actually," she said.

"What's your name?" asked the man.

"Rachel Lin. One minute I was asleep, and the next I was here," replied Rachel.

"I can help you. Come over here," said the man ushering her over.

Rachel paused for a moment and then proceeded.

As she drew closer, the expression on the man's face changed. His eyes grew bigger and turned a yellowish hue in colour. His complexion began to pale, and his mouth widened to a grin that exposed two fangs. Rachel screamed. The man grabbed her and pulled her until she was up against him. The man opened his mouth and moved his head forward to bite her.

"Let her go!" yelled a voice.

Rachel was released as the man looked over to see Sashin walking towards him.

"You should keep away from that parasite – he's an energy vampire," said Sashin.

"Who do you think you are?" snarled the vampire.

Sashin's eye began to glow with white sizzling energy as his astral body became super charged.

"The Traveller," he replied, smiling.

A look of fear appeared over the vampire's face as Sashin shot forward in a stream of light.

Glossary

Akasha – Sanskrit word for the space where the Akashic records reside

Akashic records – The collection of universal events, thoughts, words, emotions, and intent ever to have occurred in the past, present or future

Astral body – A non-physical body that some believe can separate from a person's physical body and survive after death. It is also known as the subtle body, body of light, and spirit body. It has been elaborated on in esoteric, occult, and mystical teachings. The astral body is related to astral projection/travel, which is an out-of-body experience (OBE) that is believed to happen when consciousness functions separately from the physical body and travels through the astral plane

Astral plane – A non-physical realm of existence that is believed to be where spirits go between death and the spirit world. The astral plane is believed to be inhabited by various entities that are negative and positive, and can be reached through astral projection, meditation, near-death experiences and lucid dreaming. It consists of lower, middle, and higher planes

Chakras – A Sanskrit term meaning 'wheel' or 'cycle', referring to energy centres within the body, believed to be spinning wheels of energy that regulate physical, emotional, and spiritual well-being. There are seven chakras:

Base or root chakra – located at the bottom of the spine, known as Muladhara in Sanskrit

Sacral chakra – located a few centimetres below the navel, known as Svadhisthana in Sanskrit

Solar plexus chakra – located at the solar plexus, known as Manipura in Sanskrit

Heart chakra – located in the centre of the chest, known as Anahata in Sanskrit

Throat chakra – located in the throat area, known as Visuddha in Sanskrit

Third eye chakra – located between the eyebrows, known as Ajna in Sanskrit

Crown chakra – located at the top of the head, known as Sahasrara in Sanskrit

Beta – A term of endearment used by Indian parents towards their child, meaning son

Jivan Sanjivani – An Indian medicine oil used for cold and flu

Kali yuga – In Hinduism, Kali Yuga is the fourth, shortest and worst of the four Yugas in a Yuga cycle. A period of darkness, characterised by ignorance, corruption, materialism, and chaos

Satya yuga – Is the first of the four Yugas in the Hindu Yuga Cycle, and is considered the golden age of humanity

Mayavirupa – Another term for the astral body that emphasises its nature as a temporary, vehicle for consciousness

Plane – A distinct level or realm of existence within a wider metaphysical or spiritual framework. There are several planes often described as dimensions or layers of reality, each with unique characteristics, energies, and inhabitants, that represent different states of consciousness. These are:

Physical – Our earthly plane

Causal – Just beyond the earthly plane where the Akashic records reside

Devachanic – A higher astral plane where one returns to reincarnate

Sushuptic – A spiritually higher astral plane

Nirvanic – Believed to the be the highest astral plane, for example as attained by the Buddha

Printed in Dunstable, United Kingdom

82758023R00178